CRIMSON QUEEN

Mephisto's Magic Online Book Two

CHRISTOPHER JOHNS

MOUNTAINDALE
PRESS

Dedicated to those who like to read. And those who like to read my works.

Seriously—you all keep me having fun and doing something that, without you, would be impossible and not nearly as fun.

Thank you.

CATCHING UP

When Seth—Kyvir Mageblood—logged into the latest and greatest game of the century, Mephisto's Magic Online, with his guild, and streaming friends, Mona, Al, and Sondra, nothing was what they had thought it would be. The world was amazing, so detailed and insanely fun that it felt real. Too real. But they weren't together so it was hard to really enjoy that newness while Kyvir had to get through the tutorial to get to his friends.

Mona Hart — Monami Sunfur, a dps fighter whose ability is Allure. She's Seth's best friend from since before they were born thanks to their parents being close.

Al — Albarth Remell, the other dps fighter whose ability is Fire Dart and former healer for the group. The group found out that he's actually the world-famous fencer Alexander Remell, who retreated into video games after the loss of his own dearest friend and unrequited love.

Sondra – Sundar Strongtusk, the former tank-turned-healer whose ability is Totem. A noncommissioned officer in the army whose love of gaming and structure led her to start a guild in other games that welcomed new players.

The four of them entered the game expecting to do what

they had always done after the tutorial, but the biometric and psychological readings that the portals, the systems each player enters to play the game, had other ideas. After finding out that their usual roles had been swapped out for new ones, their goal became figuring out their new powers, surroundings, and abilities while preparing to stream the game for their fans.

They geared up, made some friends with the local army, crafters and even some of the city guardians. Unfortunately, when it came time to show off the levels and knowledge they had gathered in a short time, they found out they couldn't due to some other genius attempting to stream something they shouldn't.

So, with nothing better to do, they attempt their first dungeon. Undead abound, but it really wasn't that difficult for the crew of veteran gamers. No—what was hard was the fact that an admin of some sort seemed to be goading them into leveling up and getting stronger faster.

Because "Not everything was as it seemed." Or whatever that meant. It wouldn't have been so bad if Mona didn't have reason to think that the admin may be, or have some connection to, her father who disappeared years ago with no word and no trace.

Due to some small inner squabbles, the group dynamics were a little tenser than they ever have been, and now they have to travel East to reach the mysterious city of Belgonna's Hold in order to unlock the other half of Kyvir's magic.

All while the real world seems to be growing…stranger and stranger. Seth explained to Mona that he thinks the game may be affecting reality in strange ways and isn't at all sure what is going on, but the race is on for the group to grow more powerful and figure out what is happening. In-game, and out of game.

CHAPTER ONE

SETH

Sunshine lit my face as the great fiery orb lifted to begin the new day. I knew I'd have to leave soon to make sure our preparations were complete. Traveling from one city to another in territory we had no idea what to expect was both exhilarating and terrifying. Granted, dying here was easily done and fixable, it was a game. Having to earn back twice the amount of experience lost just to get back to where you were? Yeah, that wasn't so awesome, hence the need to prepare.

"Do you have to go right now?" Thea groaned at me. I glanced over at her, sweat having built on her face and shoulder, her light green training shirt sticking to her athletic and toned body around her chest and midriff. She moved toward me once more and speared her sword toward my head so fast it was all I could do to bring my glaive up in time to parry the blow away from my face.

Panting, I eyed her some more, not angrily or anything because we had spent the majority of the night sparring. "I did say we would be leaving today."

"I know," her grin a touch pouty, her golden skin peeked out from beneath her shirt, glistening, and I found myself distracted long enough to end up on my back. She'd swept my feet out from under me, and I could only groan and chuckle painfully.

She helped me stand, shoving the top of her wooden blade into the ground by her feet so she could brush her long blonde hair behind her elven ears. "Sorry, can never resist that opening."

"I know, that's the sixth time this morning I've been on my back because of you." She raised her eyebrows provocatively, and I rolled my eyes back at her. "Come on. Mind out of the gutter."

"Where would I put it otherwise?" we both laughed at her response, and she stretched herself out. "What do you have to do this morning?"

"Go to Ori's smithy and see about collecting the others' weapons and my shield. That sword I ordered too." I scratched my head, "I might see about going to Ophira's and collecting some more of the stuff she uses to make dyes. What was it she called it again? Tinctures! That's it."

"What do you do with these tinctures?" Thea frowned curiously at me as she plucked her sword from the ground.

"I add them to something with the color I want, then let it sit until the tincture takes on the desired hue." I shrugged after that, it was very simple to do, but the thought of making my own dyes sent a thrill down my spine. I loved colors, specifically bright ones.

"That's all?" She raised her eyebrows once more. "The witch doesn't teach you anything else?"

"Nothing yet." I shrugged again, suddenly confused. "Why?"

"Just curious is all." Thea shrugged and tossed her hair behind her back as she stepped out of the circle. "I've heard rumors that she practices odd types of magic. I thought she might be tempting you toward them."

I snorted. "Nah. Nothing weird. Going to take a shower?"

She stopped and turned back to look at me over her shoulder, her grin returning. "I am. Are you coming?"

I grinned ear to ear. "Yes, ma'am."

She turned, and I chased her inside as she shrieked with laughter.

CHAPTER TWO

MONA

Ugh, where is he? I thought for the tenth time since coming to the forge. The other smiths watched me with kind, somewhat knowing smiles. They were nice guys, but they had no idea what was going on with me, and my irritation wasn't with them. Not really. "What do you guys say we try to get some work in while we wait?"

Master Ori, his mountainous bulk lumbering forward swiftly, said, "Yeah, that's the idea, girl!"

His human grin and friendly demeanor made him approachable, though a lot of people seemed to take a look at his enormous size and muscles and discount him as a muscle head.

I'd only known Ori to be a kind—but firm and harsh— master. He expected great things because he gave great training.

"Don't forget to let Kyvir know that we ran out of ore to make his elven sword," he nodded to the half-formed sword. "The other more senior smith, Regan, had overestimated how much of a lighter ore we had available to make the sword, and it fell far too short to make anything that would be worthwhile."

"I won't, Master Ori." I smiled as he had Alvor bring out the piece of iron we would be working. It was a simple metal, and easier for me with my lower level in smithing to safely work.

"We're going to make a sword with this," Ori instructed us all. Smithing in this forge amounted to a group effort, typically overseen by Master Ori or by Regan. "And we're going to have you working the metal, Monami. Are you ready?"

I nodded, and he motioned for Alvor to put the ingot into the forge. Falo, the junior smith, worked the bellows to stoke the flames. All the men in the forge looked like they could be training to be Olympians, their physiques matching that of most dedicated bodybuilders. Alvor was on the smaller side, but that was mainly because he was still young, but he'd grown up mining, so he had muscle.

I used my metal magic and tentatively reached out to the metal in the flames, "A little more heat." Falo stoked the flames more and Alvor dug the iron into the coals and coke to gather more heat about it. I didn't even need to see it to know that the metal had taken on a cherry-red color. Perfect for manipulating. "Now."

Alvor pulled out the metal ingot, and we began to shape it, Regan and Falo striking with smaller heavy hammers as I attracted it toward me. One of my seven bars of Aether depleted, but with that, I could pull the shape of the sword we made together out faster than the others, though it was still tiring work.

Each strike of the hammer assisted me in bringing the impurities of the iron forth to be beaten out, and the shape began to truly take. I could feel the metal cooling past the safe working heat and nodded to Alvor. "Heat!"

Alvor immediately pulled the forming sword off the anvil and swung it into the fire. The other smiths rested, Master Ori watching silently as he supervised our work. This was a far less detrimental piece of work, simple make, simple materials. This was his test to see how we could work together and how well I managed my magic.

Rumors and legends stated that people with my affinity could make weapons without the forge and hammer. They could shape the metal with only their minds, magic, and will.

I wanted to get there so badly, but Ori was a traditionalist and refused to let me try it on my own without understanding the basics of the craft.

He'd earned my respect with that, so I would listen to his wishes. Even if he was an NPC.

"That's enough heat," I called, and Alvor reappeared next to the anvil with the metal on it. We beat the shape into it, and as I envisioned the sword, I started to see the design shifting in my head. I fought against the design, but the more I fought, the more the metal bucked against my attempts to mold and manage it.

"If it's showin' you what it wants to be—don't fight it." Master Ori instructed from behind my shoulder. "Throw it in the flames, boy. Let's have another go. Monami, you make what you see. Aye?"

"Yes, Master Ori!" I replied in a barked intensity that matched the other smiths. I could feel his approving nod behind me, and he moved to stand on the opposite side of the anvil from me.

The cherry-colored metal was back, and the others pounded the metal more. Another bar of Aether gone, and I plucked and pulled the metal with my mind and will, bringing the shape I saw in my mind to fruition by ordering Regan and Falo to hammer in specific places.

Folding the metal on itself to thicken it, then reheating, beating it again, and reheating. Folding. Heating. Another bar of Aether spent. Finally, the true shape of the weapon began to form. It thickened near the spine to create a broad, flat area that thinned closer to the beveling. The edge would stay dull until the smiths could grind it, but I curved it halfway up to make the belly of the cutting edge that led to the point. The broad spine was flat for about half a foot before it tapered in as well, leading down toward the tip where it would meet the point.

It looked more and more like it would be some kind of long knife or a short sword at this rate, it almost seemed as though it couldn't decide what it wanted to be. We put it in for a final round of heating, sweat pouring from my face and arms as the heat intensified and then brought it back to the anvil. Regan and Falo beat the hell out of the blade, the tang lengthening where the handle would go.

Finally, I could see that this design was what the metal wanted and ordered the heat treating. The blade was longer, more than the initial shorter blade that I had seen within. Ori stopped Alvor before he could put the piece into the forge again.

"Excellent work gentlemen, and lady." His discerning gaze eyed each piece of the blade that he could see, then he took the tongs away from Alvor and showed it to Regan. "What could you say might be a problem about this weapon?"

"If we heat treat it now, it will likely be brittle if the wielder parries a blade off that spine." His deep voice was contemplative, but he knew what Ori wanted, so he continued, "We need to use some clay to keep the spine of the blade cool so it will make a more flexible core. This way, the weapon can take the impact of a strike and not shatter under the blow. It's not something a lot of smithies will do for the fact that the process is odd, and they prefer dual-edged weapons."

"Very good," Master Ori handed the tongs back to Alvor and looked from the apprentice to Falo, then me. "Anything to add?"

I shook my head, and Falo looked to Alvor, the boy putting the weapon on the anvil so Regan could apply the moist clay. "I think using the weapon as a means to parry without an alloy or something else to act to soften the blow like a different metal for the core, it might be a bad idea to do it too often. What if we were to do this with a softer metal and a harder metal with the outside?"

"That's an excellent idea, good form!" Master Ori grinned and turned his gaze to Falo. "And you?"

"I like his idea, and it would be a good way to help with the flexibility and durability of the blade, but I would also work in making the striking of the spine worthwhile." He shuffled over to a shelf and grasped something, then brought it back. He held up an odd-looking guard that had a flat spike on it. "I would make a trap to help the wielder tear the attacker's weapon out of their hand."

"Both are excellent ideas." Ori nodded approvingly and clapped both men on their shoulders. "I would like to see the two of you heading a project of similar design. Are you ready, Regan?"

Ori turned and his eldest apprentice pointed to the forge where the blade sat inside the flames. The bellows creaked as Ori busied himself with upping the heat, and the rest of us waited. "Idle hands are useless hands—I have no need for useless hands!" Ori barked angrily.

"Falo, Alvor, you two find an appropriate hilt for the weapon," Regan ordered readily. "I'm thinking hand and a half if we want to be able to have the user stripping weapons from someone else."

"I don't know if that will be necessary," I called. "I see a simple hilt, it'll be for Kyvir, to replace the weapon we couldn't make for him."

Ori was quiet after that and watching and waiting as we worked to make the best use of what little time the treatment took. Some people came over to talk about weapon orders, and Alvor had to handle the front. It wasn't long before a calloused hand plopped onto my shoulder, Regan nodding toward the forge, startled me.

"It's time, Monami, you can have the honor of the quench."

Ori tossed me a set of tongs that I rested on the anvil, then a heavy pair of gloves smacked into my shoulder. I fought them, then slid them on my hands, their length going all the way up to my elbows. I tossed my mane out of the way, grabbed the tongs, and turned back to my work.

CHAPTER THREE

SETH

Thea opted to join me for the walk to Ophira's and the smithy, Al and Sondra, having given me the heads up they were on their way to Ori's already. As we walked to the dye shop, we saw that most people were still eating right now, leaving the streets less crowded than they could have been.

I knocked on Ophira's door, the multi-colored windows and sign making me smile. The door was still locked for some reason, but I saw motion inside, so I waited patiently with Thea behind me.

"Welcome back, Kyvir!" Ophira greeted me in a newer looking dress, this one a bright and vivid purple that made her skin look almost sallow. But it was amazing. The dress whooshed around her ankles as she moved from the doorway toward her counter. "How can I help you and your guest?"

"Thea Oberon," Thea greeted her with a smile, though it was a little tense.

"A pleasure to make your acquaintance, Ms. Oberon."

Ophira's smile never faltered. "Would you care for any dyes? Feel free to peruse while I speak to Kyvir."

I watched as Thea turned toward a section of greens, her eyes shifting in such a way as to keep an eye on her back and the door.

"How can I help you, Kyvir?" Ophira's smiling, pastel pink covered lips quirked at the sides, and her blue eyes wandered over me. Her eyebrows were different colors today, an exotic cream color for the right side, and a deep mauve for the left. "I take it you are leaving?"

"Yes, I am, and I hoped to take some more tinctures to help with my dye-making if you could spare it?"

"I can, how much would you like?" She cocked her head to the side, her customer service smile coming to bear. "If you open it, you've bought it!"

Her called statement made Thea flinch and put a phial down hurriedly, before going to another section.

"How about two gold worth?" I selected the amount from my inventory, the number subtracting from the thirty-six gold pieces I had.

She grinned, winked, and turned to go into the back, then stopped to point at Thea with raised eyebrows. I got her meaning and turned to watch my new friend. Lover. Things between her and I were fast approaching delightfully complicated. I liked her, she was fun and vibrant, appreciated my humor, strong and seemed to be caring. Capable.

She was a mystery to me, and putting a name or title to what we had seemed to… cheapen it almost? As if, if I were to try and claim it by naming what we had, I risked losing her, too.

And after one too many losses lately, I wasn't sure I wanted that. Not right now. And definitely not without her input. I'd already done more than enough without clearly knowing what a person I cared about wanted.

A clanking of glass grabbed my attention behind me, and I turned to find Ophira lovingly lugging a lot of vials toward the counter in a special tray designed to hold them at the bottom and middle with little metal cages. "Each one you bought before would cost about a silver to make, I'll give you a bulk sale discount as well as your apprentice discount. You have seven phials now, but here are another twenty."

I frowned. "That math doesn't add up."

She eyed me, a small smirk on her face as she grasped my shoulder tightly. "Never correct someone when they're being generous, unless you mean to pay full price for that generosity. Think of it as encouragement to become more adept, if you have to."

I grinned at Ophira, and she winked mischievously. "Take these, and bring me back the products so I can see how you've grown."

I nodded and touched one of them when a notification populated in front of me.

Would you like to collect all of the phials here? Yes / No?

I selected yes, and they all disappeared into my inventory, only taking up one of the slots. "How convenient for you wanderers."

I could hear a hint of jealousy in her voice, but I knew Ophira was likely only teasing.

"Thank you." I offered her my hand, and she shook it cordially. "I'll be sure to keep an eye out for anything interesting."

"See that you do," she said in a purring tone, and took the tray off the table. "And do see that you come back safely. I know that you cannot die permanently but die as little as possible."

"I'll try, it's only two days' worth of travel there, right?" Thea chose that time to come up to the counter and press two phials of deep emerald green onto it.

"Two days through open wilderness." Thea sighed knowingly. "Only way to traverse it safely is in numbers. Even then, you risk your outriders being picked off by vultures, bandits, and other dastardly creatures. You have horses?"

I thought for a moment. "No, I don't think we do."

"Probably better that you don't, though that may add half to a full day to the journey." She saw me frowning at her.

Ophira interjected, "There are creatures out there that would kill you to get to the horse. And you would be out a mount, money and time."

"So, we travel by foot then?" A half a day could be all right, I guessed, but a mount would have been nice. I'd never ridden a horse before. I tried to pay for Thea's dyes, but she raised a brow at me, and I knew that look from Mona. She had it.

"That's a good idea but keep an eye on the sky." Thea winked and put the amount of money that Ophira had asked for on the counter and collected her items. "Thank you for your hard work."

"And you for your patronage." Ophira nodded back. "Good luck to you, Kyvir."

Thea and I left Ophira with a wave, turning toward the Fire Square and the smithy. The streets had filled with citizens, and their daily lives carried them to and fro, into our way and out of it again. That was okay. It was still early, after all.

I could tell at a distance that we had come close to Ori's smithy, the pedal grinder screeching across the metal of some poor weapon, sparks likely flying and flinging all over the place. The smiths and Mona stood about watching Alvor as he ground out imperfections in the face of the weapon and sharpened the blade.

I went to say something, but Thea grasped my arm tightly, whispering in my ear, "I've seen this before." She motioned by tilting her head at the scene before us. "This is important, I think. Let's wait to see what they do."

I tucked my hands into my pockets and watched as Alvor handed the product to Ori. From what I could see, the blade was beautifully crafted, and the handle was simple. The cross-guard of it had what looked like half a handle on the back that stretched up it opposite the blade's edge.

The handle of it was hidden in Ori's meaty palm, he nodded to one of the older smiths, and they brought out what looked like a sword blank. It had the form and shape but wasn't fully sharpened.

Ori stepped back and the other smith held the blank up as if he were about to attack. They eyed each other for a moment before Ori surged forward with the blade and slammed it into the blank. A peel of metal against metal and collective groan from the smiths. The blade had snapped against the blank, sinking point-first into the wooden support beam to the left of the intended mark.

"Regan, melt it down, and we can try again," Ori ordered, handing the broken sword to the elder smith. He turned to Monami, a scowl on his face and my ire rising as I thought he was about to lay into her. He put a large hand on her shoulder, her body stiffened. "Don't beat yourself, girl. Trust your instincts. Fighting the metal with a gift like yours can cause fractures and impurities to lay in wait. You'll get there. Some damned fine forging you all did this morning. Get out of here before I keep you from your travels. And you." he pointed a meaty finger at Mona. "Be safe now, hear me?"

"Yes sir," Mona mumbled, and he gripped her shoulder a little harder, encouraging her to look up at him.

"You remember what I told you when I let you into my forge?" He looked to the two other men in the forge, Regan having gone out back out of earshot. "What have I taught you all when it comes to these things?"

They all intoned together, "Metal melts when tested and failed, tested mettle never fails when your will is your hammer."

"We can remake a weapon; we can remake armor. Metal melts and can be reborn." Ori lovingly tapped the chest of each of his apprentices. "But your mettle cannot be if you let doubt crack it. You know your trade, and I will see you trained properly. Trust in me, trust in you, and trust your gut."

"Yes, sir!" they all cried together.

Made me glad that Ori had taken Mona in to teach her.

She turned to find me watching and nodded to Thea and

me. "Well, you both being here for that was a little embarrassing."

"You made a weapon." Thea tried to comfort her. "That's something to pride yourself in. Failure only reinforces the things that you know are right. It can be the same way in combat, though slightly less deadly if I can say as much."

"Slightly" Monami crossed her arms, the fur there brushing against itself. Her lioness-like features looked tired and defeated, her tan hair hanging over the side of her face. "Sorry Ky, but your sword won't happen. They don't have the right kind of metal for it. We tried, but it won't take. Ori said he'd give you your money back if needed too."

"How about a trade?" Mona and I looked at Thea, she reached into her own inventory and pulled out a sword. It was like the one she had described, of elven design. The silvery sheen to it was lovely, though there were some nicks and marks on the blade and spine. "You take one of mine—I get the one they were supposed to make for you."

I took the weapon that she offered, grinning at the stats it provided, though it was on its last legs.

Elven sword
Quality: Uncommon
Base dmg: 7-9 dmg
Durability: 3/15
Worth: 2 gold

That was some nice durability. "Yeah, I'll take that trade for sure."

"Happy to have been able to help you." Thea grinned and sauntered over to the counter. "Master Ori! Would you have someone fix this up so I can give it to Kyvir?"

Alvor appeared as if by magic. "I'd be delighted."

Ori lumbered over. "Thea, how are you?"

"Good, Master Ori." She grinned and jumped as Ori slammed a dark metal shield onto the counter. "For Kyvir, hope it helps."

"I'm sure it will." Sondar's huge mitt landed on my shoulder and I grinned up at her tusk-flashing, smiling visage. The huge, Orcish woman's muscular body invaded my view and personal space as she swept me into a hug from behind before whispering, "You okay?"

"Yeah, thank you." I extricated myself from her grasp, politely because I knew she genuinely cared.

Grinding drowned out the noise around us, and Albarth joined us, a little tired looking, but whole. His deep brown skin was hidden under green clothes and his leather armor. I noted that he had a very nice rapier on his hip as we gathered and gave him a curt nod. He returned it, looking like he wanted to speak but didn't dare in current company.

The grinding stopped, and here came Thea with her sword, presenting it like one might present a weapon to a feudal lord. "For your protection."

I snickered at her and took the weapon by the hilt; the durability fully restored. It reminded me... "Hey Alvor, could we get some of the repair powder you have?"

"No." He shook his head. "We already sold it to Monami with a whetstone to care for your weapons. We won't get another shipment in for a few days, and if we have to run repairs, we will be hard-pressed. Use it sparingly. The whetstone will let you recover a little of your weapon's durability. Don't worry. Monami can explain a bit more."

His easy grin found my friend, and she grinned back, she offered her hand and they high fived. A small surge of jealousy leaked into my heart and then died immediately. I didn't have a right to be mad. She had other friends, so did I. We were still besties.

After we left the smithy, all of the men inside giving Mona pats of encouragement and smiles before Ori stepped closer to her. He held out a small parcel of paper wrapped protectively in a sealed leather container. "Take this to that smith I told you about. They'll be able to help you master your gift. Take it then when you get the chance, but don't dawdle."

Mona nodded and hugged the large man before turning and joining us.

Thea walked us to the eastern edge of the city limits, just inside the gate. The eastern sky looked bright and cheerful, players fighting sheep in the fields. Their auras blinding at times.

"Well, be safe out there, and don't worry, the investigation of the mines is almost finished." She grinned at my bewildered face. "You forgot already?"

I panicked. "Of course not! I'm just a little preoccupied is all. Thank you. If we can help at all, let us know?"

"Nah, we got it. You let the guard and army sort that out. My friends will have the trail of whatever it was that came out of those tunnels soon." Thea pulled me into a hug, then shook everyone else's hands, Mona held it a little more tightly than what looked absolutely necessary. "You all just go and get strong, so I can meet you back out on the front lines."

I paused. "You're going to the front lines?"

"It's a soldier's place." She smiled at me. "It's not like I'm shipping off today." She rolled her eyes playfully. "I was only here on leave, Kyvir. I was always going back to fight. You'll be okay. And I'll see you when you get there, okay?"

I felt somewhat numb and broadsided by the news, but Sundar looped an arm around Thea's shoulder and squeezed her, a grin on her face as she said in a growling tone, "Just remember, blood makes the grass grow."

Thea snorted. "It does make a nice fertilizer for demonic plants." She looked at me, and a softer smile replaced her earlier grin. She stepped forward and gave me another hug. "I'll be waiting for you. I had a good time, Kyvir, but I'm a fighter. A protector. My place is on the battlefield. As is a wanderer's—we will meet again."

"Sounds to me like you'll need this more than I will." I held her weapon out hilt first to her, and she just pressed it back with a shake of her head.

"Ori won't let me go unarmed, and that's an old one." She

paused, biting her bottom lip in thought. "It was a gift of sorts. if you want to give it back, bring it back with a tale."

"I'll do that." I touched her sword and brought it up to chest level. "I'll bring this back to you, I swear it."

"I'll hold you to it." She winked, and the others all groaned pointedly. "Better get packing. Bye."

I smiled and mouthed, "Bye." Then turned and followed the others out the gates, through the gently rolling hills of sheep and wanderers into a more open plains land.

"You guys ready for a whole mess of adventure?" Sundar bellowed to us good-naturedly, her easy smile and relaxed demeanor making me smile in return.

"I'll say." I bumped her arm with my fist, and she smacked me playfully.

She looked at the other two who remained slightly quieter than normal and snarled, "What the hell is your issue?"

They both jumped, Mona sliding her a glare that she usually reserved for people who had truly annoyed her. Al just looked miserable.

"What's all this moping and stuff about?" Sundar plowed ahead, motioning that we all follow her. "So, you two aren't going to be making a thing of dating?"

She was looking right at Mona and me, my cheeks boiled. Monami looked aghast, and Sundar just threw her hands up. "So what?! You're best friends! Have either of you thought to end your friendship?"

"No!" I blurted Mona doing the same.

"Then, *nothing has changed.*" She asserted. She grabbed Al by the shoulder. "You and I have known each other for a long-ass time, Al. You gonna keep moping?"

"She's gone, Sun!" Albarth snarled angrily, stepping closer to her and shoving his finger in her face. "You going to do something about this *pain?*"

She reached forward and lifted him off his feet into a bear hug, grumbling, "Yeah. You ever put a finger in my face again, I put a foot in you. You guys are my friends. If I can't escape life and game with you all, I don't want to do it."

I looked over to Mona, her face almost as red as mine. "I'm good if you are."

She looked at me, took a deep breath and let it go. "I'm good. Things have just been stressful, and it's hard to get it out of our heads. We should tell them what you think."

"I can put my deep-seated angst aside long enough to ask what the hell is going on that you think we should know." Albarth glared at the two of us as Sundar put him down.

Mona slid a glance my way, her eyebrows knitted together in an uncertain frown. "Ky, you have more experience with it so far."

"I do, but I also think talking about it in-game could be intercepted." They all looked to me as if I had suddenly grown a third horn, and I mouthed the word *portal*.

"When we log off." Sundar nodded, her eyes closing slightly, as if daring any of us to disagree but sighed. "If we log off now, we waste precious time, and you know we can't chance dying out here."

We agreed and moved on from there, traveling the plains and keeping our eyes up. We didn't see anything other than a few quadrupedal animals moving at a safe distance from us. They were too far out of the way for Albarth to use his bow and arrows.

A few hours for us in-game passed before anything of any real interest happened.

"Shadow coming in hot from southwest," Sundar grumbled, and I went to turn my head, her hand grasped the top of my head and kept it still. "Keep moving, but get ready to run if you see a shadow close to you and growing, cool? Dive to the side and get weapons ready as soon as you can."

"Why don't I try to shoot it?" Albarth whispered fiercely. "Or use my magic?"

"You confident you can shoot it down in one go, Mr. Hood?" Sundar shot back, and Albarth flushed slightly. "If we tip this thing off too much, it could run off and bring buddies. We've seen some weird shit in this game so far, it could happen. So, let's play it safe and lure it close."

It took another half an hour of walking at our normal pace, slowly moving toward each other so that we were closer together and not too clean a target before the shadow grew and moved in toward our right side.

"Steady…" Sundar hissed her eyes darting from the shadow toward the ground it had yet to make up. Thirty feet out, it still dropped but slowly shrank as well. "Dive!"

I dove away from the shadow, struggling to get my new metal shield up in time to avoid being gored by thick, razor-sharp talons.

A screech filled my ears, a ringing setting in that caused me to cry out.

Audible impairment debuff Resisted.

I would hate to see what it would really be like, I grumbled.

The shield lifted, and since it was strapped to my arm, I went with it. I squirmed and kicked, trying to get my leg up so that I might knock the talons off my shield before it lifted me too far. An arrow bounced off my shoulder armor, ricocheting up and smacking lightly against my forearm.

7 dmg taken (friendly)

"Damn it, Al!" I howled, the man yelling he was sorry, but the bird screeched again, and the apology was lost to me.

I finally managed to free my new sword and sliced upward with it, hoping I would hit something and felt a slight give as I did.

8 dmg to Scarvenger

Lvl 11 Scarvenger – Hostile

"No crap, game!" Mona shouted, I glanced down and saw her dancing along the ground toward me, the bird's flapping paused for a moment when a twang reached my ears and it screeched, dipping low enough for Sundar to grab my legs and pull us both down.

The talons on my shield loosened a little, so I switched my

sword to my left hand and grasped the creature's foot with my right hand and poured my ice Aether into it. The talon crackled and froze solidly to my shield, two bars of my Aether gone.

"Good job, Ky!" Sundar grunted and pulled my leg harder, bringing the bird down closer to the ground. "Disable the wings! I'll try to seal the shield to the ground!"

I pulled, and so did she until I was almost on the ground, the others fighting heroically to try and keep the bird from getting away. Flames washed over a sharp weapon that bobbed into my view just as I freed my arm from the shield, and it touched the ground.

"Seal!" Sundar snarled as she slapped the shield where it laid on the ground. "Shit, it isn't working right! I only got one side."

The bird had yet to be truly injured, and the powerful wings tugged the only unsealed side from the ground, the earth rising dangerously where it was.

"Seal the other side, Sunny." I grunted as I stood, narrowly avoiding one of Monami's flying, ringed chakrams as it sliced the air by my cheek. It buried itself in the birds' wing, and Mona whooped loudly.

9 dmg to Scarvenger.

The earth beneath the bird crumbled, and the shield lifted before Sundar plunged her sword into the bird's calf and slapped the rising side, securing it to the ground herself. Her totem flashed to life, and strengthening life coursed back into me.

But the most entrancing thing was the Hell Cat spirit aura that cloaked Albarth, his flaming rapier a blur. He struck vital spots with ease, and as he moved his rapier in odd directions to force the Scarvenger to move one way, the tip of his blade would slip into a rift he made with his magic, and it collided with his enemy exactly where he wanted it to.

CRITICAL STRIKE
27 dmg to Scarvenger
Burned Debuff added to Scarvenger

6 fire dmg

Blind Debuff added to Scarvenger

My weapon slid up into the birds grotesquely scarred breast, hot blood flowing onto my hand, the scent of it almost like what a good cheeseburger smelled like.

I ignored my notifications as the creature died, my hand drifted closer to my face. My mouth suddenly went dry and my lips cracked as if from a hike in the blistering sun.

I licked my lips, my hand shook slowly as I brought the crimson-stained limb toward my mouth. Against my volition, I could clearly see my tongue snaking out just once to taste this strange delight.

"Kyvir, what're you doing?" Monami's question snapped me out of my urges, and I hid my hand like a kid caught reaching into the cookie jar.

"Nothing, what's up? Find any loot?" I blinked several times, my throat and lips still a little dry as I turned to see the others all staring at me.

"Some feathers and meat, as well as sixty-five EXP." Her frown deepened. "You sure you're all right? You look a little flushed?"

"Perfectly fine, though I'm uh…" I glanced down at my shield and smiled. "Not sure I want to use my shield to fight those birds any more than I have to. Supercooling the metal like that can make it weaker, right?"

Mona grinned. "Yeah! So, you were paying attention in that science lesson in third grade after all. I knew Mr. Dean hadn't been very fair with you that day."

"You kidding?" I snorted, rolling my eyes. "The guy was so obsessed with how bacon and alcohol were the perfect aphrodisiacs that he smelled like smoked whisky and pork the whole year. Talk about dedication."

"I love bacon." Sundar rubbed her abs longingly. "It should be a religion."

"A good port paired with some would be lovely." Albarth

smiled to himself. "I may do that later while we talk. Come, let's go."

We spent the rest of the day in-game walking East and found that as we moved, the area changed, albeit a little more subtly at first than changing zones might in other games. A new map in most of those games is exactly that—a new map. They don't always go seamlessly into the next like this, you could always kind of tell that you were in a new area. This whole place seemed like a brand-new world.

Our way of figuring this out was when the grass grew much higher than it had, as if we were in a field of long grass that never seemed to end.

"Anyone else weirded out by this?" Albarth asked quietly as his eyes scanned the chest-height grass before us. "No mention of this in the city before we came out here at all, anyone else hear anything?"

"Nope." Sundar crossed her arms and stared hard. "I can sense some animals, though. May make avoiding things a little easier, you want me to reach out?"

I blinked at Monami, her reaction mirroring my own as I grabbed a couple hand fulls of the grass for later. "Yes?"

"Okay." She shrugged and stepped forward with a chuckle. "Figured I'd ask before I did since the last time, we had someone screeching over it."

Mona's cheeks flared brightly at that, and she pointedly found something interesting to look at where we couldn't see her face.

Albarth and I exchanged a brief grin at her expense, then went back to watching Sundar kneeling down on the edge of the grass where she held out her hand and clicked against the roof of her mouth and teeth as if she was calling to a cat.

The grass before her parted slightly, and a large, green lion stepped from the grass, a short primal thrill surged down my body and into my feet, making me want to run. To dip out of there and hightail it back to civilization, but I wasn't going to leave my friends high and dry.

"Bloody hell, Sundar!" Albarth hissed, his hand on his rapier's hilt, ready to pull it and start to swing for the hills. "Get away from that thing!"

The lion turned amber eyes toward the noise-making nymph and a sort of clicking growl that you'd hear in old animal videos emanated from its chest. It turned back to Sundar and butted his head against her shoulder.

"Hey there, big fella," she greeted him warmly, large fingers dancing through his short mane and flicking back and forth to scratch him. His tail flicked behind him, and I could hear the pleased grunts, his eyes half-lidded at the pleasure of the contact. "You're not so bad, are ya? Nah. No, you're not. You want to do me a favor? Can you lead us safely through here?"

The big cat sniffed at her throat, sandpaper tongue lapping at it for a second before he turned and padded toward each of us. "He needs to make sure he knows what you smell like, so he doesn't get you killed in the future. Just relax and let him smell you."

He came to stand before each of us, his mouth slightly opened and hot breath ruffling the legs of our pants as he took on our scents. Eventually, he turned and sprayed Albarth, the nymph looking decidedly murderous as his hand flew to the rapier on his hip, but Sundar had sprinted to him and grabbed him.

"He says this will help to cover our scent!" Sundar reproached him, his seething anger making him look like he was about to begin foaming at the mouth.

"But why him?" Mona held her nose almost in disgust.

"His scent is the strongest, so he had to pay—I mean, be sprayed—to cover it." Sundar chuckled and shoved the nymph forward. "Come on, let's go."

We walked into the grass, the somewhat itchy sensation of it crawling over my skin as it grasped at my clothes, making my skin crawl where it touched. We walked on, crouching so that not all of us were visible at once, Sundar having the worst time of it since she was so tall and broad.

Every now and again, the lion would stop and scent the air, making us stand for long moments at a time before we kept moving as quietly as we could in grass that seemed to not want to leave us alone.

Our group of five stayed easily in view of each other with space no more than three feet between each person at any given time. Albarth ran lead behind the lion, Sundar after him, then Mona and me. We walked for what felt like hours, the muscles in my legs truly wearing on me when there was a commotion off to the north of our position. A loud whooping and screeched call of something before the noise abruptly came to an end made the hair on my neck stand on end.

—*The lion says that is why we must continue on as we have; so the little raiders don't catch us.*— Sundar explained through a whisper.

—*Little what?*— Albarth turned to look at us, the rustling of his leather against the grass suddenly almost deafening against the silence.

The lion perked up and turned his head north, stilling, and listening.

—*Stay very still.*— Sundar warned us all. —*We might have been made.*—

I took a slow, controlled breath in as deep as I could, and held it for a few seconds before letting it go so as to keep my beating heart from hammering too loudly.

Grass moved in the distance, slowly at first, then nothing came after that. Sundar's shoulders relaxed, —*I think we're good let's get moving again, but slower.*—

I nodded, and we moved forward when the grass shifted once more, on our northern side. Suddenly a large gazelle sprinted through the grass, the fur having a slightly green cast to it and the horns looking like long pieces of stiff grass curving up over the head, bolted between Monami and me.

Albarth's hand over her mouth helped to stifle her cry of surprise, but the swiftly moving grass told me there were more coming, and I wasn't going to stay and be impaled.

I motioned with my hand to move forward, then made a fist

and pulled it down twice to make it clear we needed to move quickly. Learning these hand and arm signals from Sundar had never been such a nice lesson to have learned before.

We began again, this time moving with a purpose that kept our pacing swift for some time.

The lion whirled to the right and bounded straight back toward me, a snarling visage of rage and death. I dipped to the left just in time to miss a small spear aimed at my heart, my shoulder numbing instantly from the impact. I dropped to a knee, turned slightly as the lion made its way past me.

The lion fell on the attacker with a snarling roar, great clawed paws thudded and slashed at something small that screamed and fought ferociously without victory.

—*Run!*— Sundar bellowed over the whisper chat. —*More come!*—

I stood, my legs pumping and stride lengthening as I pushed myself to catch up to my friends while they ran on.

More little creatures who looked like humanoid piglets with tiny spears the size of large arrows followed. But each speartip looked wickedly barbed and had an inky-black substance on them. The same substance on my shoulder armor gleamed in my peripheral vision—likely some kind of toxin.

Still, better to not let it touch my skin or a wound if I could help it. I pulled a large batch of the grass into my hand, careful to leave it clumped together thickly before wiping the majority of the gunk off my shoulder. It worked, for the most part, the deep green mixing with black and a soft breeze wafted the noxious scent my way, making my eyes water fiercely.

I sneezed once, twice, unable to fully catch my breath for a second, then I gasped and found I was on the ground with my left hand above my head, someone dragging me away as chakrams sawed down sections of grass behind us as we went.

"Move, move, *move!*" Albarth snarled as he darted into view with his rapier cutting more swathes of grass down, blood spraying into the air and oinking whoops filling the air.

"Get up Kyvir, we need you to get up so we can run,"

Mona's voice rang out against the drowsiness calling at my mind. I grasped at the Aether within my body and used a bar of it to circulate cool energy through my body, hoping to force my mind to fight the warm call of slumber.

Shivering slightly, I turned and stood moving on my own, if only slowly at first. "Thank god!" Sundar gasped audibly, a sigh of relief later, and she turned to swat a small pig-man aside. "We need to go!"

"Going!" I grunted and socked a scurrying piggy creature in the back of the head with the butt of my sword's hilt.

5 dmg to Piggmy Hunter

I rolled my eyes and ducked under a spear. My feet churned as projectiles slung in the air around me, missing narrowly as I dipped and rolled through the grass. A pounding of feet thumped along with us, the lion stormed along our path with us, his eyes forward and an injury on his left shoulder.

My shield flashed out and slapped one of the little things trying to jump onto the lion from my left, no damage notification coming as I batted it aside into the steadily growing grass that crowded and surrounded us.

"Coming to the edge of the grass!" Sundar roared back to us.

A soft light in front of us grew, the grass had grown taller than our heads by now. The lion started to slow down, falling a little behind, and I stepped aside to shove Mona forward.

"Hey!" Her complaint making me growl at her before she moved forward.

"We don't know what's ahead, and I'm not going to let them catch one of you!" My voice took on a harsher timbre than I meant. An arrow arced just over my head and narrowly missed a Piggmy that had attempted to gore Mona.

A dart of flame slammed into its face, and it cried out, slapping and slamming fists and palms into its head like a child throwing a tantrum. I slid my sword between the arms as I moved past and ran the edge across the throat as I lifted and tossed it back.

24 EXP

I ignored the other notifications coming from the fight and homed in on what was needed. The light had grown larger now, and we were on our way out of danger. I pushed my legs a little harder so that I could keep up with Mona and Sundar.

Breaking the line of the grass, my heart pounded faster in exhilaration—we'd made it through!

"Shit!" Sundar grabbed my armor and snatched me to the left of my exit, my momentum forcing her to gasp and cry out as she swung me bodily out of the way of a drop. She let me go, and I rolled onto the ground with little grace at all and watched as she turned and did the same thing with a slightly more cautious Albarth.

He went to say something to her, but she placed her big, meaty palm over his mouth and pulled him close against the line of her body as we waited with our backs against the grass. She looked to Mona and me where we panted, motioning for our silence as the sound of footfalls carried on toward us.

One of the piggmies had been smart and came through cautiously but didn't look left or right to see us until he was well outside the grass. By the time he did, I'd held up my hand and sent a small shard of ice spiraling into his eye. He howled in rage and anguish as the projectile gored his pupil, his cries of pain summoning the others who sprinted straight out of the grass into him with spears raised.

Their hurry saw them over the cliff, screeching and plummeting to their death as a dozen notifications of similar value flooded my sight.

Lvl 8 Piggmy Hunter died.
24 EXP.

312 EXP! I shrieked internally. "You guys get a ton of experience for that too?"

"That was convenient and lucky." Sundar sighed in relief, Albarth struggling in her arms. "Sorry, Al."

She moved her hand, and he spat. "Your hand smells and tastes like cat."

A growl behind him made him yelp, the lion limping over toward us from inside the tall grass. Sundar shoved Albarth toward the grass to get over to her newest friend, making concerned noises.

"You're hurt, we can heal you and then move on." She insisted, but the lion butted his head against her shoulder where she knelt down. "No, I'm not leaving you like this, you're coming with us."

The great cat hissed at her, but she just stood. "You can come with me willingly, and we can avoid more of those things in the grass, or I pick your ass up and *make* you come with me. Try to fight back."

The challenge wasn't lost on the lion, his ears flattened and teeth bared at the woman in front of him. She put her hands on her hips and just did the same at him with her own teeth, her eyes narrowed.

The cat finally relented when echoed calls of more whooping sounded in the distance, his tail sank, and he stood and marched off past us. He limped down a downgrade leading to a lower bit of rocky ground. With how low the sun was beginning to get in the sky, we decided that staying here with the cliff at our back as compared to leaving and trying to find safety out in the open plains would be a better idea.

We "slept" there until morning. Each of us took shifts to watch for something that could eat us while the lion healed and slumbered next to Sundar.

My shift was uneventful, though I did sit and wonder what it would have been like to taste that blood while I made dye from the grass that I had collected. Though those three bottles of grass green dye did little to suppress my revulsion at myself. The thought of the blood making me salivate a little, my stomach churning at the idea of it. Why was I being so weird right now? It was an ability. It wasn't a way of living. Right? Then I caught myself wondering if the piggmy blood would have tasted like bacon and shut the whole train of thought down.

Other than feeling exceptionally bad about myself wanting

to experiment with my ability, which was odd in and of itself, Albarth replaced me with a nod and I set an alarm to wake up at dawn.

Laying down on the grass was easy enough, made better by watching the half-moon and stars for a moment before I fell asleep, I marveled at both how realistic the stars looked above us. How they seemed to mirror our own back home and how I almost preferred this sky.

CHAPTER FOUR

SETH

I woke up slightly before my alarm when Mona grasped my sword and pulled it from the sheath with a loud hiss.

"What're you doing?" My bleary eyes noted the dawn beginning to rise behind her as I glared about wondering what could be going on. I realized that it was her, and let go of her wrist, though that didn't mean I wasn't still concerned.

"Checking your weapon's durability, it looks like it will need sharpening." She pulled out a small stone and poured water onto it before running the cutting edge of my sword over it at an angle. She grunted at the sound that it made, adjusted the angle, and began again, this time a little more at ease with it.

"Thanks, Mo." I sat up with her as she worked and watched the sunrise in companionable silence.

"So, Thea seems nice." Mona checked the cutting edge by holding it up to the light and inspecting it, finding some flaw to work out, and beginning again.

"She's been very helpful, yeah." I shrugged it off.

"You seem pretty attached." I glanced at her, but she was very carefully looking away.

"I mean, she has been teaching me how to fight, acting as a guide for us, and she even tried to help me out with some personal issues." I shook my head, finding the grass suddenly very interesting. "She's a good friend."

"She's an NPC, Kyvir." Mona offered my weapon to me by the hilt and took out her chakrams, working on them too. "Data made by someone at a computer. Or by an AI. She's not real." Her whetstone scraped a bit harder as she growled and said, "I am. You should come to me with your problems."

"We weren't exactly seeing eye to eye at the time, Mo." I chuckled, she glared at me, and I rolled my eyes. "So, I'm supposed to come to you when I'm not sure how to feel about you? When I'm not sure if the feelings I have for you are because I feel that way or because you are accidentally using your Allure on me?"

"I told you I didn't know." Her furred cheeks reddened again, and she scraped her weapon a little faster. "And besides, you said that you weren't sure what you were thinking, why *not* just come talk to me? We've always come to each other with our problems, what makes this so different?"

"The fact that it's you, Mona." I sighed, the scraping stopped, and she stared at me in confusion. "I came to you and said what I said, asked if you wanted more, and you couldn't even be bothered to give me a straight answer. You said it was an idiotic idea that someone must have put into my head—I know not in so many words—but still, you said it."

I held a hand up to stop her from interrupting, "Our whole lives, you and I have always had each others' backs. When your dad left, I was there for you. I fought for you to help you with your depression because I cared about you. When my parents were gone for weeks and months at a time, you kept me from being lonely. Taking me into your family without so much as even a thought, Mona—I love you. I will always love you. But having to be that vulnerable with the one person in the world I thought I could always depend on to shoot it straight with me, and have them call what I was thinking and feeling idiotic was painful."

She touched my arm, hurt in her eyes. "Seth, I'm so sorry." She pulled at my arm to make me look at her again. "You weren't wrong to come to me, I could have handled it better too… I just didn't know how. I'm sorry."

"And you know what?" I shook my head, "I was a real asshole about it, too. To you. To Sunny and Al. Acting like those assholes who used to bully you in school when you didn't want to date them—I was no fucking better."

"Don't you dare compare yourself to them!" Mona spat, her fist cocked and ready to fly at my head. "You know you're nothing like them, and I should beat you for that!"

"Hit me, I deserve it." I goaded her, lifting my chin to give her the perfect target. "Do it to me like you had to learn to do it for yourself. Knock the stupid out of me."

She rolled her eyes and laughed. "I'd break my hand before I got it all out."

"God gave you two, girl." Sundar sat up and winked at us. "I think Kyvir had a point, though, right?"

I nodded, giving her a thumb up. "My point is that right now, there's more to worry about than my stupid wounded pride and petty distrust—but *you* never have to worry about me not coming to you as a friend. You and I are always there for each other, Mo. We're best friends, siblings even, you don't ever have to worry about Thea taking your place as my best friend."

Mona stared at me for a moment longer then, smiled her same soft, knowing smile. "Okay."

"Glad that mess is sorted out," Albarth grumbled groggily, "I know that we are all partially at fault, but as apologies typically mean penitence, I will not be giving one."

Sundar, Mona, and I all glanced from him to each other before Mona snickered. "Typical Al."

"Yes, haha, typical me—can we go?" He rolled his eyes before he stood and shook himself out, eyeing the still slumbering lion. "Are we going to be bringing the king of the grassy jungle with us?"

"Sundar? What do you think?" I asked with my eyebrows raised.

"I think it's his choice." The lion arched his back and shook himself out, his display much more gratifying than Al's, then looked at Sundar and then us.

She stepped closer to him and sat down, butting her head up against his, his tongue lolling out of his mouth, as if he were panting. She scratched his ear, then stood and turned toward us. "He likes me, but this is his territory. He can't leave it undefended."

We all waved to him as he turned and sauntered away, circling the cliffside and padding back up it.

"Sorry about your breakup, dear." Albarth winked grotesquely at the orc who just rolled her eyes at him. "Ugh, I'm learning from you. Come, let's go."

We packed up, really just picking up some of the things from our persons that would have made sleeping on the ground harder.

I grabbed my shield, tied it to my hip with a leather cord so that I could carry it more easily, and it was more accessible. I could put it in my inventory, but that would require precious seconds, and I couldn't justify that as the tank.

I made sure that my sword was at full durability, and my shield was good despite the exposure to my ice. My glaive set in the quick slot for my back. I glanced over at Mona, her own prep for the rest of our journey settled and whispered, "Thanks for the assist, Mo."

She turned and grinned at me. "Any time, Ky."

We moved on from there, the sky a cloudy gray that made me think of rain. "Think we should jog?"

"I'm good with a little morning run, hoo-ah!" Sundar's tusks flashed at all of us.

"Why are we going to jog?" Mona seemed skeptical about it, to say the least. She knew how much I hated to run.

"Because I smell rain." I glanced pointedly at the sky, and she hung her head.

"Okay, let's go." Sundar jogged off first at a brisk pace, the rest of us joining her.

"I'll take point, keep your eyes up and on the horizon," I ordered, making my way to the front of the group. "Our normal diamond formation is enough for this portion of our travel."

The birds in the sky no longer seemed to want to trouble us as we made our way through the softly sloping hills as the clouds continued to churn overhead. Winds of almost gale force whipped at our clothes and threatened to topple us over as we pressed on.

Our sure progress slowed after a couple hours taking breaks when we were tired of jogging just to walk, but we kept on moving. We had a marker placed on the map by the guild to help guide us, but it was pretty general. Mainly just showed up in the corner of the map as a green marker.

Travel grew almost treacherous when sparks of lightning in the clouds above us sparked, and all the world faded to dyed grey and bleak. Wind howled past my ears annoyingly, moaning in the distance before roaring towards like an angry dragon in some of the games we had played before.

"If we die in this, we're screwed!" Albarth screamed over the wind. He motioned toward where we headed, nothing in the distance but more open areas. "We have to move forward and hope for the best! The storm should keep the local wildlife at bay, hopefully."

Twenty minutes after that droplets of water flecked against my cheek, the wind carrying some of them aside. Ten more and the downpour came. A deluge of water that seemed almost like some kind of tropical storm that threatened to devour anything in the plains that wasn't growing from the ground itself. It was no wonder no one built here, no one dared.

We pressed forward again, the water stinging our skin so much it was a miracle that I hadn't taken any damage.

"There's something in the distance!" Mona shrieked, her forearm up to protect her eyes and open mouth. I risked a slight peek under my own forearm and found a growing mass far in the distance that appeared to grow up into the clouds and disappear in the rain but stretched for miles.

We moved on, the water at our feet rushing downhill toward the center of the plain. We tried to steer clear of it, but there was a divot where I planted my foot, and my ankle rolled, toppling me over and sending me down toward the foot of the hill in a small tide of muddy water.

I sputtered and cursed wildly as the water continued to drag me, then stopped as something grabbed my armor and tugged it upward. My head whipped up in time to see Mona held by Sundar and Albarth. Her hands stretched out toward me, and her teeth clenched tightly in a grimace as she motioned me toward her, using my armor to pull me up in small increments.

Mona breathed heavily, her panting forcing her chest to rise and fall quickly, and I couldn't understand why until I looked back and found a gaping sinkhole in the ground behind me.

I clawed and scrabbled with my legs and hands, dirt crusting my fingers as I fought for my life. I could die here and be fine but having to earn all the experience I had gained, then earn it all again just to be back where I was could not happen without a fight.

With Monami's help, I reached a safer point, panting myself, and climbed to my feet to find Monami had passed out with a severe nosebleed.

"What happened?" I rushed toward her and Sundar slapped her hand onto my wet armor to stop me stepping in the same divot.

"I think she ran out of Aether. We need to get somewhere safer—now." She motioned with her head, and Albarth tugged on my right to lead me away. "More of those sinkholes are opening up all over the place!"

Our way forward grew spottier and spottier as more and more sinkholes dotted the landscape moving east. We dodged the ones we saw, one of them opening up and almost swallowing Albarth into it immediately. If it hadn't been for Sundar and I both snagging him by his shoulder armor, he would have fallen in and had to catch up with us in another couple days in-game, and that would be really shitty on his own.

We tread more cautiously, the storm intensifying above us. Crashing thunder made me jump, and vivid lightning slammed toward the ground in the distance seconds before another scorched the air next to me, some of the splitting arcs sizzling my armor.

3 lightning dmg taken.

The lightning tunneled into the sinkhole and lit it up like the day-lit sky and what I saw made my heart lurch and my steps less careful.

"Run!" I ordered, my feet working against the mud on the ground. "Run!"

Albarth almost turned on me, but I pushed him forward and put a hand on Sundar's broad back, Mona still in her grasp. "The hell are you on about?"

"Bugs!" I cried as the first of more than a dozen centipedes as long as I was crested the lip of the sinkhole in a wave of chittering frenzy.

Our legs carried us faster, water splattering the back of my legs and armor in our hurry to be away from the beasts who stormed the ground behind us. Their chitinous black exoskeletons reflected the lightning in the sky until another blast of the elemental energy speared the ground in the middle of seven of them, charring them and scattering the others.

"There!" Sundar pointed at something that moved along the ground next to us, traveling quickly, it looked like a cloud of black. "Get to them!"

I doubted her thoughts as the creatures looked like large, wild buffalo, but she still sprinted toward them. We followed as swiftly as our feet would carry us, and chittering greeted my ears.

I didn't look back; I didn't need to—I knew one of the

centipedes followed closely enough for its breath to lick at my heels. I reached back with my left hand and willed my Aether to freeze it in place.

An unearthly squealing shriek pierced my ears as I moved away, two of my Aether bars eaten away. Another of them crossed before me and I jumped as high as I could, stepping onto its back and hopping off onto the other side. By now, the creatures we ran toward had begun to realize the danger that approached and ran off away from us.

"Please help!" Sundar shouted loudly, the wind pulling her voice away from us. Two of the beasts slowed and fell out of formation to trot that way, just not so quickly as the others. "Hop onto their backs."

Sundar's orders surprised me, but I was a little confused as to how we could. Being as close as we had come now, they were massive and towered over us, their shoulders almost as tall as Sundar herself.

Their matted fur or wool lay thick on their hides, great horns on their heads jutted out like a bull's would. Sundar threw Mona up onto the shaggy beast's shoulder like a sack of potatoes and began to climb up it herself. Once she was on, she clicked her tongue and the animal surged forward at a gallop like a horse.

Albarth had already leapt up onto the other creature's back. He turned and held a hand out to help me do the same, my feet flailing as I clambered up his back. Albarth *hupped* loudly, and the trotting beast kept plodding along.

He kicked, and the thing still wouldn't listen, so I clicked my tongue twice and patted his side gently. The beast surged forward, and angry chittering filled the air behind us.

They galloped northeast for a time, then Sundar convinced them we were finally safe and told us that they wouldn't take us East. She thanked them for us, their great tongues sliming her face affectionately before they turned and trotted away from us.

"They said that we're about a couple hours away from the place where they cannot go." I frowned at her cryptic message from the two animals, but she shrugged. "They said that many armored people come from there, but none of their kind dares travel farther into that place. Says that flying creatures eat them there."

"There's no way that those birds could kill them outside of being grouped together," Mona said, then groaned as she came to. "I miss much?"

"We almost got eaten," I offered helpfully. She blinked and looked around, likely noting we were safe. She frowned. "It's getting late in real-time, let's get to the new place and call it a night."

I nodded, the others agreed as well, and we were off once more.

CHAPTER FIVE

MONA

Clouds parted slightly in the eastern sky, filtering light shimmering with a rainbow over a squat, walled city built into the mountain that we had observed in the distance on our way here.

"That has to be it," I muttered as I scanned the wall, wishing I had Kyvir's ability to see auras for the dozenth time.

Other than the three evenly spaced towers, the wall was the tallest structure toward the outside of the city, and even toward the well-protected rear of the city, the tallest building appears to just barely come above the wall. It was more difficult to make out the details from here, but it was a fine-looking city.

"Must be." Kyvir strolled over to me and grinned. "You going to lean a little more into the normal style of play you have?"

I frowned. "What do you mean?"

"Well, you're normally all for role-playing, and you do have the most presence of all of us. If anyone is going to talk us into the city, it'll likely be you."

"I agree." Albarth grinned at me and nodded his head. "It would be nice to have a little more normalcy in light of what the two of you are keeping from us. Whatever it may be."

I turned to Sundar in the hopes that she would stop this foolishness, but her grin just solidified it. I mean, I love to role-play, but things were heavy right now.

Their gazes pleaded with my heart, and finally, I growled, then said, "Fine. But only if it's necessary. Let's go."

We moved down the hill at a trot, the rain having quelled hours past, tired and soaked as we were, there were new things to see that drove us on.

It had been hard to make out at the time due to it being covered with grass, but a small wall protected the outermost portion of the city, protecting the people and their livelihoods. Crops of varying types grew and prospered inside the lower wall; I could imagine that this wall was a preliminary defense, but it likely stopped the majority of the wind as well.

The people in the fields working in the evening sun, likely finishing up their work, stopped and stared a moment at us, some human and dwarven faces poking out of the crops, a tanner stopped and watched after admiring her work. Children playing in the fields were called in for supper rather loudly. Such an intricate design on the programmers' parts. I had to give these people their props. This was an amazing setting.

We carried on forward so as not to cause too much of a fuss. Past the farms and gentle hills grew a wall so immense it was like it had been pulled from the earth and formed by a giant.

Upon closer inspection, it looked to be made from finely hewn stone stacked and mortared together so the seams were almost invisible, and it had to stand more than a hundred feet tall. More than ten times larger than the wall that had been around the farmlands.

It was another twenty minutes of walking before we came close enough to the gate to see the guards in the towers had weapons trained on us.

—*Seems a mounted platoon is en route to us. Who wants lead?*—

Kyvir's whisper brought my attention from the walls until I caught sight of the movement at the gate. Sure enough, figures rode toward us on the backs of large goats, their horns encased in black metal as if to protect them.

I stepped up to the fore, Kyvir, and Sundar closer to me as Albarth stood behind them.

The riders all had beards, their armor red with a claw emblazoned upon their chest pieces and shields, and beady black eyes pierced us from within their red helms.

"Halt!" The first of them ordered as the rest of them surrounded us. His body rigid where he was seated, the spear in his hand pointed directly at my throat. "Who be you? What be yer business in Belgonna's Hold?"

"We are a group of weary wanderers from Iradellum," I began, my arms spreading to show I held no weapons, though I adopted a more friendly tone. "We have one among us in need of his magic being awakened, and we seek to gain strength for the war effort far from here. We mean this fine city no ill will."

The leader looked to his men before standing in his saddle. "What magic would that be?"

"Summoning magic," Kyvir answered, his gaze on the smaller man in the saddle. "I was told I need to come and speak to the Crimson Queen?"

The riders muttered to themselves for a moment before the leader cracked his spear against the right horn of his mount. The goat bleated loudly and dug a hoof into the ground. The others quieted swiftly, and he slid out of his saddle. He came to about dwarf height, and as he took his helmet off, things were confirmed.

These were, in fact, dwarves. Swarthy looking and clad in some of the finest armor I had yet to see in the game so far, I had to appreciate the craftsmanship. I'd definitely learn something here if I could.

"What the Crimson Queen does with her guests is her business, but ye'll not be seein' her this eve." He whistled twice, two sharp and short blasts, and his men fell into formation around us. "I will see word sent to her that ye have come an' she can decide when to receive ye. I will need to see yer guild pages if ye would be so kind?"

I was the first to show mine, he nodded and inspected the others, eying Kyvir a moment longer oddly, then shrugged. "We will see what the gate captain thinks. Onward march, lads."

The goats' clip was easy for us to keep up with, and we made it to the gates soon enough. Rather than doing anything to get someones' attention himself, the dwarven leader tapped his mount, who unceremoniously stepped back twice and charged the door. The resounding, crashing knock echoed, and a red helmet appeared over the gate.

"What's the password?"

The dwarf on the goat's head tilted back, taking in his breath and shouting, "Ye open this bloody door afore I come up there an beat ye with yer own helmet an' drink yer mams swill beer, Gildrir, ye idjit lad!"

The helmet stayed there a moment longer. "That'll do it." Then disappeared over the edge.

A moment later, several loud grunts came from the other side of the gate. More than twenty feet tall and more than fifteen feet wide, thirty feet wide for the both of them, and it moved slowly, inch by inch.

It took ten minutes for them to open the door wide enough for the mounts and us to get through one at a time. The leader went through, then three of the riders and the others waited for us to pass through before joining us.

The four mounted dwarves who entered last turned about and used their mounts to close the door more swiftly. Once the door closed fully, the dwarves dismounted and stood near us. Their weapons drawn, but not actively pointing at us. Which was nice.

The leader spoke to another dwarf inside a small hut who seemed to take every word he spoke very seriously. He nodded, his beard waving back and forth and motioned toward all of us.

The goat leader came back out of the hut and motioned us

forward toward him. "I'll be taking you to the inn in the center of the village. We will send a missive to the Queen so that you might speak with her upon her earliest convenience."

"Thank you." I bowed my head for a second. "If I could ask for it, what is your name?"

"Oh, sorry, 'bout tha'." The dwarf grunted and shook his head. "My name be Blothl, and I be leader o' the Herd this evenin'. Follow me."

He turned and marched himself off toward the center of the city, the main roadway itself. All of the buildings close to the wall appeared to be stout and made of a similar stony composition of the wall. The grey stones smaller than the ones outside, but no less expertly crafted.

"So, Blothl, what's the story of this city?" I asked, my friends snickering at my expense, I ignored them and hoped that the man would tell me something. "And what inn will we be staying at?"

"The Tilted Keg, be a meadery an' inn in the square o' the city." He smiled back at us. "A wanderer wants to hear a tale? I do nae know much o' yer ilk, but word from where you hail casts a pall on yer kind. Impatient and petulant at times. Sure ye wanna be wastin' yer time on tales?"

I grinned. "We try not to let what other wanderers do affect us. And we *love* a good tale. Possibly over a pint?"

He stopped and whirled on me, a big grin on his face, splitting his dark beard nearly in half. "Ye said the magic word, lass. Aye, then a tale ye'll have. Come along."

It took us little more than fifteen minutes of purposeful walking to reach what had to be the center square of the city. This portion of Belgonna's Hold had buildings made of a mixture of wood and stone. And in the center of the large circular square stood a large fountain of water. The pool had to be about sixty feet in diameter and the fountain more than forty feet tall. A dragon's arm clutching an egg, all of it cast in gold and water ran down the top of the egg, down the arm into the water.

"That there be a portion o' the tale, but it requires some time to tell the whole o' the history o' our fine city, patience please." He held up a hand to stop my excited questions from bursting forth and halting his progress. I groaned, and it only made him smile more. Glancing at the others, I knew they could tell I was intrigued and it was only going to get worse when I just *knew* the story here would get so much better. "Let's get ye settled first."

Who designs a game where NPCs aren't throwing themselves and their stories at you right off the bat? I rolled my eyes and followed the little man and my friends onward.

He led us around the right side of the fountain where children chased each other in the dusk light, laughing and playing. Giggling and screeching happily as they struggled with each other. Reminded me of the times that Seth and I had gone to the water park and splashed each other incessantly on the sides of the pools there. Our parents had thrown us in the pool to make us stop splashing innocent bystanders.

The building he led us into was large, brightly lit, and busy. The people inside were a raucous sort, their noise filtering out into the square and reaching my ears even thirty feet away.

The bottom half of the building seemed to be the stone half, likely due to foundational integrity and the heat of the kitchen hearth, and the top half was made of wood. The sign on the wall between the two windows showed a large dwarven man lifting a keg and pouring it sloppily into large tankards with a grin.

Inside, humans, dwarves, some gnomish folk, and the occasional halfling looked to be enjoying lively music, games of chance, food, and drink with nary a care. Quite a few of the dwarves looked up to stare angrily at Sundar, but since Blothl was with us, they seemed content to mean mug us from where they sat.

Blothl stepped up to the bar, slapped his hand against the thick wood four times, then waited patiently.

"What's with the stares?" Sundar leaned down to the dwarf

and whispered.

"They hate orcs, dwarven thing really." Blothl shrugged. "Be in our history a bit, see—they don't know ye be a wanderer, so they hate ye. That may or may not go away if they find out what ye are. Cause what do we dwarves hate more than orcs? Fuckin' *demons*."

He hocked a big loogy in his throat and spat on the floor. Several other dwarves who were close to us followed suit enthusiastically.

"Warding off evil?" Albarth raised an eyebrow at the other man, and Blothl simply nodded once. He saw our quizzical stares, and he sighed. "I have very superstitious relatives who do the same sometimes."

"Smart folk," Blothl muttered, then looked to us. "Ye wanna learn now?"

I nodded, but the others looked at the clock. It was nearing one in the morning in real-time.

"How can I help you lot?" A chipper voice greeted from behind our dwarven guide. She was a smart-looking woman, her clothes pressed, and her apron, while dirty, was well cared for. Her dwarven features reminded me vaguely of the dwarf on the wall out front.

"How many rooms have ye available?" Blothl asked politely with a nod of his head to the woman.

Her fingers tapped the bar a few times before she stroked her soft red beard. It was shorter and parted at her chin with bows holding the two small braids firmly. It looked very soft, and I was curious as to why she had one. Most of the dwarven women in games I played didn't have them, though there were some bits of lore where they sported beards themselves.

"I have seven rooms available, two to a room, though." Her hand dipped down behind the bar and pulled a mug out. "Drinks and food?"

I checked and saw that we were nearly at a starved debuff. "We should eat before we go to sleep. How much is it for a few days?"

"Friends of the Herd?" She eyed Blothl, his eyes falling on us, then returning to hers with a brief wink. "Five silver a room for three days. A silver a room for meals. Drink is by tab, paid nightly."

I glanced at the others, and they seemed to find that agreeable. Kyvir paid the fee for the lot as he had the most coin, and we sat down with Blothl. He winked at me.

His easy mannerisms and mischievousness reminded me of some of the other NPCs we had come across so far. They *were* so lifelike.

He cleared his throat and nodded to the waiting woman who blinked at me. "Uh, yes, a round of your, uhm…"

I couldn't decide on what to drink, and Blothl seemed to take pity on me as he tapped the bar with his finger. "Start 'er cheap—I owe the lot a story o' our fair city, Nildy."

"Cheap beer it is." The woman, Nildy it seemed, turned with two mugs and deftly began to fill them until all five of us had a frothing mug of darker liquid before us.

I started to speak, but Nildy placed a surprisingly soft hand on my forearm. "The first drink is always drunk before any sort of tellin' dear. Let him drink his beer in peace first."

I closed my mouth and looked to Blothl, his bushy eyebrows pressed toward his hair, and he nodded once to us all. He lifted his mug in a toast, and we mirrored the motion before he knocked it back, pouring the bitter liquid into his gullet.

He came back with a sigh of relief and pleasure before clapping the bottom of the mug on the bar for a refill. "Thank ye, lass."

He motioned to a table that had just emptied and motioned to Nildy that we would be moving tables and to bring food. She nodded with a smile and walked off after refilling his mug.

"Ah, to the tellin' then." He stared at all of us as we came to the table and stood. "Sit, sit! This be no place to stand on ceremony."

We all chuckled, and he sat down at a corner so we could all see him. Sundar procured another chair from a nearby table that had emptied thanks to our presence and sat with bated breath.

Blothl took out a pipe, long and slightly curved along the stem, before packing it lightly with a small bit of herbs. He tapped his body for a light when Albarth took out his rapier and used his magic to set it ablaze. Chairs scraped across the floor, and harsh words came our way, but when they realized he wouldn't be stabbing anyone, they came back. Nildy glared at him and shook her head.

We got the message.

"Thank ye, lad." Blothl grinned, holding the pipe in his teeth as he clapped. "Eons ago, me people carved their homes out o' the bones o' the Fire Brand Mountains, this range of stony crags and cliffs above us. Dwarves o' all ages come to prove they could mine, mason an' settle above the ground so that more resources could be spread from our ancestral homes under the earth. For a time, we knew peace an' prosperity the likes o' which no dwarf ever had a right to know, as we can be a stubborn lot."

He took another deep draft of his drink and stared ahead of him as if gazing on the time itself. "After a time, other races began to appear to the dwarves, some meaning to aid like the gnomes and halflings. Others, like the orcs, meanin' to intimidate and take from us. This was after our homes under the mountains had been besieged by great, terrible beasts. Forced us above ground for good, then, but the orcs? They were almost as bad.

"After several small-scale skirmishes with orcish outriders, my people built the walls that you see now. For a short time after that, peace returned. Finally, a siege by orcs leadin' goblins in droves o' thousands came, the orcs meanin' to take our people and do what they would with our lands, mines, and creations. More than a week, our forces held the line, and still, they came at us for little reason in our minds. Our king slain in battle, our men exhausted and starvin—all looked lost."

He finished his drink, scowling bitterly and glancing at me, I waved a hand as he called Nildy over to order more beer, but I held up a hand. "Something better for him, please." She smiled and rushed away. "Please, Blothl, continue."

He grinned and returned to his telling, "Me ancestors had prepared for one final assault as a way to try an' get them to run when they began to batter our wall with fell magic. No matter how much we tried to beat them off our land, they were goin' to win."

Nildy returned with a lighter drink that Blothl raised to me and drank from, moaning once in delight. "Thank ye, lass. Now, all looked lost until a black cloud speared across the sky. Everyone looked above, expecting to see some sort o' omen from the gods that this was to be the way o' things now. Me ancestors' faces fell when a hulking dragon dove from the clouds toward the ground. Scales o' blood barely returned a glimmer o' light as she fell like a meteor o' rage and snarlin' hatred, her wings flared, and she breathed hellfire on the orcs heads. She landed and crushed them, their mightiest warriors culled in her first pass, eaten by flames.

"Smoke clouded the sky and nearly blotted out the sun, the stink o' cinder and ashen flesh was said to have been so thick that you could almost taste burnt orc in the air. So merciless had her slaughter been, that my ancestors thought they were next, but she was nowhere to be seen. Then the sound of large wings and a gust o' air reached the onlookers mannin' the wall, the billowin' smoke clearin' as her blood-soaked head appeared over the wall. She called for their leader, as she had an urgent matter she needed to discuss with them. When none came forward, she asked for the elders o' the city, those most trusted and wise, to come forth and listen to her."

Oh no, was she going to devour them? I found myself gripping my seat and leaning forward, hanging off his every word. Our food arrived, and he took a bite, motioning that we should do the same. I was so interested in the story that I could barely taste the food, minced pie, or whatever it was. I wished that my dad could hear this. And how that sudden wish left me feeling so hollow.

He spoke on, a slight smile on his lips, "When they gathered, knees quakin' from hunger and fatigue, she asked one question, 'Have you need o' a protector?' The dwarves were gobsmacked. They listened to her as she explained that she were lookin' for a safe place to raise her clutch, away from the dragon wars that had yet still been in their prime, and she felt this place would be safe for them. For exchange o' her aiding in their protection, the dwarves could provide gold and well-made creations as nesting materials for her clutch. After some deliberation, the deal was struck, and she came to be a part o' our people. Years turned into decades. Decades into centuries and the dragon wars had finally ended with a tentative truce. But rather than leave, Belgonna stayed.

"The dwarves had come to trust her wise and intelligent council, and she had come to love me ancestors in her own way. While she did not know much in the way o' leadership, she knew that without a strong hand to guide them, any people would fall to their foes. Together with a council o' the eleven clan chiefs, and a representative of the non-dwarves, she has led this keep since."

"But what of the egg in the center of the city?" I blurted, my hand flying to my mouth like I was a child who had said something terribly out of turn. That hollowness began to build as thoughts of all the things that I had missed in life, thanks to someone not being there.

Blothl's generally jovial face fell, his shoulder slumping as he took a sip of his drink. "That be the Lost One. See, Belgonna had her clutch, and in that clutch were three eggs. A fine male was born, a warrior if I ever see'd one. And a female with an innate talent for magic that would put any studied magician to shame. But the last egg... never hatched."

My eyes watered at the tale. "Why?"

He shook his head, "No one knows. Belgonna was inconsolable for more'n a decade after that. Until a wee lad came to her, abandoned and frightened. No home o' his own. She decreed that her still egg be taken, bathed in gold, and put where everyone could see it. Then, my ancestors were to build an orphanage to house the lost and unwanted children."

My breath faltered in my throat, and I felt a hand on my shoulder, Kyvir's concern evident as his eyebrows raised warily.

"Yer question be plain on yer face, lass," Nildy spoke, making me jump. I turned to see her soft gaze resting on me. She put her hand on my shoulder and motioned to all of the people in the building. "The claw is her hand lifting us from our sorrows, and the egg is a reminder that we are all her children."

Tears fell from my eyes slowly. "That's so beautiful." A groping moroseness clawed at my heart, memories of not having my dad. Even though I had been an adult when he had... was no longer there. It still hurt knowing that he could have been there to see me doing things that he had always wanted for me. Graduating college. Doing something with myself. Being there for my mother, me and Seth.

"Me apologies for makin' ye cry, lass. An after ye bought me booze, too." Blothl ran his hand through his beard and gave it a tug worriedly. "Right improper, that."

"No!" I sniffed and wiped my eyes with the heel of my hand. "Your story was so beautiful I couldn't stop listening. Thank you so much!"

"Oh?" He looked genuinely shocked. "It's just a history, lass. Nothin' to be worked up over."

"It was a well-told history." Kyvir smiled charmingly. "You could be a storyteller for how well you do it."

"Don't fill his head with shite." Nildy snorted. "Me friend's head be harder than his goat's!"

We all laughed at that, Blothl swatting at her with a spat curse. "Well, I can tell that the lot o' ye be tired. If ye be needin' anythin' talk to Nildy, and she can send for me. Aye? Ye folk been kind. Don't do nothin' to get in trouble an' we'll be square, aye?"

We nodded, and I slipped him a silver coin for his time. He

winked at me once more and turned to whistle himself out of the building.

Sundar footed the bill for the drinks and food, then we decided to head off to bed and log out. I stopped before I was fully up the stairs and called out to Nildy, her face tilted up to me. "Hey, if we get any kind of word or anything, could you slip a note under our doors? We might be gone tomorrow."

Her beard moved as she nodded, and I smiled at her. Sundar and I would be bunking together, as things were still a little awkward between Kyvir and I. Both of us ladies taking a bed in the sparse rooms, though hers just barely allowed her to rest on it. Her legs from the calves down hung off the edge of it like watching an adult try to play in a child's room.

I laughed with her, and we logged out.

———

I came to in my portal and glanced out into the room. It wasn't austere like Seth's; I had decorated mine with posters and paintings. But that was mainly due to the fact that this was the guest house and also my living room. The lights had turned on thanks to the timer that I had set, and a post-it note had been stuck to the glass of my portal.

—Come have some food when you finish.

Mom.

I sighed and opened the door, toweling off before grabbing the sweats and sweatshirt I'd wear to bed tonight. I pulled them on before stepping into a pair of old tennis shoes. I stepped out the door into the warm night air and walked the fifty yards to the main house.

Three stories tall, white with gray trim on the windows, the house looked like a cookie-cutter home for the neighborhood. The only difference from our house to the others was the fir trees we had planted and nurtured there when I was five. People hated how different it made things look, but we were way too wealthy for the homeowner's association to try and mess with us.

I pressed my code into the back door, then my middle finger against a dimly flashing light so it could scan my fingerprint as well, to be safe. The security update had been installed after my father's leaving. Disappearance. My heart pounded in my chest as I fought to truly understand and decide what had happened to my father after these last few years. I hadn't given it much thought before, in anger and denial, but now I wondered if he had left of his own accord. I perished the thought from my mind with a violent shake of my head and focused on just getting into the house.

Mom had gone a bit overboard but as the only daughter of a billionaire professional football player-turned-sports-analyst-tv personality with a beloved granddaughter in the house to protect, you have the money to throw at a problem you think you have. She liked to live in this neighborhood because people minded their own business and didn't hound her about grandad, but I tried to live on my own money. Grandad and my dad had loved each other, and both men believed in working to achieve things for yourself.

That work ethic had seen me through school on exemplary grades, graduating with honors and as valedictorian of my class. Scholarships and grant recruiters stomping up my driveway months leading up to graduation trying to get me into Ivy League schools for next to no tuition out of pocket. I had gone through two years of classes just to get my general education out of the way. I'd had plans to follow in my dad's footsteps and take up game design.

We'd spent hours on the weekends together gaming and discussing plots and quests and what he liked and didn't like as compared to my favorites and most hated aspects of some games. He had cultivated my love of gaming since I had been old enough to hold a controller. All the classic systems and games at my fingertips, and his relentless enthusiasm for a well-crafted story.

If I was being honest with myself—I got that from him.

I looked on the island in the kitchen and saw a foil-wrapped plate with a note from mom saying she loved me and that she looked forward to dinner tomorrow with our little family.

I rolled my eyes and got a notification on my phone from the others that they had started a group video and booked it back out to my place.

The least they could have done was wait for everyone to get a shower!

I slid through my door into the living room and the door locked behind me. I pulled up my laptop and projector, sliding the video chat onto the wall where the others already waited.

"Finally!" Alexander sighed tiredly and ran a hand through his long hair, his dark skin shining slightly as though he had just showered himself. "This silly wanker refuses to speak without you; will you please tell us what's going on?"

His intense brown eyes stared into the screen, and his tank top was a little distracting over his muscular frame. "Well?"

"Come on, Alex—she just got here." Sondra huffed as she came onto the screen with a smile, her tanned skin crinkling around her storm-grey eyes. "We should be ganging up on Seth."

"Why me?" Seth groaned comically. His own multicolored hair wet from a swift shower, which was almost unheard of.

"Because you're you!" I teased, and the others chuckled. "Before we get down to business, how's that hand I recommended to you working out, Sondra?"

She held up her left hand, and her smile turned into a grin. "I love it! It works almost better than the hand I lost in the jungle. The leg is getting there, but the VA is a little slow on getting people better equipment if they have something usable."

"You know, I still have some pull with a friend I had from getting my degree." She arched an eyebrow at me as I spoke. "Synthetic Kinesiology and Advanced Robotic Synapse Sciences was a very competitive degree program, and he's already working on his doctorate. Guy's a genius, and I was really lucky he took me under his wing and helped me a lot. He's all about helping people who fought in that farce of a war."

"He also tried to hit on you a lot," Seth said, then growled, and I shot him a withering glare. He really had never liked the guy.

"Can you blame him?" Sondra rolled her eyes. "I'd hit on her myself if I wasn't a good ten years older than her."

"Age is only a mental state," I teased her, and she chortled as both Al and Seth groaned. "He was young and stupid, he has an awesome fiancée now, and has really grown in the two years since I've seen him."

"People don't change." Alex grunted, and Seth nodded at him. "I'm assuming you will be talking to this gentleman with or without Sondra's consent, so we can skip all the goodie-goodie shite and get to brass tacks—what the devil is going on here?"

I glanced into the camera at Seth, and he began things. "Here's my theory, and I have evidence, so don't interrupt me, okay?"

I nodded, and the other two looked exasperated, but they assented so he would begin.

"The game is somehow affecting real life," Seth began, causing Sondra and Alex both to almost bust a gut laughing at him. "I should have expected this."

"Of course, you sodding should have!" Alex grabbed his stomach as if in pain. "You die in the game, you die in real life. Wasn't there some kind of movie about that? Seriously, mate—stop taking the pi—"

"Al—shut up." I snarled; my fists curled into balls in my lap as I stared at him. "You wanted to know what was going on? We're telling you. Shut up so he can finish. Sonny? You too."

"Yes, ma'am." The older woman's smile cleared instantly into a blank mask that she must have collected from her time in the armed forces.

"As I was saying, *we* think that the game is affecting the real world," Seth corrected himself and motioned toward me. "Just after playing the game, I began to be able to see auras like my character can. They were faint at first, Mona's and this guy at Bill's diner, too, that same night. The dark figures attacking hospitals, parks, and stuff? Seems like a play for demons."

"Apparently, I can use my Allure ability outside of the game as well, which had been affecting Seth too." I shook my head, still wondering if I hadn't gone crazy alongside him. "And then I found out that my mom had cancer."

"No, Mo." Sondra's face came closer to her camera, concern all over her features. "Shit, that's no good, I'm so sorry."

"How long have you known?" Alex sat back and hid his mouth with his hand.

"Not long, but she went for a check-up to see if it was spreading like it had with my aunt, and it was gone." They both gasped, joy and surprise battling over their features. "I know. They ran several tests and couldn't find a single cell of it left. It disappeared almost like…"

"Magic." Seth finished for me. The word seemed to hang in the air as if held aloft by some unseen force, weighing down on all our minds. "And, there's more."

I blinked over at him, and he scratched his neck nervously.

After trying to figure out how he was going to put it, he sighed and just admitted, "I died again in-game. The night before we left for the hold, and instead of coming right back, Mephisto came to me as if in a dream."

"He's an AI—what could he possibly want?" Alex frowned deeply, a tinkling like a bottled drink being opened, reached my ears and both he and Sondra pulled a bottle of beer from the bottom of their screens and drank while eyeing Seth.

"It's almost creepy how in sync you two can be at times." Seth shook his head, stalling for a moment. "He's not an AI. He's the leader of the demons, and he wanted to congratulate me—us—on figuring things out first."

"But how is that possible?" I almost shouted at him. "He

can't have figured that out. And even then, he should have killed you for knowing anything like that, right? Isn't that what the bad guy is supposed to do?"

"That's not how he works, Mo," Seth corrected gently. "He feeds off the chaos and strife that our conflict with his people brings. Hell, he even bragged to me that no one would believe me about this, and even if they did, all it would do is give him more strife to feed off of. It was like he just wanted to have a good time. He gave me the ability to drain magic from things and store it to see if I could gain that magic for myself, or some other prize like it as a sort of reward for knowing."

"Why?" Sondra's eyebrows knitted together, and she rubbed her forehead with the butt of her right hand. "Why would he give you an edge like that?"

"Because I think he feeds off the demon's strife, too," Seth asserted, he looked to be thinking, I could hear his fingers drumming on his desk. "It makes him stronger, and while I don't know what he's planning, whoever it was that told us we needed to get stronger faster had the right of it, I think."

"So then, what do we do?" Sondra sat up and put her now-empty beer bottle down.

"Mona and I have dinner with her mom tomorrow." He looked my way, and I nodded at him to let him know it was still good to go. "We're going to do a bit of snooping, but I suggest that we amp up our playtime after a full rest tonight. I'm talking four-hour naps between sessions at most."

"We talking about the old raid grind?" Alex grinned, for the first time I had seen in a while. Like, truly grinned. He loved our raid parties.

"Old raid grind," I affirmed, and Seth nodded once. "We kick the questing into overdrive, dungeons, and anything else we can manage and go for it. We need to learn what we can about the demons and their leader. I don't know how we will get that information, but we can always try."

"Leave it to the lore queen to want to dig up info on this supposed demon god," Alex said, then snorted and shook his head. He looked to me, then Seth. "I don't know what this could mean for anyone, but try to make dinner short tomorrow, okay? I still think you both are off your rockers, but if it means we go to raid mode for a couple days to get it out of your system, I'm in. I'll stock up on food today and energy drinks to keep me fresh."

"You'll be in a pod, man." Sondra almost choked as she opened another beer. "You can't drink that while in it."

"Before is fine, though." The brit's grin almost made me shiver as if he were a wolf. "I'm going to sod off then. You lot be safe."

His portion of the screen went blank, leaving us with Sondra who eyed us both with a slight frown and skepticism plastered all over her features. "You're both serious, aren't you?"

"Sondra, if you take nothing else I say seriously again, I don't blame you." Seth looked almost sad as he spoke. "But I would *never* try to induce panic on my dearest friends like this. And I won't lie to you over it. This is probably the realest thing I have ever said, and I'm scared."

She blinked and nodded almost to herself before looking down and slamming back her beer, guzzling the rest of it down and sighing after. "Most warriors are nervous before going into a war zone. I know I was. Sent us into South Pyongan after things went tits up with North Korea. They lulled us into a false sense of security that no one thought was any sort of precursor to an attack."

I blinked, trying to recall what I had learned about the war through the media and brief historical lectures. The second time we had gone up against North Korea, we had been victorious, and they had attacked us on our own soil, too, so the anti-war sentiment was lost after their bombings near Hawaii. Our action and justice had been swift, though, and shortly after the Marines had landed, they'd integrated army units to go in and fight too.

"I was your age when they sent me to Seoul, then we crossed the country border and into hell. The night before I left on a plane to South Korea, I cried because I was nervous." She smiled at the memory, now. "I'll never forget what one of my sergeants said to me. She said, 'Hey warrior, you know what makes a demon a demon? The ability to turn that nervousness into excitement. You get to go somewhere and prove that you're the best of the best. I wouldn't have you here with the Legion if I didn't think you capable of realizing the demon in you.'"

"What did you do?" Seth asked quietly. This was the most I had ever heard her speak about her time in country. She had stories, sure, but she was always careful to avoid this very thing.

"I went and protected my brothers and sisters in arms." She chuckled to herself. "They sent me and a fireteam of Marines to take an enemy bunker, small thing with heavy machine gunners mounted in slotted windows. I thought those crayon eaters were going to get me killed, but I'll never forget them. They fought so damned hard that it was easy to know why they had earned their titles over the years. I had to compete and show them I was one of the Legion. I fought harder than all of them to prove myself."

"One of 'em got hit by a potshot from one of the over-watchers in the trees when we had finished our mission." Her face contorted in rage and disgust. "They had lost the bunker already and just wanted to kill us. I grabbed him and dragged him into the brush to escape line of sight and found an impro-vised claymore waiting for me. Killed him and one of the other Marines who had happened to be in the way, took my arm and leg with the shrapnel. Luckily we had guardian angels there, and snipers had been able to clear out the few remaining ones who came for us."

She shook her head, lifting her left arm, the prosthetic flexing with her thoughts, then ran it through her hair. It looked very much like her avatar in-game. "I got medivacked out of the zone after that, and a few years later, here I am. I under-stand your fear, Seth. I've dealt with it myself. The best thing we can do is to embrace the suck and do what we can to move forward and keep as many people as we can safe. We need to find out what's coming, and soon."

She dipped her head toward the two of us, then her screen went dark too.

"I think that went, kind of well?" The left side of Seth's mouth quirked up, and his cheek raised with it. "Or at least better than us telling mom she's going to be joining us in-game."

"She is *not* going to love the idea of that." I rolled my eyes. My mother hated games, and she didn't understand why I still played after my father had… gone.

Other than because of my friends, I wondered at times too.

"But there's no telling what will happen, and if we can get her into the pod, at least she will have a chance." I stared at Seth as I spoke, my nerves jangling as panic rose at the thought of losing my mom, too. "Right?"

Seth's shoulders dropped, and so did his head. "I don't know, Mona. But I can't take the chance that it will, and we did nothing. I don't even know why we have to get stronger in the first place, but we will be."

He looked up and smiled at me. "I'll see you around noon, Mo."

His screen went dark, and I stared at myself, my long red hair still sort of gelled to my head from the portal and worry making me frown heavily. I resolved to take a shower before bed, but I would eat first.

Mom's cooking, even cold, was amazing. I scarfed the food down with gusto and then stripped down to go take a shower. I kept fighting back the urge to hyperventilate and obsess over the fact that this might be solved soon. That tomorrow we would find out whether dad had really left or not. Hopefully.

All we needed was the key to get into dad's office, and we could snoop before talking to mom.

I ran a shaky hand through my hair once more and settled against my pillows for one last full night of rest.

CHAPTER SIX

SETH

Throbbing pain was all that I knew throughout the morning, it felt like my head was going to split in half, and I might vomit everything up. Then, as soon as I took my first step out of bed, it stopped, and I felt better than ever.

I groaned and wondered what it could have been making me sweat and feel like death all morning, but I just played it off as a fluke and shuffled into the shower for some hot water therapy and old-fashioned cartoons from before even my parents' time.

The screen played the cat and mouse duo chasing each other with mallets and dynamite, and it just made me laugh. This was my Saturday morning routine, granted off by a few hours, thanks to feeling like I was going to die, but it was okay for now. I'd make my way to Mona's, then we would put this thing with her dad to bed and be able to move on. Hopefully.

Though having to tell Emma that she would be joining us in-game would prove a *significant* challenge if she didn't box my ears for suggesting it first. She really had always disliked games, and that had only been amplified by her husband's absence. It had gotten to the point where Mona had threatened to leave and never return if she came home to find her games and consoles butchered again.

That had made Emma, and her sledgehammer stop for a while. Though she had been thoroughly disappointed in me when I had suggested Mona join me in streaming. She still worked, though she really didn't have to all that much, and her streaming with me was fun. It let us continue to bond and hang out. Though we hung out often anyway.

Mona and I had always been… inseparable. Even when she had gone to college, we gamed and chatted almost daily, and the only time she wasn't online with me was when she'd gone on dates or had tests to prep for. Even then, she would send me the tests to ask her questions to help prep.

Ours was a simple and awesome relationship. I'd always loved it. Loved her. It was simple. And this complication of it sucked. The worst part was that even though I was pushing to get over it—I couldn't seem to get past it.

I'd have to work through it on my own, Mona needed me, and I needed to make sure she was going to be okay.

I turned off the cartoon and sighed as I stepped into the slightly clouded air of my bathroom to dry off and change clothes. I couldn't go to Emma's home looking foppish, she would beat me even though I'm an adult.

I threw on a pair of nicer dark-colored jeans, a green and black t-shirt with a guitar-playing demon on it and stepped into a pair of neon yellow converse.

I stepped out into the drive, a brand new red 2037 Kia Ether, reminded me of a boxy car they had in the early two-thousands, but this one was a little sleeker. Not quite an SUV, but definitely not a full sedan either. Could've been a compact SUV but I really wasn't all that great with cars, and I loved it so I'd take care of it.

The car started at my approach since the key was in my pocket, and the seats automatically warmed to my usual preference, which was just barely heated. My phone automatically connected to the Bluetooth in the car, and my music began, something funky pulsed through the speakers, and the bass crashed into my body deliciously.

I backed out of the drive and onto the roadway to head to Mo and Emma's. On the way through the area, one of the more affluent areas in the county, the grounds and trees looked more lush than usual. The already weirdly green lawns that had a certain cultivated fake appearance seemed much wilder and more unkempt. The trees had new blooms, and the leaves appeared to be that much greener and crisply colored against the blue backdrop of the sky.

My dash buzzed at me to jolt my attention back to the road-way, I was being a careless driver, and the vehicle knew it. I loved that feature. After crashing my last car into a pole to avoid a family of rabbits, I thought this feature worthy of the extra cash cost.

A few minutes later, I entered the cul de sac. I hated this place. The uniformity, the crazy attention to the lawns and everything having to be exceedingly well kept and manicured. It was a gross misuse of the people's money toward the devilish HOA, but those old coots could stuff it if they wanted any money on my account. The music in my car lowered in volume at a certain point so that Mona and her mother wouldn't be fined for loud noises—I liked that feature as well, but I wasn't enthusiastic about needing it.

I parked in the spacious driveway only to be greeted by Emma opening the garage and standing there with a fierce grin that I recognized.

Exhaling forcefully, a rueful grin spanning my face as I poked my head out the now-opened window of my car. "Seamus got out again, didn't he?"

Her smile only widened as clawed paws scrabbled against the concrete driveway to my left, and I ducked quickly to avoid getting speared by the huge Pit Bull.

The sound of paws on pleather grated in my ears, and I

turned to see one of the single most massive dogs that I had ever known glaring at me with calculating black eyes. Muscles bunched in his chest, back and shoulders that I *wished* I had as he lunged forward and shoved his paws onto my chest. His whining for my affection lessened only when I gasped for air and tried to push him away.

"He only gets like this because you don't come around as much anymore," Emma chided, her slightly-reproachful voice all I could make out over Seamus' happy whining and the constant whapping of his tail against my windshield and seat.

I kicked and spat as his tongue gouged my mouth and growled wildly as I fought to get him off of me, finally Emma took pity and whistled one sharp note before issuing her commands, "Seamus, *pfui. Hier.*"

Her Germanic commands wrested his attention from me, and he clambered out the window carefully.

One thing you could count on for Emma, she had *complete* control over her animals. She loved dogs dearly, their loyalty, and incredible talents drawing her attention enough from a young age that she had made a go of training animals for all kinds of different things. Police dogs, security dogs, protector dogs—vastly different from those meant to run security and perimeter from what she would always explain.

Her prized dog had been Seamus's sire, Caesar. That dog had been massive, a true specimen of breeding and careful cultivation. Studding him had put Emma into even further monetary gains as his progeny were some of the most sought-after dogs in the world. Outside her fee, she asked only that she have exclusive rights to any puppy she chose at any given time from any given breeding. She had chosen five. Seamus, this wonderfully idiotic creature. Losa, a mix of Pit Bull and Great Dane. Brom, a Pit Bull and German Shepherd mix. Remi, a purebred Pit Bull and finally Tialca. Tialca was the odd one out. She was purely just there for Emma, but though she was Pit Bull and Cane Corso mix, she was the kindest creature you would ever meet. Until you were around Emma or Mona—or me at times.

Then she watched you like she could see into your soul. She was the head honcho of the pack, the eldest and wisest of all of them. And they all knew it.

Seamus sat rigidly by Emma as she stood there waiting for me to extricate myself from my car. Luckily, her dogs were always groomed to perfection and his claws weren't designed to destroy; otherwise, my seats and me would have been further pulverized. Other than some short reddish hairs from his hide— the car was fine.

I came out of the vehicle and scowled menacingly at the dog. "You seem so *painfully* well behaved when she wants you to be. Awfully suspicious."

He just panted happily, his long tongue licking his jowls until Emma moved forward. Seamus very carefully shadowed her, his side never leaving her leg as she moved. This was so well practiced she may as well have had dogs for her shadow.

Arms pulled me into a fierce hug that I returned enthusiastically. I loved Emma dearly and getting a hug from her was awesome. I worried that I would never get to feel my own mother's hug again, and Emma's was the closest I could get.

A pang of sadness filled my heart with longing to see my mom again.

Emma's red hair brushed against mine in the wind. "We miss you being over, sweetheart."

"Thanks, Ma." I chuckled a little as she kissed my cheek, her sparse makeup really unnecessary. Even in her forties, Emma Hart could knock most men for a loop. Her jeans and shirt were a typical black and white combination, and her smile decorated by a light red lipstick. Her green eyes crinkled at me in delight.

"Come on in now." She motioned for me to follow her up the drive into the garage. "You can help me feed the dogs."

I scowled down at the happy looking dog trotting by her side; finally, she looked down at him and barked, "*Haus!*"

Seamus's ears perked up, and he immediately sprinted through the doggy door to the back of the property. There was no need for a fence in the traditional sense. The dogs could roam the neighborhood freely and never get into any trouble, but each one was chipped, and there was a beacon app on Emma's phone that alerted her to when one of the dogs left the property, and that tracked his or her movements. Necessary for prized animals like this, she had explained to me when I was younger.

The kennel was in the backyard, really it was a part of the main house since there was access to the house in it for each of the dogs to come and go as they pleased. This was the area they went to eat their meals since even the most highly trained dogs would fight with each other for food.

Each dog received a balanced diet of raw chicken—deboned for their safety, carrots, and peas, and in the winter months all-natural rice. Their diets changed occasionally to ensure all of their nutritional needs were met, but they were like kings and queens, and they knew it.

I took the freshly thawed chicken from the fridge and marched down the row of kennels separated by concrete walls. In each one was a bowl held aloft by a wire on each wall that I deposited my meaty prize into. The dogs sat at the back left-hand corner on their beds and waited patiently. No dog ate while the others waited for their food. This was a pack feeding, and the alpha and beta would be doing the feeding.

Emma followed close behind with the other fixings and a kind word to each dog before they were permitted to stand before their bowl. Their discipline and training shining through as they eyed the food with their peripheral vision only, listening for the command to eat from their master.

When each dog had the right amount of food, we exited the last kennel and stepped into the small hall where Emma depressed a button that closed the doors with a soft clinking.

"Pack!" The dogs all stood and went rigid in front of the food. "*Essen.*"

Growling snarls and the sound of crunching and food being wolfed down swiftly reached my ears and made me smile. I missed having a dog. Maybe I would get one myself? Have Emma help me train them, too.

Her hand brushed my cheek lightly, my attention turning from the dogs to Emma where she watched me knowingly. "You miss them."

"Yeah, and Bosco too." My parents had taken their small Frenchie, Bosco, his little black and white-furred butt wiggling self, with them wherever they went. He was their dog by all rights, but I missed him too. With everything going on, it was hard not to think about the good times we had all shared.

Chasing Bosco out in my parents' back yard for hours just because he loved to tempt me to throw the ball and then run away with it when I tried to grab it. Mom cooking on the grill while dad handled drinks and DJing for us. We didn't trust dad around food as a general rule—not because he couldn't cook— because he couldn't be trusted to not eat while he did so. So, we had him on drink duty.

"I understand. I miss them too." She pulled me into a side hug, and we were on our way back up to the house when Mona jogged across the back yard toward us. I sighed in relief, Emma was usually pretty insightful, so it wouldn't have been long before she worked a lot more out of me than I was ready to give right now. Especially concerning what we had found out.

"Hey, guys!" Mona greeted us cheerfully, her denim shorts rubbing together halfway down her thighs, and a crop top shirt moved in the wind as she moved. Her hair flew back from her face, and she skidded to a stop before plowing into us both. "Already fed the dogs? I told you I would help."

"It's okay, it's good for the pack to see Seth in a position of power now and again; besides, I know you two have some plans before we eat." She eyed us like we were trying to be sneaky about something and smiled gently. "I'll leave you two kids to it then. Also, remember to be safe, okay?"

I had a slightly confused look on my face as I stared at her, but the heat rolled off Mona in waves, her cheeks burning brightly. "Mom, what the *hell*?"

Emma just rolled her eyes and walked away, chuckling.

I turned in time to see Mona glaring at her mother as if she would catch on fire then and there.

"Why is she like this?" Her growling question just made me laugh. She turned on me and smacked my arm. "Come on. Let's get a game plan going."

"You don't already have one?" I raised a brow at her, and she shook her head. "What happened?"

"Mom moved the key to dad's office to Tialca's collar." I shrugged and made to speak, but Mona pressed a hand against my mouth. "Not here."

She took my hand and tugged me toward the guest house, and inside before she sighed in relief.

"What's going on?" I frowned at her before sitting on her couch, it was about ten feet from her portal, and the proximity made me feel weird for some reason. "Tialca is the sweetest, most kind dog I've ever met. Bosco would bite me before she would."

"You don't get it, Seth—she's not the same Tialca when she's guarding something." I couldn't register that thought before she must have seen the look of incredulous doubt on my face and continued. "You remember how protective Caesar was?"

I nodded, the gigantic beast of a Pit Bull had been likened to Cerberus, as viciously as he guarded things and people.

"She makes him look like a puppy." She shook her head and threw her hands up in frustration. "She used to guard you and me as kids, are you telling me you don't remember Satan standing guard over the room when we would have sleepovers and play video games all night?"

"Don't call her that. She was a good girl who made sure I found the bathroom okay at night and side-eyed the hell out of the tub to make sure I was safe." I crossed my arms over my chest as she glared at me with a disgusted look on her face. "She slept by me on the floor!"

"Because she was guarding *us*," Mona insisted loudly, and I snorted. "You want to try and get it from her?"

"No?" She grinned and it felt a little more real as I realized I didn't want to be on the angry dog's bad side. She really was a sweet girl. Though I hadn't seen the key on her collar earlier, she had been about ten feet away. Her collar was thicker than the other dogs'. This was getting complicated.

"Let's see what we can do." Mona pulled up a blueprint of the house on a hologram screen, simple tech, but expensive. She'd bought it to help with her work, but it was a good idea for this case, too. "Outside of the house and doors are rigged with alarms and security codes, and the second they're tripped— mom will know."

She enlarged the back half of the house near the kennels. "This is mom's office, and it connects directly to Tialca's kennel."

She swiped away every portion of the house that wasn't Emma's office. "There's a bottle of tranquilizer pills in her office that will put the dog out for fifteen minutes."

"What the hell is that for?" I stared at her in shock.

"We have to clip their nails, and these dogs are *very* unpredictable when it comes to their paws." She shrugged and shoved my shoulder. "We give them to each so that we are safe caring for their needs, and they don't get hurt either. It's nothing nefarious."

"Until now," I interjected. "You want me to go in there and get one to give to Tialca so that we can get the key from her collar."

"If it's just hanging there, then why don't we just take her collar."

"Because the second either of us approaches her for her collar, she's going to go into a defensive stance and won't take anything from us." She pulled the image up to enlarge it, and the room came clearer into view. "The pills are in the top desk drawer here."

The drawer flowed red as she tapped it. "If I go in to get it, my mom will suspect something, so I'm going to go in and help her in the kitchen for a minute while I tell her that you're looking at my streaming equipment before we eat."

"What exactly is it that you told her is wrong?"

"I told her I wasn't sure, but you would be able to test it and find out what is wrong." An evil grin spread over her face. "I've also developed this *really* nasty habit of questioning anything someone is showing me thanks to her trying to teach me how to cook. The second she hears that you kicked me out so you could work in peace, she will believe it instantly."

"You are so evil." I shook my head at her. "Let's get to work."

––––––––

I left the guest house and skirted the garden twenty minutes later to try and get into the house through the kennels, by way of Tialca's doggy door to Emma's office. Mona had let them out and opened the doors as was the normal thing for her to do so that the dogs could roam. They all knew me, so other than some pats and "good doggie, get the stick!" I was golden.

I slipped into her kennel and noticed that she was there waiting, eyeing me strangely. Distrustingly, almost, her big brown eyes following my every move. She was big, much bigger than a dog her breed should be, almost a hundred pounds of well-muscled intelligence. She opened her jowls, teeth flashing for a second before she licked her lips and sat down.

"Easy girl, I just want into the office." I smiled at her and acted as if nothing was wrong. She seemed to not pay me any mind, so I knelt down and opened the flap to the office. Luckily for me, Tialca was a big girl, or I may have gotten stuck. I squeezed through easily.

I made sure I watched everything for a second before

proceeding into Emma's office. The room was well decorated, if overly lush for my tastes, but that was likely due to the various certifications, trophies, ribbons, and awards that she and her pack had won over the years. Some of them older even than Mo and I were. I found the drawer that Mona had pointed out to me, and found both the clippers and the medication.

I took a single pill and the clippers and clicked my tongue to call in Tialca. She came without hesitation and found me standing there with the clippers and the tablet. I checked her collar again as nonchalantly as I could but still didn't find anything.

"Time for clippies," I raised my eyebrows at her like Mona had explained and presented the medicine. I tossed the pill into the air, and Tialca hopped up after it, catching it easily before laying down.

God these dogs are so well trained, I shook my head and sat in her chair to wait until Tialca's breathing regulated, and she began to snore softly. I took the collar off her, the key wasn't there and instead, there was a small box that looked like it was some sort of safe? I tried to get into the box, but it wouldn't open. It looked like it was some kind of either a puzzle box or something.

"Why won't this open?" A soft hiss of frustration escaped my lips the same time the door opened, and Emma stepped in with a bemused look on her face and her arms crossed over her chest. "Uh… I can explain?"

"I sure as hell hope so." Her severe look of displeasure made me feel five again. "To the dining room with you, mister."

I hung my head low as I made to march by her as she snatched the meds from the desk by the door and the collar out of my hand.

She followed me down the hall and to the dining room where the pack sat watching Mona.

She had always joked about feeding us to the dogs and now she may do it.

"Sit," she commanded me, but the dogs looked at her as if

to say they were, but she moved to the head of the table where she put the meds and collar down carefully.

She stared at us both for a solid minute and a half before asking, "Well, I hope you both have a *very* good reason for drugging my prize-winning baby? Any of my dogs, for that matter—outside of it being for their express care?"

She looked from me to Mona, neither of us courageous enough to speak at that moment. She lifted the collar and pressed her thumb to it, eliciting a soft clacking sound before it opened and showed there was nothing inside.

Mona and I both blinked in confusion. "These few years I knew you two were snooping in your father's office, and yet I said nothing because I felt that you would find some sort of closure in the act. I knew that if I let you have the key on your own that you might think I had gone in before you to investigate or hide things, so I allowed allowed you to find it and snoop so you might eventually let it go."

"But Ma—" Mona began, distress and shame coloring her features bright red.

Emma held up a willowy hand and silence fell again, her stern face suddenly seeming older, "I found out that you were planning to swipe it again when I noticed you looking for it the other day in the places that I had kept it hidden. When I saw that, I knew nothing good would come of it, so I made a show of hiding something with Tialca to 'guard' it. I had hoped this would dissuade you from your goal, but it seems I misjudged your drive. To think that you would stoop so low as to drug a dog who has guarded you with her life—who would kill and die to protect you. Mona Lisa Hart, I am surprised at you!"

If it hadn't been for the fact that we were both grown adults, she likely would have cried, but she didn't. And I wasn't going to either, but when Emma turned her fury on me, I felt about three feet tall and all of two pounds.

"And *you* Seth Andre Ethelbart." She slammed her fist down on the table hard enough that it made me jump, and all the dogs around us growled. "If you had grabbed the wrong medicine out of that drawer, you could have *killed* Tialca. How am I ever to trust either of you around these animals again? As much as we depend on them for their skills, they trust us to be their guides and caretakers. You have betrayed the pack, both of you."

Still, our silence persisted, and the dogs growls' finally died down, and it seemed so did Emma's rage. "Tell me what is going on."

"I think I found dad," Mona spoke softly but firmly. "In a game that Seth and I just started playing."

"Sweetheart, I know that you look for him everywhere, but your father left." Emma shook her head, but Mona slapped the table at the same time and grabbed her attention.

"This admin in the game called me Red, mom—that was a nickname that dad had for me. We've been getting all these strange messages, and it has me wondering if dad might have been taken by someone." Emma stayed quiet, absently reaching for a dog to stroke, and Seamus stepped forward. "It's much too weird a coincidence *not* to look into, so I want to check dad's office—I *need* to check it. To know for sure."

Emma blinked and then turned to me. "And you believe this as well?"

I did my best to be supportive, but voiced my skepticism anyway, "It does seem like a stretch, I know, but it's a very odd coincidence. If it bothers Mo, that much, I have to help her. I have to." I looked down at the pack and sincerely whispered, "I'm sorry we had to go to such an extreme, but we know that this hurts you, and we needed to know. We would never hurt anyone to get to the truth like this, much less the pack."

Emma remained quiet for a moment then set the key on the table. "Dinner will be ready in half an hour. We will speak more then. Do not touch my dogs until I tell you, or until they force you to." She looked both of us in the eye before growling, then saying, "Either of you."

She stomped away, a snap of her fingers, making the pack follow her in an orderly line.

Mona was up and moving before she was even out of view, her path dead set. One minute later, and we were in his office space in the garage. The large area was as meticulously clean as he had left it, several computers collected dust in the corner attached to four monitors that Mona and I would stare into for hours to help her father along a quest arc or something else fun.

A shelf of painted miniatures from tabletop games that had gone through a resurgence before the twenty's had rolled 'round again. A hoard of dice that Mona and I would play with for a while when we grew bored covered another shelf.

Everything was as I remembered it, the wall of posters lining the shelves, hundreds of source books with monsters, lore, game design work, and other books lined a whole wall. The place was *exactly* as we had left it, but we turned the place upside down anyway. Almost desperately, in a way. As if nothing had been meant to be found before now.

That meant booting up the older computers, checking under the carpet, knocking on walls—everything we had seen in a spy or thief movie ever was used for this, and still, we found nothing. Not a single speck of evidence to support her claim.

Finally, we prepared to leave, Mona nearly in tears when the screens of her father's old computer monitors flickered to life with a very cryptic message.

On one monitor, it said: *The past is a lie.*

Another read: *Look beyond the known.*

The bottom left ordered: *Pick up the dice.*

And the final one flickered wildly, but we could make out: *To look for the throne.*

"A clue," Mona's sides heaved before she sobbed, "We found the clue!"

CHAPTER SEVEN

SETH

I took a photo of it just in case, then turned to my best friend, who had begun to hyperventilate. I heard footsteps and paws clambering down the hall, the dogs invading the space before Emma did.

"What's going on?!" Emma bellowed over the din of her dogs' savage growling as they patrolled the room for the threat. Mona pointed to the screens as they flickered and threatened to fade. Finally, she growled and barked, "*Haus!*"

The dogs perked up and stalked out of the room, Emma rushed to her daughter's side and pulled her against her. Shushing and other sounds of her trying to console her in this find as I looked around the room for the die that it could have been. In a glass case on the shelf next to all the painted figures of characters from the games we had played with as children, was a single red icosahedron—the common and all-powerful d20.

Most rolls in games involving dice would require rolling one and adding or subtracting modifiers to get the desired number. It was old school gaming, and it wasn't going to be easy to get to. The case was sealed and looked to open with a key on a padlock.

"Think I found it, is there a key?" Emma and Mona looked at me in confusion before shaking their heads.

I shrugged and picked up a bronzed figure and used it like a small club to break the glass furthest from the die itself. The glass shattered after the third—hardest—strike, and I blew the shards away from it as best as I could before pulling up on it. The glass tinkled away onto the wooden board beneath the case, but what truly surprised me was the click coming from the furthest and smallest of the bookshelves.

It swung open to reveal a small hole with a well-preserved metal ladder in it. As soon as the secret entrance swung all the way open, a small light in the cubby clicked on.

Mona wiped her tears with her hand and frowned in thought. "That wasn't in the blueprints."

"If they were from the building at the city hall, then they are more than twenty years old and likely wouldn't be." She pressed a hand to my chest and moved me back. "I'll go down first to make sure it's safe."

"Emma, no—come on—I should go first." I put a hand on her shoulder and tried to move by her, but she just held out her hand and stared me dead in the eyes.

"Your parents would flay me if I let you go into danger without knowing what was going on first." Her voice was soft, almost friendly, but there was a steel to it that brooked no argument from me.

She moved forward and ducked into the room onto the ladder and was out of sight for mere seconds when she came back up shaking her head. "It's safe as far as I can tell, but there's no sense of it that I can make."

Mona stepped over to me and grasped my hand. "Me first, then you come down, and we will see what we can learn."

I pressed my lips together and nodded before glancing at

Emma. She looked genuinely confused, and if I looked close enough, I could almost see the strong and collected façade she presented to the world crumpling bit by bit.

She had just found out that there was more to her husband than she knew, and she had no answers.

"Seth!" I jumped and scrambled down the ladder after Mona. The room was a tight fit for both of us, but I could see why it had been so confusing. It was just a three-foot by three-foot room with posters of old-time Dungeons and Dragons along with some drawings of creatures and characters that we had done as kids. Mona's huge red dragon—a dragon-shaped blob if I was candid, she was never that great with art—with golden eyes staring out over a hoard of items and in the center of the room was a simple map. Not like a normal map, but one a group might use as a prop during a game at the table to denote a room.

It had walls that stood about six inches high made of cardboard colored to look like stone. A thick hallway led to the larger room, and in it looked to be a golden throne with smooth walls and cloth banners in the back. Studying it, it was simple and beautiful all at once. And along the side of the wall closest to me, the right side of the throne, was a single stone that stuck out of the wall next to a golden suit of armor.

"What could it mean?" Mona muttered. Trying to make sense of it. "This makes no sense, why be so secretive about this? What's going on?"

"I can't tell you, but I can't say as anything nefarious went on here, just something he preferred no one know about?" I shrugged and pulled her close, my arms squeezing gently. "We're going to figure this out, okay?"

"Damn right, we are." Emma scowled at us with her head hanging over the lip of the hole in the floor. "Get your asses up here and tell me *everything*."

We marched up the ladder, into the dining room while she went into the kitchen and slammed things around for a moment. She came out of the kitchen on the phone and nodded and grunted before turning to us.

"Pizza is on the way—you have twenty-five minutes to tell me everything you know."

Mona and I scrambled to fill her in, in full detail—even the stuff that we theorized on in the outside world.

She crossed her arm as the doorbell rang, and she marched the pizzas in. "Eat."

We dug in, burger pizza for me while Mona had a taco and BLT pizza she shared with her mom. We ate in silence for about ten minutes before I broke the silence, "A portal will be installed for you on Monday. We want you to play with us. To prepare."

She scowled, standing and going to the kitchen to bring back a large pitcher of tea and a tall wicker cask of rum.

"Cold sweet tea?" She barely looked at us as she poured four shots of rum into her own glass and three into ours before watering it down with the tea, the glasses *thunking* onto the table in front of us.

She mulled it over for a moment, taking great gulps of her drink before I realized that her hand was shaking; finally, she set the tea down and grimaced. "If it means that we can all get to the bottom of this? Fine. I'll call them myself and see to it that the order is expedited. And that there is plenty for them to do to make sure that it is so."

"What do you mean?" Mona frowned and glanced from her mom to me.

"My annual donation to the local community center?" She smiled, and it looked a little more feral than I think I had ever seen. "If they will get that device to me faster, I'll buy fifty of them and donate them in a lottery to the community center."

"What?!" Mona and I stood up, almost spilling our tea.

"Mind the tea darlings, that's nearly six-thousand-dollar rum." I frowned at her, and she sighed. "This was Stalwart's favorite rum. I never had a taste for it, but I think I needed this.

Each shot would probably cost quite a bit. More than half alcohol, so drink up."

"No, no, about the donation thing." I smacked the table, and her gaze flicked to the glass next to my hand.

"All I need to do is make a call." She shrugged nonchalantly. "I have enough pull and resources here to ensure that I am heard anywhere in the world. If you believe this a true threat and I can find my *dearest* husband and answers, what's potentially a million dollars or so compared to closure?"

*I mean, if you have the money to throw at a problem—throw it…*I shook my head and handed her my phone with the call already ringing on the line. She took it and sipped her tea as she waited for someone to pick up.

Two seconds later, she gave her best business deal smile. "Ah, my apologies, this is Emma Hart, not Mr. Ethelbart, but I did have a request?" I heard a slight pause before someone asked what that might be. "See, Seth—Mr. Ethelbart—ordered me a portal so that I could play with him and my daughter, and they have said *nothing* but amazing things about this game to me. I was wondering if we might be able to make a little trade?"

She listened, her face thoughtful for a moment as she listened to the other end of the line, "Yes, I'll hold while you get your manager."

I frowned, they hadn't even heard her out on her offer, and now they wanted a manager involved?

A couple minutes later, Emma's smile returned. "This is she." She listened and nodded along for a moment. "You would be exactly right, that is what I was going to request. Though I did have a hefty offer in return for the express service, would you be interested in hearing it? I do take it that you would be able to negotiate and haggle as I was given to you directly."

Her smile deepened, and she almost purred, "Wonderful. My proposal is an offer to buy fifty of your portals to be donated to our community center as a raffle, seeing as though there is special work to be done on homes and whatnot before they can be used."

"That's correct. Set up is already complete at my residence, and all of my electronics are up to snuff." She looked to be triumphant for a moment before she frowned. "Yes, he is. One moment."

She turned to me and passed the phone my way. "The manager would like to speak with you for a moment."

I took the phone with a look of surprise, "This is Mr. Ethelbart, how may I help you?"

"Ah! Good afternoon Mr. Ethelbart," a familiar, almost German accent greeted me. "I am not sure if you recall, I am Wilhelm, we spoke just the other day?"

"Ah, Wilhelm, glad to talk to you again, what can I do for you?"

"We have *special* orders to pay attention to your needs as our... *mutual* benefactor has an interest in you. You surprise him greatly with your faith in others. Wonderful." My blood ran cold, and I could tell that the others knew something was wrong. "Now, now—I know you told them. And so does he. Let us have our fun, yes? This shall be a delightful experience. If I could be returned to Mrs. Hart?"

I nodded dumbly. "Sure."

She took the phone from my hand. "What was that all about?" She listened intently before nodding. "I understand, and you can't do seventy-five? Fine, one hundred of the devices and coverage of any and all renovation fees will be fine. I expect to see your crew here in the morning, Wilhelm. Good afternoon."

She hung up and pressed the phone back into my hand. "What did he really tell you?"

I blinked and answered honestly since she would know if I lied. "He admitted working with Mephisto and being in contact with him. That he was surprised I would tell you all, but that they were happy I had."

"Then, I need to be wary of this one?" She raised an eyebrow.

"I think so, maybe having the pack nearby will help?" I

wasn't sure. If this guy had an in with demons, maybe he was one?

"Then tomorrow, I will be in the game," Emma asserted. She whistled shrilly, and the whole pack came out of the back, Tialca sluggishly moving behind the others. "Before I can allow this business to go on, Seth, you must apologize to the pack. Tialca specifically."

I knelt down outside my chair and looked each of them in the eyes steadily. "I'm sorry, everyone. I didn't mean any harm to any of you, and it was for a worthy cause."

Emma snorted. "They don't understand anything like that. They're simple creatures. Either they love you, or you've made some enemies among them. Call to them and see if they will come to you."

She whistled for their attention and said, "Free."

The dogs all relaxed visibly and began to pace around, some sniffing excitedly at the table since the pizza was there.

I called out to them, and one by one, they came to my hand and licked it, Seamus going to town on my palm and then face like the lovable idiot he was.

I turned to Tialca, her sluggishness worn off as she wagged her tail and wandered the room. I stepped closer to her. "Hey girl." She sat down right where she was and raised her paw making Emma and Mona laugh. "What? What's going on?"

"She's showing off her nails because after we clip their nails, they get a treat." Emma almost snorted, her cheeks blazing red from the booze. She tossed me a small brown morsel to offer to the gigantic dog, and she came directly to me to fetch it. She ate, and I patted her shoulders and told her just what a good girl she was.

"Well, Ma. Time for you to get ready for Mephisto's and Iradellum." Mona winked at me. "We need to get back on here soon, but I'll guide you through what to expect when you make your avatar and everything. Seth, when you log in, I need you to see if we can find a space mage who can port us back to the starter city. If not, I'll have to go help her power level on foot, and that won't be time management at its finest."

"Space mage?" Emma groaned, her eyebrows tightening as her hand swept through her red curls. "I'm already out of my depth, I thought this was some kind of medieval game!"

CHAPTER EIGHT

SETH

Getting home had been uneventful, thankfully, and when I logged in, Sundar and Albarth waited downstairs in the inn for me.

"Mona is going through some stuff to help her mom prepare for tomorrow, she should be on any time now." They looked at me blankly, and I frowned, "All in all? We found out a lot and nothing today at her house, secret room in her dad's office. Weird I know, we drugged a dog for a key that wasn't there, *stop* smacking me, Sunny."

The orcish woman growled at me as she socked me right in the shoulder before I could continue. "Turns out that the creators of the game may be in league with Mephisto—or at the very least some of the upper echelon folks are."

Since Mephisto and his lackeys already knew everything, I went ahead and filled them in on the details and then it was their turn to give me news, "The Queen has given us permission to come to her once we're ready, though we have to have an escort from something like the order of the fang?"

"Order o' the Claw," a rugged voice behind me corrected politely. Looking back, a stout dwarven warrior in plate armor dyed fire-red sat at the table next to us. He watched us with one eye, the right one closed with a grasping draconic claw that held a small patch over it, a thin leather strap braided into his long, reddish-brown hair and under the opposite ear. "Me name be Greldan, an' I'll be yer escort. I heard tell there be another o' ye?"

"Yes, sir." I motioned him over and pulled out a seat. He raised his good eyebrow and plopped onto the floor before walking over to us, the armor protecting him not as quiet as we had hoped. "She should be here soon. Can you tell us what to expect?"

"I can tell you to mind yer manners around her majesty." He smiled a little, his brown-red beard lifting at the sides. "Other than that? I be sworn to secrecy as many o' me kin be. Me apologies. Once ye meet her, ye'll understand."

"Is she really a dragon?" Sundar asked quietly. "Should we know that?"

"Oh, aye—that be fine." He waved her question away. "Be hard to come here and not think that, aye? Knowin' our history is common when ye come here, only fair really. But as to *how* she is, that is the secret we protect."

"Oh, okay. That does seem fair, I suppose." Albarth frowned and then sighed. "She's here."

Not a moment later, Mona careened down the stairs with a huge grin on her face. "Hey guys, who's this?"

"Greldan, an' I'll be yer escort to her Majesty." He bowed once to her and marched toward the door, then stopped and turned. "Ye do be ready, right?"

We nodded, and he turned back on his way out the door. We followed along closely behind him. Some of the folks backing out of his way in deference and staring with open curiosity at us, and even some with open hostility at Sundar.

"You okay with all these glares?" Albarth leaned close and asked quietly.

"I spent time in a country where people hated me because I was killing distant relatives—I can handle some mean mugging." She raised her voice slightly so that Greldan would hear her, "Though it would be nice to know that if anyone attacks me, I have permission to defend myself?"

He stopped and glanced back, seeming to take in everything in the time it took to actually look at her before replying, "Lass, not one person on these streets be brave enough to face her Majesty's ire by harmin' a guest in the presence o' her Talon. If they come for ye—we would have a coup on our hands, and loads'd be dyin'."

The leering crowd dispersed after his show of calm devotion to his orders, but he did walk slower so that he didn't leave too much space between us.

The city along this Main Street was beautifully carved, whereas the buildings at the front of the city had been masterfully crafted and well designed, the masonry on these lent more to beauty and station over function. Sweeping archways over gated fences letting out onto the street that seemed to have horns or small dragons clambering over them carved of stone. Whole buildings that appeared to have small veins of precious ore shooting through the stones made spectacular artwork.

This city was truly breathtaking, and the majority of her citizens appeared to be dwarves. The occasional halflings and gnomes ventured through with humans here and there, but no elves that we could see.

Finally, we entered the shadow of the mountain, where a large, fort-like structure had been carved into it. Ramparts stood taller than the wall outside where archers and cross-bowmen peered through telescopes, eyeing the city with bells nearby. The stone here was dark, almost black as pitch, and the area felt almost uncomfortably hot.

Four guards stood stoically stationed at the large doors nearly thirty feet tall, their spears held in their hands almost lazily, but their eyes gleamed at us excitedly. If we made one false move—they would likely skewer us where we stood.

"Four to see her Majesty," Greldan said, then grunted at the others who peered at him, their black armor almost melding with the stone behind them. One of them lifted his spear and stabbed the butt of it into a spot on the wall with an incredibly well executed and well-practiced motion. I thought I heard a small click, and then his partner joined him as the two of them turned some sort of device using the spear to wind it. The cranking opened a smaller, eight-foot-tall door in the right-hand door and allowed us all entry before the cranking stopped, and the door slowly closed with a resounding echo down the wide hallway we stood in.

All along the side of the hall in neat and orderly rows hung paintings of various dwarves of different statures and shapes. Some warriors, others scholarly, some smithing, and yet more doing all manner of other things.

Mona was dying to ask a question, but our pace wouldn't allow it. The hall was a mere one hundred yards long, and we had crossed it rather swiftly for having been just walking.

He knocked on the door to the next chamber, this one wooden, thankfully, with two guards stationed outside who were happy to ignore us.

He heard nothing then frowned at the guards who shrugged in return. "Piss off, then!" His voice almost a bark, and they muttered evilly. "I swears I'll see 'em flogged, lazy bastards!"

"What's wrong?" I asked with a scowl at the other guards as they left.

"Nothin' just don't know what the queen be doin'." He scratched his beard before a deep, guttural roar of pain rang out from the other side of the door.

Greldan and I launched ourselves forward, shoulders banging painfully into the thick wooden door and shoved together with Sundar behind us. The wood bowed slightly and gave way to us as we rushed through in time to see a large mound of red scales reeling back from some unseen force, clutching at her heart with her eyes closed. She fell, her body cracking the stones beneath her bulk and her tongue lolled out of the side of her mouth.

"No!" Greldan bellowed, his hand falling to his left hip as he raced towards his fallen queen. Suddenly, one of the large eyes opened up, the slitted golden orb taking the dwarf in.

"Ah, my Talon Greldan!" Her head lifted from the ground, and she blinked at him cheerfully. "Welcome back, I didn't expect you so soon."

Greldan stammered and stuttered until we all heard several child-like giggles from behind the massive dragon's leg. "Oh, you lot are in for it now!"

"Do be gentle with my children, Greldan," she chided as more than twenty children, dwarves, humans, and a small little gnomish girl filed out from their hiding spot.

"Gentle ain't me aim!" He howled, her eyes widening at his outburst. "Nearly gave me a heart attack ye did! I'll see all of ye swinging weapons until *I* be tired!"

The children groaned loudly, but some of them seemed to have expected this.

"Do we have to go with Talon Greldan, Momma?" The little gnomish girl pouted pathetically, her bottom lip quivering like a professional.

"Oh yes, I expect all my children to be able to protect themselves." Belgonna reached down with the tip of one of her massive clawed hands and nudged her softly. "Run along now, my beloved. We will play again soon and remember not to swing at anything you don't intend to kill, maim or massacre!"

"Yes, Mother!" The group groaned together, and she watched them lovingly walk out behind the still howling dwarf, the small side door closing behind the last dwarven child through.

"Forgive my antics, I take playtime with my children *very* seriously." The large red dragon stared down at us for a moment. Her teeth flashed in the dim torchlight of the room, her monstrous size meant that each of her teeth was likely human-sized and capable of puncturing metal with ease. "I am Belgonna, and you are here to see me?"

It took us a moment to gather our wits as we stared in open shock at her. "Forgive me, I forget how truly daunting it can be to meet a great wyrm. Allow me to make you all a little more comfortable."

Her eyes closed, and a blast of heat so strong that it felt like being on the receiving end of a napalm bath washed over us, my eyes closed instinctively just to try and stay moist even as they watered.

When I could finally force them back open, I stammered at the sight before us.

A more than ten-foot-tall elven woman stood before us. A glowing red dress that looked like scales or sequins covered her shapely figure, the bottom of it moving around her feet as she trod forward slowly. The same golden dragon eyes watched us from behind a swath of fiery hair—literal fire that flowed down her back and over her shoulders and face. Gloves that matched the dress covered her arms as she motioned to us. "Is this a little less foreboding for you all?"

We nodded and she seemed pleased. "I am Belgonna, the Crimson Queen and mother to all of this city. Again, tell me— who do I have the pleasure of hosting?"

Friends be damned, this was too good an opportunity to look good to pass up. I bowed before I spoke, "We are but humble wanderers, Your Majesty. I am Kyvir Mageblood. With me are my dearest friends and compatriots, Monami Sunfur, Albarth Remell, and Sundar Strongtusk."

At the sound of their names, each of them bowed and curtsied as they would.

After I finished speaking, it was suddenly warmer, and someone stood before me. "Rise."

I stood and craned my neck to see Belgonna staring intently down at me, her face growing nearer before her eyes half-lidded, and she inhaled deeply a foot or so from me.

"Ah, it is your magic that I can awaken." She smiled. "You

have known much love in your life, yet I can smell confusion and pain on your skin—in your heart. Tell me, where are your parents?"

I was almost a little angry at the intrusion, who was she to make those assumptions about me and ask such a personal question?

The woman who can unlock your magic! Answer her, my common sense won out, and I opened my mouth, "I don't know. They work out of the country a lot, and they can't tell me where they are for safety reasons."

She growled softly to herself before cupping my cheek with her surprisingly soft hand and moved on to stand before Albarth.

She did the same to him, her nostrils flaring wide before she spoke, "The stench of loss exudes your whole being, child, but I sense that there is yet cautious hope in you. Tell me, to what do you cling?"

Albarth's mouth quivered for a moment before he whispered, "My friends."

"See that you continue to do so." She ruffled his hair gently and moved to Sundar.

"You." She stood to her full height, her nostrils taking in whiff after whiff of the large woman's scent before she stepped back. "You poor, dear. Tell me, do you see them at night? The people who haunt you? The parents you never knew?"

Sundar just looked away, suddenly my cheeks burned, and I found myself angrier than I had ever been before. And in her silence, I could see that Sundar was reliving some of those things she had fought so hard to hide from the rest of us. Her teeth clenched painfully as tears threatened to fall down her cheeks.

Rather than lashing out, or moving on, Belgonna's arms swept out into a hug and she pulled Sundar close as the woman's pain fell from her eyes. Her fury and anguish shook her whole body as the rest of us stood by, uncertain of what to do.

After five minutes of tearful silence, Sundar stepped back and wiped her face, turning from the queen.

Mona was the only person left, and she looked to be more than a little apprehensive about what she knew was coming.

Belgonna stopped in front of her and looked her in the eye. "I could smell you as soon as you walked into my chambers. The stench of your determination that borders on obsession. If you are not careful, you will lose all you hold dear to it. I can smell the loss you feel, I can sense that you search for answers, and you may yet find them, but you must learn to harness your emotions first."

"My determination and my family are all I have—but your advice is appreciated. Majesty," Mona's voice sounded almost harsh to me as she spoke. "We came here in hopes that you could awaken the magic in my friend."

"I can," she said after a moment spent watching Monami like she was deciding what to do with her.

She turned and walked toward her large golden throne, sitting upon it before addressing us again, "But I will not do so for free."

"I hadn't thought that you would, Majesty," I spoke, but she held up a hand.

"I require that you," she said and pointed to us, "Assist me in a quest for the good of the city."

We waited, and she smiled. "You can learn, good." She sat back in her throne and closed her eyes. "My city has, of late, been plagued by a ring of some sort of lawlessness. Murders, thefts, kidnappings—things that had up until recently been unheard of. Certainly, we have had crimes of passion, but never this. This level of seemingly organized crime perplexes my guard and the law keepers of the city. I request that you find out why these things have begun to happen, and get me information on who could be responsible. Do this, and I will awaken your summoning Aether for you. Bring me evidence of their wrong-doing and reasoning, or proof that some of them have contacts helping them, and I will reward you further how I may."

Quest Received – Find out who has been running the only organized crime in Belgonna's Hold in more than seven hundred years and bring information to her. If you succeed, Belgonna will awaken your summoning Aether. Find any evidence you think credible as proof that may give a reason why they do what they do or what they may be planning in the future, and she will reward you further. Failure: Not doing the above will result in the dormant Aether in you remaining so until you find another capable of awakening.

I didn't bother reading the rest because I accepted it outright. "That sounds an excellent accommodation, Majesty."

I bowed as I spoke, her warm gaze upon me.

"Sundar, child, step forward for me?" Lifting my head, I saw that Sundar had indeed stepped forward. Belgonna observed her from her throne for a moment before she stood and wandered forward. "I feel your pain, and it breaks my heart. I have come to know so many children, loved them as my own, for I too know the heavy cost of the loss of family. You never knew yours—tell me—have you a desire to belong to one?"

I couldn't see the other woman's face, but the skepticism in her tone and her shaking head made it clear her confusion clear, "I had one—two, actually. I was a part of the army, and now I have my guild. I don't know what you're talking about."

The almost-indulgent smile that graced Belgonna's pseudo-elven face almost made me think her matronly as she explained, "A chance to truly belong to someone who will love you and give you the things that only a mother can. That true siblings can. I can give you that. I *will* give you that, all you must do is accept."

"What does that mean for me?" I could still hear the confusion in Sundar's tone, but now I heard suspicion. "For my friends and me?"

"For them?" She motioned to the three of us and shrugged. "They would be deemed your friends, and I would treat them as such. My children are revered here and treated like the royalty that they are. My people have long memories as well, and they are not so soon to forgive your kind even though racial tensions are not as they were centuries ago. Come, let me mother you, and I will bestow *many* gifts upon you."

Sundar stilled for a moment as Belgonna slowly crept closer, one foot moving before another, her towering height making it so that Sundar's face was almost breast height for the dragon queen.

"And if I were to refuse?"

Belgonna's lips pulled down into a pouting frown, her right hand reaching out to stroke the orcish woman's cheek softly. "Then my heart would ache for you, not knowing a mother's love. If you feel this to be too sudden, I understand. If you feel it also unearned, then I will allow you the opportunity to earn my favor and matronly graces."

Her hand lingered on Sundar's cheek, and I would swear that she leaned against that hand slightly.

I felt eyes on me from my friends who stared around at each other with apparent unease. This was weird. I couldn't under-stand why it was that Mona wasn't enthralled with the level of story and care taken in this aspect of the world-building and lore. Nor did I know why Al looked like he had seen a ghost, and being here made him uncomfortable, like he would rather be anywhere else.

"As a token of my goodwill and honesty in my offer, I will bestow upon you proof of my affection." Belgonna took her hand and reached into her hair, where she pulled a single, red strand of flame away.

She took it in her right hand and twirled it around one of her fingers until it looked like a thick band. The heat in the room intensified around us as she took a deep breath, her chest glowed a deep orange, then blue, then white before she blew across her hand. A small burst of white-hot flame filtered over her hand and finger for a moment, almost blinding us until everyone in the room was forced to look away.

She spoke words in a hissing language I had no hope of understanding, before the room darkened significantly.

I strobed my eyes, trying to rid my sight of the dots swirling around in my vision before I heard, "Sinistella!"

A crack like thunder echoed through the room, and a heartbeat later, another woman stood next to the queen. "Mother."

"I would like for you to enchant this ring." Belgonna kept her eyes on Sundar as she held out a small object.

"Very well." The woman turned and marched over to the throne, a hand waving in the air, and a ripple of bright blue flaring around her hand. As she did, a sort of veil parted, and a golden hue lit the room. Mounds of treasure, precious gems, and armors lined the walls and floor behind the throne.

Her hair, a sort of fiery orange, flung over her shoulder as she knelt beside the throne, using one of the broad arms as a workbench. She pulled out a small tool and tapped at the object in her hand while muttering under her breath.

"While she works, allow me to tell you what it is I would like for *you* to do, dearest Sundar." Belgonna leaned down, her scaled dress sliding low and smiled, "I would like for you to prove you can defend yourself. If you and your friends can figure out who it is running whatever obscene, criminal element is invading my city, I want you to bring me their head. No matter who it is, I will accept their head and allow you to join my family if you so see fit. Does this sound like something that would give you peace enough to finally feel a sense of *true* belonging? Of being loved as unconditionally as you should be?"

Sundar remained quiet for a moment, and Belgonna looked hopeful. "Unless you wish to take me up on my offer here and now?"

"Why are you doing this?" Mona finally blurted.

I heard a chuckle from the back of the room where Sinistella worked over her piece, without looking up from her work she shook her head and answered, "Mother likes to collect broken things and give them a home because it makes her feel like she didn't fail her lost egg." She glanced up, one golden and slitted eye like her mother's stared at us. The other eye held a deep crimson iris that seemed to burn a hole through each of us. "No offense meant, young orc, but I speak the truth. She knows it's not her fault that her egg didn't hatch, but she refuses to not take it out on the rest of the world. She knows that it was not her fault that I was born deformed, but she still seeks out the broken and mistreated to offer succor."

She slapped something from the ground onto the ring with a grunt and breathed on it while chanting.

"Please, forgive my daughter." Belgonna's placating smile was a bit tighter. "To answer your question on my *own*—" She turned quickly to hush Sinistella, who merely rolled her eyes. "I care deeply for the downtrodden and those whose parents did not know the joys of parenting as I have. I take those gifts for myself and allow them a place to grow and thrive as I wish that my children could. There is nothing wrong with my children."

Her last statement sounded like it was a little thin—holding a slight hint of obsession, maybe.

"There's nothing wrong with being an orphan," Mona pressed as she stepped forward to stand closer to Sundar. "It doesn't make her any less than anyone else. If anything, she's stronger for it."

"Oh?" Belgonna stepped around Sundar so fast that I thought she was going to attack Monami. My feet moved on their own, and I found myself held back by some sort of force. I glanced over to see Sinistella shaking her head with a finger over her lips in warning to be quiet. "Then tell me, Monami, if not knowing your parents is such an easy thing to live with, then why can you not live with the absence of one?"

Mona flinched as if she had been struck, but Belgonna pressed on, "Why is it that you obsess over finding him? Why cloud your mind and aura with the desperation you feel to find someone who cast you and your mother aside?"

"You don't know that!" Mona snarled evilly; her fangs bared at the queen.

Belgonna chuckled loudly. "No, I don't. But I know that you think it." The dragon queen inched her face close enough to maliciously whisper in Mona's face, "I know this because it is what is written on your heart. This worry that causes you to doubt everything and everyone around you to the point of hurting them and lashing out when you feel vulnerable. This *seed* of poisonous doubt and uncertainty within you demands answers that you may never find, and you have the gall to tell someone that they shouldn't feel lesser for being an orphan? That their not knowing who they are, where they come from, or who they could have been if they had just been wanted or loved enough is not valid enough to warrant thought or validation?"

The two of them had come so close that if Belgonna changed forms right then, she could have eaten Mona in a single bite, and that would have ended it, but suddenly, Sundar was there. Her hand around Belgonna's right arm and tugging.

"That's enough," she insisted with a look of pleading on her face. "Please, stop."

Her bottom lip quivered slightly, and I was at a loss for words. I'd never seen her so shaken from anything in all the time I had known her.

"I'll do it." Sundar sniffed, her left-hand wiping at her face and nose quickly. "I'll do it, just leave my friends alone. Okay?"

"Sunny, you don't have to do this." Mona started to step forward again, but the look Sundar shot at her quieted her then and there.

"She was right." Her jaw set, her tusks flashing a little as she spoke. "You have your mom, and you had your dad. You had everything since day one, and all I had was a cot in a place where they hated kids. Then I joined the army, and all I knew was how to kill and take care of my soldiers. You don't know what it's like, Mo, and I'm not mad at you for that. I know that what happened to me isn't your fault, but right now, you don't get a say in this."

Mona backed off, her head downcast, and her eyes averted. I stepped closer to her and offered her my hand in support, but she slapped it away and turned on her heel, fleeing from the room with Albarth behind her. I wanted to follow her, but I couldn't just leave Sundar alone with this woman. This dragon.

Once they had disappeared into the hall, Belgonna muttered, "Impudent," then turned her gaze on Sundar. "Since you have decided to take action, will you accept my gift of love?"

"I'll earn it." Sundar let go of the queen and stepped back as Sinistella stepped by with her hand out to her mother. "I don't know you well enough to take anything from you for free."

Belgonna took the item, and the other woman walked on with a cool disdain for the rest of the events in the room. I turned to watch her go, her similarly styled dress swaying as she walked to the door and ducked out of it behind my friends.

"Clever girl." Belgonna reached out and touched her shoulder and offered her a ring. "This is my signet ring, given to my adult children. This will allow you free run of the city and any who see it will see my child. You will need to be careful with it, as it may hamper your quest. But it is yours, and should you prove yourself worthy of my affections and attention, I will embrace you as family and give you *so* much more."

"Thank you, Queen Belgonna." Sundar bowed her head, and the queen looked a little stricken as she tucked the ring into her pocket.

"That will not do." The Queen tittered at her, stomping away to a section of her hoard where a statuette of a knight stood by the wall, familiar-looking golden armor decorated with silver and red filigree along it. She snatched a leather necklace off of it, breaking the poor thing in the back and tossing whatever it was that had been on it aside. She touched the torn leather pieces, and they melded back together as if welded shut by the touch of her fingertips.

She held out her hand and made a grabbing gesture, the signet ring appearing in her hand to my and Sundar's surprise. She looped an end through it, then the other side through so that it would hold the ring and then placed it over Sundar's head with a smile. "There, now the symbol of my offer is closer to your heart so that you know I will always treat you well and adore you as you were always meant to be."

A half-smile crept onto Sundar's face, and she bowed her head. "Thank you, Queen Belg—"

"Enough of that," Belgonna ordered as she pulled the woman into a bear hug that made her grunt twice. "If you will not call me mother, you might at least call me Belgonna until you are ready to do so."

"Very well." Sundar nodded once, and the queen stared at her expectantly. "Belgonna."

"Wonderful." She grinned crazily and turned to walk toward her throne. "Sundar, you may come here at any time. And your friends as well, especially this one. I am happy to host those who will free my kingdom of the rats that plague it."

We both bowed at the waist and turned to leave the room then, hoping to be able to catch up to our friends.

CHAPTER NINE

MONA

"That *evil* bitch!" I seethed once more as I paced halfway down the hall from the throne room. Her telling everyone everything that was going on in our lives like that just made me see red so much deeper than someone getting on my friends or someone attacking people I loved.

"Mona, stop, please." Albarth chased after me. "We should wait for the others."

"Who does she think she is?!" My teeth gritted together and growled in frustration, suddenly needing to do something or be anywhere but near where that... that *child-stealing monster!*

"You know, anyone else who has tried her patience like that has died," a cool voice greeted me from the chamber, Sinistella's figure sashaying toward us with a small smile. "That required either great bravery or foolishness born of ignorance and little care for survival. You wanderers should prove to be much fun."

"She had no right to say any of that cockamamie bull crap she was spewing back there." I threw up my hands in frustration as I glared at her. "I mean—what the hell does she know?!"

Sinistella actually laughed then. "She knows a great deal more than she lets on. She is an adept mind reader, and the fact that she can play it off as reading scent alone is startling to some. So much so, that they lower their guards and allow her to delve deep into their memories. She speaks the truth that she sees and makes assumptions and educated guesses based on her findings."

I stopped and stared at her. "How can she do that?"

"Draconic magic is very strong and being a great wyrm means that her powers are at their peak and that she has more than a thousand years of experience at her disposal." The woman shrugged. "The why is most interesting to me, as it allows her to manipulate the people around her to a more advantageous nature for herself."

"So, she was lying in there?" Albarth frowned deeply. "About how much of it, though?"

"Come with me, I have much to speak to you of." She turned without seeing if we would follow and walked straight toward a wall. I had to admit that I was curious and looked to Albarth and shrugged before following.

She did another one of those waves with her hand, and the wall before us disappeared and opened into a hallway, thinner than the main hall that appeared to lead toward a single door.

Albarth informed me via whisper, —*I sent the others a whisper telling them we were with Sinistella and that we would meet up later to discuss some things.*—

I held up a thumb to let him know I wasn't ignoring him and continued to follow the large woman. Looking at her now, there seemed to be more dragon about her than her mother. Her dress of scales seemed a little more scale than fabric, and there appeared to be smatterings of scales on her shoulder blades and the backs of her arms.

We came to the door where she muttered a single word under her breath that I couldn't understand, and it opened inward. Inside was a small room with a mirror in it. She walked up to it so that I could see her reflection in it and grinned at me before stepping into it and sinking in.

The silvery pool rippled as if it were water in a pond that you tossed a rock into when it met the edges of the frame it bounced back and stilled again swiftly.

I walked forward until a hand on my wrist jerked me back. "Hey!"

Albarth glared at me. "We need to be careful. You may not like her mother, but this one seems shady too."

"Listen, if you're gonna back out of following a cool mage back to her rooms, go ahead, but there's more to Belgonna's story, and I'm going to find out what it is." I snatched my hand out of his grasp and pointed a finger in his face. "You will not do that again. I am capable of deciding things on my own, and that bitch has got *something* planned for our friends. She's probably going to try and get us killed somehow, and I'm going to figure out how to protect us from her one way or another."

"I'm not trying to control you or keep you from doing that, I'm just saying that we should be cautious!" He hissed back angrily, shoving my finger away from him. "You've been acting off lately, more bonkers than normal, and it's starting to make me worry. Are you okay?"

I glared at him and growled. "I'm fine, but it seems that whatever she was planning worked as it's turning us against each other."

Rather than wait for him to get over his shock, I stepped back into the mirror and into what felt like gelatin. The world around me shook and shivered, and then cool air brushed against my back and I took another step.

"I was wondering if you would be too frightened to follow me," Sinistella greeted me with a smile to her tone. The room we stood in seemed almost like it wasn't a room at all. A large section of the wall to my left was open to the world, the view of the mountain and city below both spectacular and terrifying. Like standing at the top of a skyscraper and looking down. "Quite the view, is it not?"

"It is," I breathed, wondering if it was awe or fear keeping me from forming a more complete thought.

"Welcome to my tower."

I turned to see her standing over in another side of the room that actually had a wall. She looked over the desk beside her, notes and papers scattered all over it in neat piles and held down by shiny baubles. A chalkboard of a more basic design covered the wall behind the desk, surrounded by bookshelves with books that had well-worn spines. Finally, she walked around the desk and sat, watching me casually.

"Your friend will be here soon." She must have noticed my look of confusion. "The pathway to my chambers can be as swift or slow as I please. I desired a small amount of time with you to discuss things, and I figured with how you acted when he addressed you about me, you might appreciate the ability to think for yourself."

I winced at her unapologetic look toward my wrist. "You heard all of that?"

"You know that I did; let us not waste any more time on frivolous questions." She leaned back in her high-backed chair and stared at me. "What my mother said was not a lie, much as you believe it to be, but a culmination of her experiences, intellect, and the information she obtained from you. Had it not been for your orcish friend, and maybe the Kin, she would have slaughtered you where you stood if you had questioned her so alone. They saved you."

"Death isn't a problem for us." I crossed my arms stubbornly. "How do I keep her out of my head?"

"*You* do not, the trick is staying away from her." She stood and walked to the side of the desk closest to me. "She wants you to out this criminal element because she rules the city, and it displeases her to know that there is someone undermining her authority. I want it done so that it does not undermine mine when I take the throne."

"So, you want the same things then." I frowned at her.

"Yes, but I have another request in mind for you." She

grinned and I didn't like it. "I want you to find a way to make my ascendancy to the throne a tad grander. See, great wyrms are powerful, and as my mother has endeared herself through centuries of maneuvering, she has this city in the palm of her clawed hand—but she is not long for this world. Since I run the city logistically and do everything that she wishes not to, she is merely a figurehead at this point."

"You want me to kill your mother?!" I scoffed at her; she eyed me without blinking, and my heart shuddered almost to a halt. "You can't be serious. How would Kyvir be able to unlock his power if she's dead? No. I hate her for the shit she said, but I'm not going to ruin his chances of awakening his Aether."

"I don't want you to kill her." She held up a placating hand. "Despite how she seems, my mother is a wonderful matron and has taught me much. My magic was the result of her mating, but that is not something I prefer to discuss. What I want is for you to give her this potion that will make her susceptible to suggestion. Maybe the suggestion that she take what precious little time she has left in this world to spend it with her children?"

I went to speak, but she shook her head. "It cannot be you who does it. It has to be someone she can respect. She would likely kill you, and the moment would be lost. No, you will need an equally matronly woman who understands the need to put children first, though where you will find one, I'm not sure. Certainly, someone in this city may qualify, but they will not want her to abdicate the throne, perh—?"

She saw my grin, and before she could even ask, I said, "I have someone in mind—but you're going to have to work for it."

Her eyes narrowed, and she grinned. "Do tell."

CHAPTER TEN

SETH

"Where the hell are they?" Sundar asked with a grunt as we left the throne room. We had just left Belgonna's chambers, and they were gone.

—*Hey, you two, Mona, and I will be going to speak with Sinistella to find out what her mom's deal is. Let's meet back at the inn to discuss our findings.*— I blinked at Al's impeccable timing and glanced over at Sundar's scowling visage.

"Wanna talk about it?"

"S'not something I like to talk about." She sighed, and we walked on for another couple minutes. "That was really weird, though."

"Yeah, it was." I nodded to the two dwarves who stood guard on this side of the door, and they did the same spiel with the door opening. It was only slightly less shocking this time, but we got through easily.

The road we took to get back to the inn was a straight shot, so it wasn't really all that difficult to find our way back, but we took our time. Mainly because people kept throwing dirty looks at Sundar, and not moving from our path until they could bump into us or jostle us.

It took half an hour, and I was to the point where I wanted to curse at the next person who trod "unknowingly" on my feet by the time we got to the center of the city where the golden statue of the egg was.

Rather than walking toward the inn, she walked closer to it and watched it silently. I stepped close to her and reached out to take her hand in mine. A gesture that neither of us was used to as she looked at me in confusion at first, then in gratitude.

"I'm sorry that you had to grow up like that," I stated, squeezing her hand softly. "That's not a pleasant way to live life —but you did it. And look at what you made of yourself."

"Thanks." Her simple reply threw me off a little, and I wanted to probe her mind to get to the bottom of this, but knew if she wasn't ready to talk, she wouldn't. She'd been that way as long as I knew her.

We stayed like that for a little while before finally, she turned, letting go of my hand so that she could sit on the side of the fountain and stare back at the street toward Belgonna's chambers.

"I always dreamed of having a family." Her voice was soft enough that I had to physically scoot closer to her to hear her over the fountain, and the people milling through the area. "When I graduated high school, and a recruiter found me, I thought that would be it. The army would give me everything. I served my time and made a lot of friends—some I would have happily died for. But though we called ourselves family, it was a façade. Or at least it seemed that way. When I got hurt, my CO and my battalion sergeant major came to visit me and awarded me a Purple Heart for what I did to save those men. I thought that the rest of my unit would come, but they never did. And I got really bitter about that. That's what family is supposed to be for, right? Coming to make sure that you're okay? If they hadn't come, could I really call them that?"

Her whole body shook as she laughed to herself. "What was

I thinking? Those were bonds of convenience. I loved my soldiers and gave them all I had, and not one came to see me. So, I threw myself into what I had to do to get myself right. Some of the neural pathways that I had needed repairing after my injury and the folks at Bethesda suggested VR simulation to get me used to my prosthetics. It was hard, but I relished the challenge because for once—inside that game world—I felt like I belonged. So, I gamed, found support groups and self-defense classes to pay for my habit, and eventually started to come to terms with how I felt about myself. With how lonely I felt."

"You had us," I tried to offer her with a hand on hers. "We clicked almost from the beginning."

"Yeah, we did." She smiled at me, her tusks growing with it. "But I wondered when you all would leave too. You proved slowly that there were people out there who could be trusted, and I love that about all of you, Ky. I do. But this little guild we have going on? It's not the family I imagined growing up. It's not the fantasy that little girl at the home had every time she looked out onto the street and saw kids playing with their brothers and sisters before being called in for supper with mom and dad."

I sat there quietly and tried to understand her point of view. She was right; we weren't blood. We had faced a lot to get to where we were, though. She smacked my arm, jarring me.

"Don't get me wrong. I love you guys, and you'll always be like family to me—my chosen family." She took a deep breath and sighed, her body slackening with it. "But for just once, I would like to know what it's like to call someone mom and mean it. Even if it's a crazy dragon queen who adopts everyone."

"I'm not going to judge you for that." I chuckled. "You know, Mona's mom is coming into the game, and she's likely going to mother the hell out of all of us. You better be ready."

Sunny grinned. "She anything like Mo?"

"Oh, dude, Mo gets amped and so does she. You should see her with her dogs, though. Terrifying." We both shared a good laugh over Emma, and I patted Sundar's leg. "So, no judgment, but what do you want to do? Do you want to take her up on it? Do you want a crazy dragon mom?"

She turned to me and offered me a small smile. "Kind of? I mean, not to mention potential fringe benefits."

"And she seems like a hugger, so it could be a win-win for you." We both laughed at my attempt at a joke, and she pulled me into a side hug.

"Thanks for not taking what I said the wrong way." Sundar stood up and looked at me. "I know things have been tense lately, and I really appreciate that."

"You know, I found that I'm okay being the chosen family." I shrugged halfheartedly. "Emma took me in like I was her own my whole life while my parents would go off to save the world in their own ways and I was cool with that because they were happy and so was I. But I can also see how not knowing who you are because of where you came from can be a really big deal or hang up for people. I wish I had some kind of great wisdom to offer you or someone else in those shoes—but I don't. So, I won't. Just know that I'm here for you because I want to be. I see you as family even if it's hard for you to."

A tear cleared her right eye as she put both hands on my shoulders and physically lifted me into a huge bear hug that made me gasp, "Ack!"

Moisture brushed my cheek and her tears seemed to mainly be those of happiness, but her tusks did feel a little weird against my face when she gave me a soft peck.

"Gage would kill me if he found out you were giving me all his kisses." I eyed her with my best attempted lascivious gaze, and she just snorted at me.

"He's got nothing to worry about from you, kiddo." She pulled me tighter, and I swore I heard something crack before she grasped me with her arms and began to stick her fingers into my sides and ribs. I shrieked for mercy as she tickled me and barely registered that people were beginning to stare at us openly as if we were loony.

Soon, some of the children we had seen playing with the queen filtered into the area, and we stepped aside so they could play and splash in the water happily. We went inside the inn and found a seat and something to eat and waited patiently for our friends. Sundar asked after Blothl at the bar where a server raised her brow and advised that she would send for him.

It was still earlier in the day, and there was no telling where he would be, but they would try to find him for us. I tried to whisper to Mona and Albarth, but they didn't answer, and I was starting to worry a bit.

"You think they're okay?" I raised an eyebrow at Sundar as she drank a light beer from the bar with her eggs and toast with sausage.

"I think so," She belched happily and grinned as the server walking by clapped for her. "I like it here. Besides, Sinistella doesn't seem the type to kill people as much as she would manipulate. As rude as she seemed to me, she looked like the calculating type."

"You got that vibe, too?" I looked over to her, and she nodded once. The door opened and Blothl strutted in. "Hey! Glad to see you again!"

"Aye!" He grinned, his beard parting widely. "Ye have yer time with the queen? She be helpin' ye?"

"More an exchange of services," I offered in return, and he quirked his head to the side. "She asked us to help sniff out the criminals that have begun to show themselves in the city."

His beard formed a slight "oh," and he ducked his head closer before whispering, "How ye meanin' to do that? The Talons been lookin' for a month and nae found shite."

"Talons?" Sundar offered him a sausage, and he took it from her greedily with a wink. "We've heard that before, but what are they? What do they do?"

"They be the five leaders of the Order o' the Claw." He took a bite and groaned at the savory taste of the meat before continuing in a low tone, "They be the city guard and law keepers o' ours. Five o' em keep the city free o' crime. Or, rather, they were meant to. This shady business done been drivin' the lot o' em mad seein' as though they always seem to be one or two steps behind the culprits."

"When did this all start? And how?" Sundar frowned and scooted closer so we could speak even more privately.

"Started with the murder o' a Talon's clan head 'bout a month ago," he lowered his voice to a growl, the place slowly filled with workers and folks seeking a meal. "Found 'em strung up all weird, an' his blood strewn about like they were drawin' somethin'. Weird symbols and the like left all over, an' I be hearin' they found him tore up with things missin' from his innards."

I swallowed hard, that did sound pretty gruesome. "What else has been happening?"

He sighed. "Some thefts and other murders, some seemed like they was done in public as a warnin'. Others like the first, some more ugly than that, others less so."

"Who's investigating this?" Sundae asked quietly, it seemed that people still wanted to glare and glower at her for what she was, and it made this discussion a little less secretive than we would have liked. "The Talon's, right?"

Blothl nodded his head once and glared at a particular burly dwarf who had come swaggering over to our table. "Got somethin' on me face, or are ye gonna try an' kiss me, ye ugly gobshite?"

The dwarf spat onto the ground, his lips pulled back and down, the corners brushing braided mutton chops hanging down before the man's chest. His hair shook wildly, as it stood on end and appeared to be dyed red.

"I was thinkin' o' callin' after the lady first, but if the herd wants to side with the bloody fookin' orcs against his people, they're as shite as I thought they were." His broad chest puffed up and his beady black eyes fell on Sundar, unimpressed.

"Blothl, if I beat his ass, will they lay off me?" Sundar asked as if the other dwarf weren't there.

Blothl's eyes sparkled evilly, and he seemed to think about it.

"The others? Maybe not, though if you break his jaw, he won't be able to talk shite like he thinks can. May make him prettier too."

"You lot take it outside!" Nildy came out from behind the bar with a small wooden club with metallic beads all over the thicker end. "I'll not be havin' this establishment disrespected by anyone, an' ye attack me guest, without her consent—I'll brain ye."

"So ye be sidin' with the enemy too, then?" The dwarf snarled and rounded on Nildy, standing intimidatingly over her. To her credit, she didn't back down or blink at all. "Fine. I'll nae be back here. Let's go have a word, orc. Yer kind donnae belong here!"

She sighed and tilted her drink up, her throat working the alcohol down as the crowd around us watched. She finished with a sigh and began to stand as the dwarf stepped closer, as she rose she loosed a belching hot burst of air in the aggressor's face. His eyes widened dangerously, and I stepped closer to him with intent to intercept him, but Sundar put a hand on my chest.

"Let's head outside for a civil chat, eh?" She winked at me and walked outside without so much as a glance back to see if anyone was following.

We walked out into the daylight and blinked at the brightness of it before noticing that a crowd had already gathered in the area. They had to have planned this.

"So, what's your deal, nameless dwarf antagonist?" Sundar called as she walked through the crowd of faces toward the fountain in the center of the area. She splashed some of the water onto her face as if washing it and then a little through her hair.

She turned and leaned against the short wall of the fountain lazily so she could watch her opponent step from the crowd.

"Mah name be Preltan o' Clan Stonefist." At that, he raised his hands into the air and dozens of voices raised in cheer throughout the crowd. "And I be meanin' to teach ye yer place —which be far gone or dead."

"There'll be no killin' today ye limp-bearded cod swallow," Blothl blustered angrily, his face and neck flushing red. "They be guests o' the Crimson Queen!"

Preltan sneered, "She be a dragon, orcs be beneath her notice. But fine, I'll nae kill her. But she will leave, one way or another."

"Blothl, what're the rules to this little chat?" I asked quickly, as Sundar and Preltan stared each other down.

"It be a fight lad, the first to knock the other unconscious wins." He shrugged, "No beard pullin' be allowed, or magic, an' no weapons either. Interference from the observers be strictly forbidden an' will bring shame to the clan o' the cheater, and the aided side."

"You hear that, Sunny?" She finally tore her eyes away from the dwarf across from her and glanced my way. "Knock him out, and you win. Don't touch his beard."

"Why would I want to touch those poor excuses for mutton chops?" She gagged theatrically and spat on the ground. "They look like pubes."

Preltan howled and charged forward, his hands held out to grab her in a tackle with his fingers splayed like claws. Sundar laughed as she sidestepped and slapped his rump as he sailed into the wall with his clavicle. A snapping sound and short snarled gasp of pain was all that the dwarf gave us. There were no notifications for me as I wasn't actively a part of the fight, but I could see that he favored that side slightly.

That didn't mean he was going to give up the fight, though. He stalked forward with his hands up, quite the feat with a broken clavicle. Seemed dwarves were a cut above normal people on their pain tolerance.

Sundar allowed him to get closer to her before she widened her stance and lowered her center of gravity and waited for him to try and hit her. She swiped his fists away from her stomach and chest with ease, each time she slapped his right arm, he'd grit his teeth and try to attack with the other to no avail. Finally, he tried to grab her around the waist and kick out her legs from beneath her. Rather than stopping him, she let him topple her, giving her access to his neck from behind. She lifted her elbow and used her massive legs to keep him closer to her waist before dropping elbow after elbow on his unprotected head and neck until finally, he fell limp against her.

Sundar bucked her hips and flipped him over onto his side, placing his left arm under his head and the right along his body. She checked his pulse for a second, people beginning to worry and jeer from the sidelines. Calling her all sorts of dirty, creative names.

After a minute, she seemed to have had enough and slapped Peltran on the cheek hard enough that the crack from it turned him onto his stomach.

He came awake with a start and started to get up when Sundar walked away from him. Once she was more than ten feet away, he had finally made it to his feet before trying to rush her from behind, some of the folks in the crowd gasping, others cheering and a few more still shaking their heads in disgust.

"Sun!" I bellowed as he was about to reach her back.

She stopped, twisted her head and shoulders back to take in her target, and lifted her right leg in a spinning back kick that would have made a Shaolin monk smile in pride. She whipped her booted foot across his face hard enough that he spun in the air and landed on the ground on his back in a daze.

"Anyone from the Stonefist clan want to collect yer trash?" Blothl clapped his hands and cackled delightedly. The crowd dispersed slowly, people still leering at Sundar, as they moved past but none of them had the courage to speak ill of her or spit at her for now.

"We leave you alone for a little while, and you start some sort of racist fight club?" Albarth cried with his hands thrown up into the air as they separated from the crowd of onlookers still hanging around. "Why did you not tell us to bring popcorn?"

"One, I can't stand the stuff because it gets stuck in my teeth." I rolled my eyes at him and Mona who had nodded her agreement. "And two, because you weren't replying to our whispers, either of you."

"Someone wanted to dance, and I'm not one to say no." Sundar grinned at the others in delight. "What happened with the princess?"

They blinked, and finally, Albarth grasped it. "Oh! Sinistella, yes, she has agreed to assist us in this and is also willing to help us in gaining access to a fast travel feature."

"They have that?" I blurted, stepping closer to them. "I asked the mage in the castle about it, and he said that it would require a very powerful space magic-user to teleport somewhere."

"The way she explained it was that it's creating a rift between a place with no ties." She pointed with her head to a pair of stones, roughly the size of soccer balls. "These are bound to each other, and when one is touched and given a bar of Aether, they will activate, and you will automatically and instantly be transported to the other."

"This is insane!" I grinned at her. "Think of the applications! We could use it in a fight? We could use it to fast travel back to the inn."

"We could leave one of them in Gage's back yard in Iradellum and go get my mom," Mona stated, and I frowned. "That's what's going to happen. Albarth and I are going to go back to the city and help my mom power level before coming back here. Can you two handle the investigation?"

"I get that you want Ma to be ready and a part of this, Mo, but how is this going to help?" I stepped closer to her, and she put the stones in her inventory. "Splitting the party is pretty bad news in most cases."

"She's an extra body, and with Al and me there to provide DPS, she's going to be able to level up faster." She sighed knowingly. "Plus, we know people there and can help her get set up sooner and with better gear. This way, we can come back here, and be better prepared to infiltrate whatever organization this is to take them down and get your magic unlocked. Everyone wins, and we keep mom safe and close."

"That doesn't actually sound like a bad idea, Kyvir." Sundar inserted, making me glare at her. "Besides, we already have some leads that I'd like to look into, and since we can cover more ground like this, it'll be okay. How are you guys going to make it back to Iradellum?"

"Transport has been arranged as well as an enchanted item that will cloak our movements," Mona informed us. "We'll leave today so that we can get there either before or just as mom comes to the city so we can help her more efficiently."

I tried to come up with some sort of excuse as to why they should stay. That it was too soon. That we were stronger together. But this was important, and we just needed to be smarter about things and get outside our comfort zones to make the best possible outcomes happen.

"Okay then, you both be safe, and let's keep in contact." I shook Albarth's hand, and he nodded at me with a soft smile. Then I gave Mona a hug, whispering, "Be sure to tell me what kind of magic Ma has."

She snickered and gave me a kiss on the cheek before they both turned and began to walk away.

———

"Blothl, this hardly looks like the kind of place that a Talon would hang out." I glared at the darkening surroundings of the alleyway.

"Shush," Sundar squeezed my shoulder softly and whispered in a hushed tone, "Any one of these cross alleys could be used to set an ambush. Trust Blothl."

We walked on, the stone of the outer wall folding in on us for a moment before we came to a small, squat building with no outer signage or denotation as to what was inside the building or what it could be. Blothl knocked three times then another three times in more rapid succession.

The door opened, and a pair of hands flew out and grabbed him around the throat, yanking him inside and slamming the door. Adrenaline surged through my veins, and both Sundar and I, converged on the door before it opened once more, and a hand reached out and snatched us into the building as well.

"You are out of your gourd, Blothl!" The person hissed vehemently. A light flared into existence above us, then sharpened to reveal a small, older gnomish woman with thinning grey hair and thick spectacles on the front of her face that had multiple glass additions that looked like they could be flipped in front of the main glass. "How *dare* you interrupt my craft *and* bring strangers!"

"He be under me orders, Herilda." A gruff voice rasped. An older dwarf stepped out of the shadows on the far side of the room, his sharp brown eyes scanning us before looking back at Blothl. "Ye said there'd be proof they were to be trusted?"

Blothl looked from me to Sundar. "Show it to him, lass." She tried to play dumb for a moment, but she frowned when he pointed to her chest and the necklace under her armor. "It slipped out durin' that spat with the idiot. All o' me kin can recognize her touch."

Sundar pulled out the ring, it flashed red in the light above, and the other dwarf marched forward and examined it carefully without touching it. "It be true." He looked up at Sundar, stroking his long grey beard while his wrinkled features wrinkled further. "But yer not fully family?"

"She offered to let me earn it, and I took her up on that." Sundar tried to smile, but I could tell that she was a little weirded out that he seemed to know.

"Ye earn yer way?" The dwarf laughed and shook his head before looking at Blothl. "Always did be a good judge o' character, lad. I give ye tha'. I be the Talon called Qornath, and I be the thumb o' her Majesty's claw."

He motioned to Herilda. "This be our examiner."

"I'm a mage and apothecary!" The woman snarled at the dwarf who rolled his eyes. "I don't look at corpses for just *anyone*, old man!"

"I be younger'n yer wrinkled arse!" Qornath blustered as if what she said had been the most preposterous thing he'd ever heard. He wagged a finger in her face. "A whole *two years*, ye hag!"

"This happens often." Blothl rolled his eyes before clapping loudly to get their attention. "Oi! Yer both old! Now can we be gettin' to business then?"

Both Qornath and Herildas' heads snapped toward him before narrowing their eyes at him, and he shook his head. They turned to each other again and looked at each other as if saying, "later."

"What is it that you're examining?" I asked, and the gnome just rolled her eyes. "I know that they're bodies, I'm not stupid. I wanted to know what is different about them as compared to what might normally be."

"They were missing their hearts, brains, liver, and their tongues." She raised her left eyebrow at me. "Yes. There was more than one, and the latest was found just this morning."

"We be keepin' the find under wraps, as this one donnae make any sense to us." He scratched his bald head and rasped to himself. "The others were people of import in the city. People who mattered. This one were a beggar. Nice sort, an' kind to anyone what wandered by him. Protected others o' his ilk by buildin' small shelters out o' scrap."

"That does seem odd." Sundar rubbed her chin thought-fully. "Can we see the remains?"

Herilda waved us back toward the darkness, and the globe of light followed above us, weaving and bobbing to and fro as we moved. Finally, we stopped near a table with a sheet over something that looked suspiciously like a body.

"Please, refrain from vomiting on the remains." She glared at both of us.

I had seen cadavers before, dead bodies in morgues, and on

examination tables in TV shows and movies. They had always seemed so sterile—this was not. She removed the sheet and small specks of dried blood tore away from the flesh beneath in a sickening way that my mind failed to liken to any other sound.

A hairy dwarven man laid on the table, his stomach torn open by something that hadn't just gone digging, it had gone in to destroy and consume. Flies buzzed around it, despite having not formerly been there, and the stench hit me. It smelled like rotting meat, eggs, and poo.

"Oh, this is interesting." Sundar moved forward and touched the man's face, and the eye rolled to one side, the head turning to reveal that the side of his head had been caved in and picked apart like some kind of melon.

The room suddenly felt very warm, and I began to sweat profusely and it was all I could do to breathe and swallow before I turned from the corpse and my companions and hurled everything I had in me up.

"At least it's wasn't on the evidence," Blothl's voice sounded as though he were smiling, and I groaned pitiably.

"Is there a pattern?" I heaved again, this time, mostly bile coming up. I had never puked in-game before, but this was crazy.

"A what?" Qornath queried, his beard popping into view on my left.

"A pattern." I tried to stand but my stomach cramped painfully, and I had to just breathe as I wiped my face on my sleeve. "Where did each of the deaths occur, where were they found, how, and what was stolen. Do you have a map of the city we could use to plot it?"

"Aye." Hands on my shoulders, and both Blothl and Sundar came to grasp me and move me from the area.

"Thank you." We moved to a different side of the shadows and found a table with a window by it that Herilda opened begrudgingly.

Qornath supplied the map and plotted the various things that had happened of a nefarious nature. There were several small thefts of weird things. Candles, sheep, rope, chalk, and whatnot. Then some larger marks were made in three different locations in areas that made no sense. One near Belgonna's stronghold in the nicer part of town, another southwest of it, and the last almost on the edge of the city near the wall opposite the second murder.

"You said that there were strange markings and things in the area of the murders?" Sundar asked thoughtfully.

"I did," Blothl confirmed as he pulled a pipe from his inventory. He tapped it on his boot and filled it. "Weird markin's that made no sense. Runes in blood an' in chalk."

He lit his pipe and puffed it, then paused. "Ye think they be connected?"

She looked at me, and we both nodded. And if that was the case, there was likely no way that we would be able to get into this organization—because they were likely trying to summon demons.

CHAPTER ELEVEN

MONA

"I cannot believe she gave us something like this to use," Albarth said for the third time since we had left the city little more than an hour ago.

The covered wagon that we were in moved quickly with the team of four horses that pulled it. The way that she had spelled the cart was an area of effect, anything within thirty-five feet of it moved silently and without being seen. All four of the horses had been bred powerful by the driver for the task of transporting dignitaries to where they were meant to be and swiftly. We had been told that if things went well, we would be there by tomorrow morning.

"It's pretty cool, for the third time." I smiled to myself. We had been traveling only a little while, maybe a little less than an hour, and it was only slightly annoying to hear it again.

We jostled in silence for a little bit before he finally spoke again, "So what happened while I was being transported to her tower?"

I stilled and tore my eyes from the small window next to my

seat to look at him. He watched me curiously, and I could tell that he knew something was off.

"I saw the severe change in time, Mona." He explained as I worked on how to either lie or change the subject. "You were alone with her for half an hour, and I highly doubt it was just a social call with how tight the two of you seemed. I've seen that kind of chumminess before."

I blinked and raised my eyebrows at him in mild surprise. "Oh, do tell."

He grinned wolfishly, "When two boys who weren't exactly friends had tried to get me fired as captain of the English fencing team." My heart throbbed as he leaned forward. "They had concocted a scheme to try and not only get me fired but likely kicked off the team altogether because I was better than both of them combined. I found out about their little coup and ended them in my own way—but I know that look. Spill."

I thought about lying, I wanted to so badly, but I nodded to myself and told the truth. "Sinistella asked me for help gaining control of the throne from Belgonna. Before you say it—no— we are not going to kill her. We're simply going to give her a potion to make her more susceptible to reason."

"So, you're going to drug her?" Albarth threw his hands up and almost flew out of his seat at me. "Mona, that's insane. She's a great wyrm! That means she's the most *powerful* a dragon can be! And you want to try and convince her to give up that power?"

"I want to try and convince her that she has enough time left to spend devoted to the children she craves!" I snarled back, surprising him more than a little with my animosity, but honestly, him not trusting me hurt after what the queen had said. "She wants to accuse me of obsessing and becoming a monster, but she has a limited number of years left to live, and she's going to leave those kids the same way she saw my dad leave? How is that fair?"

"So, what, Sinistella takes over and reigns from there?"

"She's already logistically running the city, her mother is just a figurehead." I waved his concern away with a flippant motion of my hand. "She still wants us to complete the desired task, and when mom is ready, we will bring her back there and help Kyvir and Sundar with what they find."

"Why did you keep this from us?" He tilted his head to the side. "From me?"

"Because there was a chance you could go in front of her again, and she could glean the plan from your mind and memories." I looked back outside, the plains moving more quickly by us as we went down a hill. "I know it might seem hurtful and distrusting, but I didn't know how else to make this work in our favor with as little chance of getting caught as possible."

"It does seem hurtful." I saw his slightly defeated sigh from my peripheral vision and glanced at him. "We've been a lot closer lately, you and me. I had hoped that you would trust me."

"I don't know your full story, Al." I sighed. "We have been spending more time together, yes. But I need the same level of trust going forward."

"Are you saying that you would like to get to know me?" He actually laughed at that. "Mona, we've been gaming together for almost two years."

"Yes, we have, and as a gamer, I know you very well, but I don't know the *full* you." I insisted, thinking back to the things that Belgonna had said to us. "Sure, I pieced together that you're a famous fencer, but all of our business was brought bare in front of everyone. It just seems like Sunny and Ky both know more about you than I do. If you know my past, I want to know yours too."

He rolled his eyes and chuckled. "This is the weirdest game of I show you if you show me I have ever played."

I snorted and motioned to our surroundings. "You have better plans?"

————

"No way." Albarth rolled his eyes. "No, you can't be serious."

"Absolutely am." I crossed my arms and smiled. "I could ride on his back when I was four, Caesar was massive. And such a good boy."

"Ugh, I envy you, my friend." Al chuckled and shook his head. "My mother despised animals, and I was never allowed them when I was younger. As an adult, I find my schedule much too hectic to take care of any regardless, though I am quite inept with them and awkward."

"We love them at my house, but they have their place there." My cheeks hurt from smiling so much, with everything that had been going on lately, it felt good to smile like this. "I appreciate you being so willing to talk about your past with me. I'm sorry about Reneld."

His smiled turned tight, the corners of his eyes tightening as well. "I think discussing it as I have lately has helped me be less of a sod about it. At the mention of her name, I used to go almost catatonic, but now it's a pang of sadness and guilt that just sort of stays there for a while. Thank you for listening to me prattling on. She's gone now, and my therapist says that discussing her with friends is a first step in letting her go."

"Oh? Is that why we're just finding out about her?"

A barking laugh escaped his lips as he slapped his knee. "Oh, no. That was years ago! I've just gotten round to it."

We both chortled for a few minutes and fell silent. Finally, he looked out the window and noticed that it was now late afternoon. "I like it here."

"I agree." The world seemed so peaceful and welcoming outside the demonic threat that was coming. "I don't know if I'm cut out for this whole resisting thing."

Albarth frowned at me. "What do you mean?"

"We're supposed to be prepping for a fight against the demons in this game, right? Going to the front lines and pushing them back—that's the narrative we've been fed." He nodded and watched me. "I don't know if I'm cut out for that. And what about our world? We're defenseless there."

"We can't know that this is actually what's going on. I

realize that these crazy things are happening, and that it is a *real* concern, but there has to be something else."

"And what if there isn't?" It was hard to keep the rising panic from my voice. "My mom is all I have left, and with how I am with you guys and Se-Kyvir? If anything happened to any of you, it would break me."

"We're going to be okay," he asserted and put a hand on my knee. "Besides, none of us is going to abandon you and your family—or each other."

"I know. I trust you guys." I quieted for a moment. "Hey, Al?"

He looked over at me, and I tried to figure out how to ask this question without seeming weird. "Why is it that you're here? I mean, with me rather than letting me get my mom on my own? We've been spending a lot of time alone together, and that's not normal for us."

"Do you dislike it?" His normally posh and proper tone sounded cautious. Almost as if dreading what he might hear.

"No. Just wondering if there was a reason for it." I frowned. "Normally, we bicker, and you avoid being alone with me."

"You remind me of Reneld." A small gasp escaped my lips. "Bull-headed girl that you are, she was the same way. But you also share her finer points. Kind, protective, brave, and loyal."

"Kind of sounds like you're describing a dog." My voice sounded a little flat as I tried to cast a joke into the conversation because of my own awkwardness.

"I suppose it does." He gave me a genuine smile. "I found those things in you early on, and it hurt me to be around you so I would bicker and pick fights with you as a way to show myself I wasn't interested in becoming close to you. I missed her, and I wouldn't risk hurting like I did for her again for anyone else."

Warmth crept up my cheeks at his words, and I saw a small smile creep onto his face. "Don't worry, I have no designs on trying to pursue you. I was the one who encouraged Kyvir to try and tell you how he felt."

"That was you?!" I almost shouted, catching myself just in

time. Shadows passed over our position, three of them, and then flitted away from us. "Why?"

"Because I know what it's like to have someone you love not know how you feel, and to deny yourself that chance to let it all be laid out." He held his hand over his heart. "There isn't a moment that I don't feel like an absolute fool for not having told Reneld how I felt about her. I didn't want the same for two of my dearest friends."

"But why would you say that to him?" My eyes and chest tightened dangerously, it was a sweet thought, but it had caused so much turmoil. "We were happier. We… we were able to just be us!"

"Are you trying to tell me that you don't love him?" He shot me a knowing look as I raised my head toward him. "And don't you *dare* tell me *like a brother* unless that is all you feel for him."

That all-familiar gnawing anger and confusion that tugged at my heart chawed up my chest and out of my eyes as tears began to fall. "Of course, I do!"

His jaw fell open, suddenly shocked, and it was all I could do not to dart across the two feet separating where we sat to beat him for his part in what had happened.

"Wha—why did you refuse him then?!" He threw up his hands, and they hit the roof over our heads.

"The man that I've loved since I was *thirteen* just suddenly notices that I'm a woman who could be more to him than just a friend—who had always seen me as a sister—randomly spouts off the question of if I want to be more than a friend to him and I'm supposed to just say yes?! I don't get to be shocked or alarmed? I panicked and ruined *everything*."

My head fell into my hands, and there was a shifting before my side of the cart shook slightly, and Albarth joined me on my bench, his arms covering my back and shoulders in an awkward hug.

He was silent for a few minutes and just let me weep quietly before finally saying, "I knew it. I knew exactly what had happened, and his foolish pride got in his sodding way. If he had just listened to me, the two of you would be happy together."

"No!" I shoved him away, shock coloring his features. "No. That's something for him and me to figure out with no one else's help. And honestly, I think he thinks it was my Allure ability playing tricks on his mind, and I wasn't even trying to use it."

"How do you use it?" He asked suddenly, and I blinked at him. "When I want to cast my Flame Dart, I activate the ability by using a small button in the bottom left hand of my hud, it shows the cool down and everything."

"I don't know, I guess I just think about wanting them to notice me, and it activates. The second it activates the cool down shows up in the same place for me. But otherwise, it's when I want to be... noticed."

The realization dawned on me as he nodded. I had been doing it on purpose, I just hadn't realized that I was doing it. And now I wasn't sure if what he felt had been real or my ability either.

"Oh, god." My shoulders must have weighed a thousand pounds then because I couldn't even so much as sit up from where I was. I had caused this as much as anyone else had. Because I hadn't just been okay with what we had.

"You can fix it—I won't help!—but you can," Albarth reasoned with me softly. "I know how stubborn you can both be, but it is possible."

Finally, I lifted my head to stare at him in disbelief. "But didn't you basically just tell me that *you* liked me?"

"Yeah, I did." A smirk graced his face, and he chuckled softly to himself. "But at least this time, I made my feelings known. Besides, if you care about someone—their happiness should mean something to you, too. If you being with the lovable tosser makes you happy, I'll support you."

"That will likely be difficult for you." I sniffed and wiped at my eyes again. "I'm sorry. I like you, and all it's just that with everything going on and the things that have been happening lately, I just…"

I tried to think of something to say to soften the blow, but he shook his head. "No need; I understand. I simply needed you to know what I felt and how *you* felt. And there's no need to try and think of how to fix things right now, just wait and get your mum sorted out and then you can worry about getting your man."

I threw my arms around him in a hug, muttering into his shoulder, "Thanks, Al. You're a good man." I froze, realizing what I'd just done.

His deep laugh reverberated through my chest, and he squeezed me once before letting me go and growling, "And *don't* you forget it."

We laughed and continued on with the journey, discussing what we might be able to do with my mother to get her the help she needed to get her ready for the next leg of our lives.

CHAPTER TWELVE

SETH

"We've been at this since early this afternoon, Sunny—we need to take a break and get some food. You know—at home?" I glanced up at her and frowned. "The others have been gone for a while and they can just log out en route there."

Sundar watched the roadway beneath us without so much as blinking. "Give it ten more minutes until we can get Blothl to come here and watch for us."

A soft sigh escaped my mouth before I leaned back over and checked my side of the roadway. The light had long since died down, and it was approaching the pre-Dawn hours as we sat here on this rooftop. This was the most logical place for someone to attack based on the previous attacks, and there was traffic off of a main road nearby so we could attempt to foil it.

Five minutes later, a scuffling sound reached us from behind, and I turned to find Blothl huffing softly as he clambered over the side of the rooftop.

He limped over to us a second later with a grimace. "Likely just have to fall on 'em to stop anythin' I see. Nothin' for ye?"

We shook our heads, and he just grunted. "I hear tell ye wanderers disappear when ye go to yer home?" We nodded at him. "How long do ye plan to be gone?"

"Likely not too long. Three hours tops." Sundar answered for me and nodded my way. "We'll see you here in a few hours."

She and I stepped to the other side of the wall, where we couldn't be easily heard, and I asked, "So, half an hour?"

"Yeah, that's what I was thinking." She frowned. "That enough time?"

"I lined up a meal prep service and got some stuff ordered for tomorrow, so I'll be good with a sandwich for tonight. How about you?"

"I meal prep to save time gaming." She smiled at me. "I'm good for the next few days to a week, depending on how hungry I get."

We nodded at each other and logged out right then.

Once I was back in the world, I didn't even bother with a shower and just washed my hands and face so that I could eat quickly. The sandwich wasn't all that large since I wasn't really all that hungry, and I checked the news to see what the headlines were on the monitor in my countertop.

Miracle cure for cancer patient prompts renewed research.

Record shattering pumpkin crushes competition.

Shadowy figure flees from fire at Children's Hospital.

Beached whale spontaneously combusts.

The first one was concerning just because I wasn't sure how it would play out with magic. The second one, well—that was the least weird honestly.

Another attack ... were they actually demons? How were they coming through? I would have to see if there was some way to check, but I didn't even know where the hell to start.

I watched a video of the whale combusting, and it was as spectacularly terrible as one might think the poor thing. I had no clue what that was about, but I was almost positive that the smell had to be absolutely disgusting.

I finished my sandwich and hopped back into my portal to log back on.

Important notice from Mana, Myth, and Legend Studios: Hello all! We wanted to let you know that the portals will be receiving an important update just about four days from now. Nothing too bad, and it should only keep you out of the game for an hour since we're amazing at what we do.

Enjoy!

Suddenly the countdown to login began, and I stood on the rooftop where I had logged out.

I was alone, and my adrenaline spiked when I didn't see Blothl, so I rushed over to the edge of the roof as low as I could and scanned the area as swiftly as possible. I didn't see anything below me and looked around all over for any signs of a struggle. The dark rooftop looked fine in the dim light the growing moon shone down upon it where he had been posted up. My nose caught no scent in the air, and my heartbeat quickened.

"What're ye lookin' for lad?"

Blothl's whispered question made me flinch and yelp, "Ah!"

"Spook easy, Kyvir—ain't a good thing in this line o' work, skulkin' about as we be." His amusement at my alarm, splitting his beard with a grin. "Ain't seen anyone since ye went home, so there be nothin' to report. May have been a night where they weren't huntin'."

"Has there been any other sort of connection?" He seemed not to understand, so I decided to try a different route. "The killings seemed to be random other than the locations, but has there been anything else that could pinpoint how often they happen?"

He seemed to think about it for a few minutes, then shrugged. "Qornath'd know, but they started a month back, spaced about two weeks for the first two murders, then a week for this last one. We've had other bodies pop up, but they weren't the kind with the symbols. Those ones started showin' up two months back. City's been in arms over it. People afeared to go out alone at night for worry of bein' chosen as the next victim."

The other victims, the not marked, what were they like?" Sundar's voice startled us both, and I had to reach out and stop Blothl from teetering over the edge of the roof in surprise. He cursed vehemently under his breath and shook his fist at her.

"Ain't seen 'em, but Herilda said they looked messier." He frowned at her and raised a curious brow her way. "Why?"

"It seems like they may have been learning how to do it right." She rubbed her head and looked around. "I'm later than I wanted to be, but it's because I did some digging back home. There are old pages that talk about ritual sacrifices being necessary to summon creatures from beyond."

"Pages?" Blothl muttered, with a look of confusion on his face. "Ye mean books? Ye have books on such things back in yer world? Crazy lot, ye be."

"Yes, books." I chuckled, knowing she likely meant the Internet.

We watched the alley for about an hour in silence, the growing pre-dawn light rising slightly to eat away at the darkness above us.

Finally, Sundar decided to break the silence, "So has your city joined the war effort?"

"Oh, aye!" The dwarf clapped his fist to his beard-covered chest with a proud stare at me. "We offer warriors and material aid as well as some of the finest forged blades this side o' the demon wastes."

"So, then it stands to reason that taking you guys out of the fight would be a pretty big blow to the war effort, right?" Sundar's question came just before I could ask the same thing.

"I s'pose so, aye?" He frowned and blinked at both of us before realization dawned on his face. "Ye be thinkin' they're traitors?"

"It's entirely possible." I looked to Sundar. "If that's the case, we're probably in over our heads. We may need to go to the queen about this."

Her eyebrows knitted together, and her tusks bared to both of us. "That's fine, I guess. I really wanted to earn this on my own, though."

"Well, you gathered information that they otherwise didn't have already and have connected it to a major faction who would want to see the city burn so they can win the war." I scratched my head near my right horn, my nail butting up against the hard attachment as I did so. "We're on our own here, and honestly, if we can get more help in this, I'd say we go for it."

"Okay, when the sun comes up, let's go see her and figure this out." She stretched her shoulders and squared down by the edge of the roof. "Seems like this may have been a dead spot anyway."

"Wait." Blothl stilled, and I heard something that sounded like gravel shifting and heavy dragging.

We all crouched and peeked over the edge to see a stout figure dressed in dark armor dragging someone out of the connecting alleyway to the one we watched over and took out a long blade.

"Blothl, get the guard!" I whispered harshly, and he lifted himself and scurried away while Sundar and I looked down below. We couldn't let him do what he was about to do and decided that the ten-foot drop had to be fine; otherwise, he would start the deed.

Sundar lacked the agile nature I seemed to be cultivating, so her drop made it sound like some archangel of doom had landed in the alley and it spooked the man, his reflexes much sharper than hers as he ducked beneath her clutches.

I dropped down next in an attempt to block his path, and he juked around me with his hood up and his long dagger slashing for my ribs.

6 dmg taken.

Luckily, I took it on my left vambrace, or it might have been more. He sped past me, and I flung my hand out toward him and thought *freeze* before willing my ice Aether to strike him.

Four of my bars syphoned away, and a blast of frigid air left my hand and caught him in the back, but it only seemed to slow him a little as he plowed into the main roadway. Sundar surged by me hellbent on following our suspect, so I did my best to keep up. It was just before dawn now, and some people had begun to stir and get ready for their days, going into the streets to prepare for whatever their day held, only to be rudely shoved aside by a runaway dwarf and the enraged orc chasing him.

As I began to catch up to her, Sundar snatched up anything she could get ahold of in the streets—pieces of wood, baskets, fruit—and hucked them after the fleeing figure. One of the smaller wooden beams clattered against the ground loudly and caught the figure about the legs, his momentum carrying him forward and into the wall of a large stone building with a crash. Several small barrels and pots clattered and cascaded down around him, beating against his back, and he struggled to get up out of the lucky trap. We were closer now, but he was off again down an alleyway next to the building.

Sundar roared as she rounded the corner, and her aura sparked blue before she disappeared. I heard her roaring in fury and grunting in the distance and felt a fight had begun, so I drew my short sword and proceeded to the mouth of the alley.

"Tell me what you're planning!" Sundar bellowed to the figure she held in a chokehold with her right arm and her back to me. His hood was down now, and I could see by his beard that he was a dwarven man, and she fought to keep his other arm reaching for his weapon.

I jogged down the alley and pressed the tip of my blade against his sternum. "You go for that weapon again, and I cut you from nape to chop. Tell us everything."

He screamed in rage, his body bucking against Sundar, who struggled to hold him still, and spittle flew from his mouth. My eyebrows furrowed, his tongue worked for something in his mouth, and suddenly, Sundar grunted, then said, "Oh no, you fuckin' don't, not happening to me again!"

She turned and slammed his head against the wall hard

enough that I thought I heard a crack before his eyes rolled back into his head. She held him there by the throat and stuck her large green fingers into his mouth like she was digging for gold.

Finally, she yanked something out and threw it onto the ground, "Fucking plan B! Whoever it is that is running this doesn't want their people caught at all."

"This way!" Bellowing and shouting from the street at the entrance to the alley drew my attention as six heavily armored dwarves in red armor and Blothl sprinted down the path to us.

"Drop him orc!" One of the guards behind Blothl barked angrily, and our friend from the herd promptly turned and slugged him right in the kisser.

"Any o' ye speak to one o' Queen Belgonna's chosen like that again an' I'll brain ye an' drag ye on yer face to her Majesty meself, aye?" The others looked like they were about to converge on the dwarf when a sharp blast of a whistle caught their attention.

Qornath strode down the stones toward us, out of breath. "Get ye goin' ye lot, to the queen's audience chamber at once. The rest of ye, three blocks yonder near the butcher's—we have another body. Help Herilda collect it, and for the love o' the gods keep yer gobs shut. Go now."

Three of the red-clad dwarves sprinted away, and I stepped closer to Qornath. "How is that possible, we stopped this guy."

He looked me in the eyes, and I could see the panic and worry there. "There were three murders this mornin' lad. And they chose the best one it seems. We need to get this one to Queen Belgonna and see what she can make of him."

Qornath waved the three other dwarven guards forward, and they took the injured suspect and clamped irons around his wrists and legs before hoisting him over one of their shoulders and walking off, presumably to meet with the queen. I leaned down and grabbed what Sundar had thrown on the ground to pocket it for later. I wanted to ask what it was and if it was dangerous, maybe we could put it to good use.

Nearly twenty minutes later, we had arrived at the doors to Belgonna's chambers once more. We knocked, and the door opened as if it were supposed to be that way at all times. The damned thing nearly flew off the hinges.

We found Belgonna in the company of four other dwarven men dressed in similar clothing to Qornath, she eyed the talon and rolled her eyes, "Finally my talons have gathered. I have received word of three new deaths today? *Three!* And one of them had those cursed markings again! Why is my city being plagued like this? My children live in fear!"

"Queen Belgonna," one of the younger-looking dwarves raised a hand and stepped forward with a curt bow of his head and spoke with a very clear accent. "We have men scouring the city at all hours. Guard shifts have changed, and even the herd have been employed to join in rousting out these nefarious bastards for you."

"Fat lot o' good that's done." Snorted another of the men standing next to him, the grey-bearded dwarf rolled his eyes and shook his head. "We ought to be goin' house to house an' street to street to find the culprits. Kick in the doors an' beat 'em where they hide."

The other two dwarves roared at that and began to screech and call over the first two while Belgonna massaged her head in her tall elven form, she looked tired and stressed out.

Finally, Qornath seemed to have had enough as he whistled a shrill, piercing note that cut through the bickering and sneered, "Shut yer flappin' beards an' get yer damnable hands out o' yer trousers ye bunch o' measurement, contest slingin' cocks or I'll—"

"That's enough, master Qornath." Belgonna growled, her once human-looking teeth sliding toward draconic in her anger. "I see you bring Sundar and Kyvir to me. I hope you bring news, or I may have to find a new talon."

"Aye, they an' Blothl—me informant among the herd—

believe they found one o' the culprits, an' if I reckon right, they may have more disturbin' news."

Belgonna turned to me and Sundar, then eyed her talons. "You all may stand aside. Sundar, my dear sweet child, you and Kyvir come and stand before me. Please, report what you have found."

Sundar and I stepped forward together, roughly twelve feet away from the giant woman, and explained the morning's events to her as they had happened. She listened carefully, confirming things sporadically with Qornath and Blothl as she deigned to.

"So, I see that you bring me a possible member of this group to me?" She stepped closer to the dwarf that had been put upon the floor. "His mind is muddled by an injury, but that is an easy enough fix. Blothl, please go and fetch father Caltross from the church. He will be able to heal these mental wounds."

Blothl bowed without so much as a word and sped off out of the room before Belgonna turned to us again. "What think you of all this, hmm?"

"Kyvir and I have reason to suspect that there is a faction of people who are working with the demons in an attempt to summon either a demon or something worse here." Sundar sounded like she had been giving a report to an officer in the field. "When we came upon the culprit, he was quick to attack us in order to flee and then tried to commit suicide by poison when we caught him, and he couldn't escape. Most people who think that way are radicals or think that they will likely die worse if their superiors find out they were captured."

"And what makes you think it is the demons that they consort with?" She raised a red, fiery eyebrow at me.

"It's the only thing that makes sense based on your involvement in the war, the bodies found, and the similarities in the deaths and what has been stolen." I shrugged my shoulders and thought a moment longer, before adding, "If I could remove an enemy and cripple the front line by doing it, then I would likely come here too."

Belgonna strode forward until she looked over both of us and muttered, "Barely two days." She turned back toward her talons and snarled, "Not even a week, and already they have proven more competent than half of you in centuries!"

She stopped where she stood, her shoulders rising and falling where she was and dragged her hands through her flaming hair. She turned and smiled at us almost sadly. "Forgive me. The stresses of my people tax me, and I am not normally so volatile. I love my city. I love and trust my people. I trust my talons and forgive their failings as they are useful and highly skilled. Please, forgive me my outburst, all of you."

The talons all knelt down onto a knee as one and barked, "Forgiven!"

She pinched her nose and looked about. "I have been remiss, it seems, I'm not inquiring after your friends. Where are they?"

"They've returned to Iradellum to prepare Monami's mother for joining our party," I explained, her features grew pinched.

"I see." She stepped forward and reached out. "You have completed my quest, it seems, or at least a portion of it. And for that, I will uphold my bargain and offer a new quest as well. But first, your rewards."

She looked down into my eyes, "Summoning Aether is one of the rarest types in this world, and for me to activate it, the toll is heavy on you. I do not know exactly what it will take, but it will take something, I fear. Are you willing to make this sacrifice for power?"

What on earth could it take that would be so bad? I fought not to smile as I remembered the cost for Trickle, the water guardian of Iradellum, to awaken my ice Aether. She had taken my first kiss in this game world. If that was all, or something similar, I could deal with that. "I will make this sacrifice for power."

"As you wish." She motioned for me to kneel, and as I did so, she joined me. She was still much taller than me, and when I was fully on both knees, she took my shoulders in her hands and rested her forehead against mine. A sharp pain lanced through my body and every fiber of my being burned, aching, and screaming for me to be away from this creature who tormented me.

The burning ended in my heart and mind, fading almost as soon as it began, and I looked up to see that Belgonna wept above me. She pulled me into a hug so tight that it was all I could do not to pass out from both the heat of her body and the rough contact.

"I am sorry, Kyvir. I am so sorry." She continued to sob against my head and shoulder, her tears moistening my hair and armor to the point where I had to push against her chest to get away so I could draw breath.

Huffing, I panted. "What... was taken?"

"I cannot tell you." She sniffed, and her golden eyes looked bloodshot. "It is against the laws of the Aether. You will find out someday. And when you do, I hope you will be able to forgive me."

She pulled my head to her lips and kissed my forehead in a motherly way that made my whole body warm before she stood and stepped closer to Sundar.

Sundar pulled out a handkerchief from her inventory, handing it to the large woman, and she smiled gratefully. Belgonna dabbed her eyes and smiled sadly at Sundar.

"I had hoped this would be a more joyous occasion, but alas, I cannot say that it will be for now. Normally, there would be a feast and a celebration for days over what I offer you." She raised her hand and pressed it against Sundar's cheek warmly with a small, sad smile. "I feel that would be unsightly due to current events, but I offer it to you all the same. I offer you the chance to become my child in truth and not only in title."

"What do I have to do?" Sundar stepped closer to the dragon queen and looked up into her eyes. "If it means I will be able to have something I've dreamt of for so long and be able to help my friends—I'll do what I have to, Mother."

When the orcish woman called Belgonna mother, you would

have sworn that the queen had gazed upon her first-born child then and there. The love and adoration in her gaze was so intense that it made me miss my own parents so fiercely a tear crept into my eye.

"Survive." She lifted her wrist and bit into her flesh, her teeth sharpening as mine did, and blood welled up to the surface of her skin. "Drink this, and survive."

My mouth began watering as the crimson droplets fell to the floor, but movement caught my attention, and I broke from my narrowing vision.

"I'm a wanderer, of course, I will." Sundar's confident grin widened, and she opened her mouth wide to allow several large drops of blood to enter her gullet and swallowed. Her hands flew to her throat, and her eyes widened in panic just before she screamed, and Belgonna shifted into her massive draconic form and hid my friend's body from view.

CHAPTER THIRTEEN

MONA

"Okay, Ori, I get that you wanted me to deliver that parcel to a smith that you trust in Belgonna's Hold, but we had precious little time there before we were taken to see the queen." I held my hands in front of the angry man's face in a vain attempt to ward off and stay his outrage. "Plus, I found out that my mother would be joining me here in this world, and I had to return to greet her and help her."

He slowly leaned back and folded his arms across his chest. "I take it that means you'll be wanting to make gear for her? Using *my* materials after you failed to do a simple task?"

"If it makes you feel better, I can make the trip back and do it *right* now, but I'll still require your help." I tried to reason with him, but he still eyed me in distaste. "I *swear* that I meant to do it, but I have to take care of my mom, Ori. She's all I have other than my friends. The only family I truly have."

He held out a massive calloused hand. "Helpin' family is one thing, girl. But if your ma is all you got, then you helpin' her is fine by me. You'll pay only twenty-five percent less than cost of materials for her gear, and you'll be working harder than ever to make up my esteem of you. As soon as you deliver that parcel, I expect you'll appreciate my wrath now. You hear?"

I snapped to attention before him and barked, "Yes, master!"

He snorted and plopped a massive hand onto my shoulder hard enough that it threw me a little off my feet, and I had to catch myself to stay upright.

"You know when she's going to get here?" He raised a brow at me.

Doing some quick math in my head, I guessed. "Likely a day or two? Time moves funny for us." We were about to take a break for food anyway and then in a few hours, we would break for a four-hour nap.

"Then get your sorry behind in here and start to work." He growled affectionately at me. "You'll earn every damned swing of our hammers!"

Nervous laughter escaped my slightly smiling mouth as I bolted into the place and began to do my part with the others. I told them of the weapon maintenance I had done and what I could of meeting the queen, though they asked more, I told them I couldn't say because of magic, and they took it at that.

While I toiled away, Albarth went off to secure the best quests that he could find for us to take and give to my mom so we could level her up as swiftly as possible. Our goal was to get her to level ten and up to speed as quickly and painlessly as possible.

The work was hard and long, toiling like this only making me hungrier somehow, and this time I used tools in conjunction with my metal magic. The amount of focus it took was beyond me at first, and Ori had a hard time relating something he wasn't as familiar with to me.

"Working tools and magic simultaneously is draining work, and I wish I knew more, but all I have for you is theory." He groused and looked over my work, pointing to a flaw in the metal. "Melt it down and go take a break, you're beginning to get sloppy."

"Yes, master." A heavy sigh escaped my lips, and I looked about for a smelting bucket to put the ax head into when I got a whisper from Seth.

—*Something big is going on, and we've been rewarded for our part in the quest. Sundar has been adopted, but she's going through some kind of change, I don't know what it is. We need you here ASAP with Ma if we want to have a chance at things.*—

I frowned, found a bucket, and dropped the axhead into it, and pressed it into the forge before walking out of the smithy and into the cool air. We had been gone a few hours in real-time. The carriage sped our travel exponentially, and it only took us a day to get back. How had they managed to get themselves into trouble so soon?

—*What the hell happened?*— I sent back as soon as I had read the message a third time. —*Do you need us back now?*—

It took a second, but the response made my jaw drop.

—*There's someone here trying to summon demons or something. We aren't sure how many of them there are, but we need all the help we can get. Nothing active except the Sundar thing. Make sure you train mom well, we may be in for a hell of a fight.*— Cool air flooded my lungs, but I still couldn't grasp what he was talking about with Sunny.

—*Is she going to be okay?*—

—*I don't know. Belgonna is using her wings to shelter her from sight, and she was screaming for a good minute or two before finally falling silent. It's been three minutes.*— I could tell he was worried. —*She's not telling me what's going on, and I don't know if she's going to be okay, but this seems to have been somewhat expected? She keeps gently pushing me away and telling me not to worry.*—

I gritted my teeth and tried to decide if that was reason enough for me to go back there. It was earlier in the morning here in the city, so it would still be morning there. I could take an hour and go back to Belgonna's Hold to investigate, but that would take me from here for at least an hour, and Seth had said Belgonna wasn't worried. I didn't trust her, and I could deliver that parcel… but I'd still be gone if I was needed here.

—*What do you make of all this, Al?*— I ran my clawed hands through my hair and waited as calmly as I could.

—*I assume you mean Kyvir's message?*—

—*Duh. I'd like to go and check on them, but I don't know if that's a good idea.*— I frowned before adding, —*I even have a delivery quest back there to meet a smith in Belgonna's Hold, but I don't know if that will start some kind of training that will keep me there super long.*—

—*Don't go then, Kyvir and Sundar are gamers, they can fend for them-selves, and if the queen says that it's okay, then we would only be putting your own quest in danger by being in her presence.*—

I hadn't thought about that at all. And here I had been ready to march straight back into the room with the big lady to try and grill her about Sundar. Damn.

—*Then I'll hold off.*—

—*Seems that you can learn after all.*— I could almost hear his smarmy British smugness in the message, but just rolled my eyes and tried to reel in my anxiety. Time to eat.

I turned and walked back over to the guys at the forge. "I'm going back home for a little while. I'll be back in about three hours or so."

They waved and grunted, turning to grab the bucket from the forge to check the metal within before I turned around to log out.

I opened my eyes to see that the lights in my living room were on, and my mom stood there with her back to me cleaning something. I blinked a few times and opened the portal door, making her turn and smile.

"So, this is how they are supposed to work?" Her hands gently touched the machine, feeling it as if she were trying to memorize the touch of it. Or as if she were someone leaned over the edge of a cliff and making sure they wouldn't fall.

"Don't worry; when you get yours, you'll go through a tutor-ial, and it will explain everything." I leaned down and picked up some jogging shorts and a loose tee from the ground to put on, not caring about the need to towel off with her here. "Have you thought any more about what you want to make your avatar be? Please tell me it won't be human like you were thinking about."

She frowned at me and put her hands on her hips. "And just what is wrong with human?"

"Other than the fact that it's the most vanilla thing one can possibly be in a fantasy game like this?" I raised my eyebrows and motioned to myself, then her. "They're possibly the weakest race in most fantasy games. They likely won't have the most beneficial stats, and you'll need every edge you can get. Every edge we can give you."

I didn't want to tell her about all the internal drama going on for now, she would likely figure it out sooner rather than later.

"I will consider carefully, what I choose." She rolled her eyes and pointed to the table where two plates of hot food lay ready for us to eat and chat. "Figured you would be hungry, and I wanted to clean a little before they come in the morning."

"It's fine in here!" I insisted as she sat next to me.

"Last time, they had to shovel your clothes out of the way." She picked a discarded shirt off the floor with a knowing smirk. "An intelligent mind makes for a cluttered space, a cluttered space makes for a suffocating space. Without fresh air, we cannot grow."

"Dad used to say that…" my eyes fell to the floor at her feet, and she lifted my chin, forcing my gaze to meet her own.

"Where do you think he learned it?" Her eyes softened, and she smiled softly. "He was always somewhere off in his head, his fantasies, and worlds. I never knew where I would find him from one moment to the next, but I could always tell when his office was a mess by how irritated he was. I would remind him to clean, and he would always tell me, 'Em, you know me too well. Thank you, my clean queen.'"

I couldn't help the snort that escaped from me as I tried to imagine that. "Seriously?"

"Oh, yes. He was the most inventive and creative man I had

ever known, and that was his nickname for me." The sides of her eyes crinkled in delight. "You know, all this time not talking about him, I never realized how it affected you because of my own pain. I realize that now, and I wanted to apologize."

"Mom, it's fine. I knew you were hurting, and I had other places to go to talk about it." I looked at her, and she raised an eyebrow expectantly. "Or not. Seth listened when he could, but you know how he can be."

"Trying to help by talking and attempting to solve the issue?" When I chuckled, she laughed and rolled her eyes. "Sweetheart, that's not a Seth problem, that's a man problem. A lot of men are like that. Got a problem? Solve it immediately. That can't always be done. They just don't always get that."

We laughed and ate a little. The chicken marsala she brought out was two days old, but delicious. We loved leftovers in this house, and it was because my mom's cooking was always the best.

"Speaking of Seth," she began, making me still. Her gaze lifted to me, and I carefully made myself go back to eating. "I see you two are up to more together than usual. And I've also seen the way you look at him. The way you lean on him for support. When are you going to just realize that you love him? Confess it."

"I do."

"Just come out with it and let him know how you fe—I'm sorry?" She stared at me as if I had a horn suddenly growing from my head.

"I said, 'I do,'" I snarled at her without meaning to. The admission seemed sudden, even to me. "Sorry. I'm still coming to terms with it at the moment, and my normal anger at you pushing for answers came out."

"I don't blame you." She grinned like she had just won some vaunted prize. "When did you know? Sorry, when did you finally admit it to yourself?"

"Forever ago, but more recently too." Not wanting to get into the details of it, I checked my phone and saw that I still had more than half an hour and rolled my eyes. "But it doesn't matter because I ruined that."

"You didn't panic and accuse him of something, did you?" My face radiated warmth like the sun, and she cursed vehemently. Violently enough that I stared at her in shock. "You're so predictable at times that it's like watching your father screw up our relationship when we first started dating all over again."

She stood and began to pace the room in front of me. "He loved me, always had, and when I asked him about if he wanted to date, you know what he told me?" I shook my head, flabbergasted. "That he was in love with Meredith."

"Seth's mom?!" My hand flew to my mouth, and she cackled crazily. "No way. How? Why?"

"He panicked, and since they were such good classmates and lab partners, he thought of her first because he was around her all the time."

"What did you do?" It was so hard to hear the wonder in my voice and not cringe. This was the gossip I never got because I always hung out with Seth, and my mother hadn't been this talkative in so long I had almost forgotten what it was like.

"I marched up to her in the hallway at school and asked her right then and there if she knew he loved her, and she snorted in my face." She stopped and threw her hands into the air. "I loved this boy so much that even her apparent dismissal of it wounded my pride for him, and I told her that she had better let him down gently or I would be making a visit to her locker. She looked me dead in the eyes and said, 'listen girly, that boy loves *you* and makes it known to me all hours of the day. You better get to him before someone else realizes what he has to offer and never let go.' So, I walked right up to him and told him I knew he lied, and he admitted it. Told me he had been nuts for me since day one. And we'd been an item from then on."

Warmth filled my heart at the gushy tale, and mom's face

filled with reminiscent joy turned to me, smile slowly fading. "And here I had almost let him go."

I patted the sofa next to me, and she sat down. "You truly believe that your father may have something to do with this game?"

"If he doesn't, I'll be at a loss as to where he could be." The thought of not knowing ate at my soul, hopelessness threatening to cloud my mind. "I have to know."

"I do too." Mom reached out and patted my hand lovingly. "I do too, sweetheart. It's all that is getting me into this freaky contraption. And without my precious dogs."

"Oh, my god, the pack!" The alarm in my voice surprised her, and she looked askance of me. "What about the pack? We will be playing for hours a day—who will feed them and care for them?"

"My assistant will have that covered." She waved it away. "And Diego has been quite some help with them while we are on vacation. He will see them fed and put through their paces."

"Okay." I shrugged. "Then I guess it's time for me to get back into the game. I'll likely be out in a couple hours to take a nap before the workers arrive. My notes on the game so far should help you in the beginning area, and I will come find you as soon as you finish the tutorial. Okay?"

"I've been reading over them, and I'll be completely candid with you, I have no clue what the hell it is that is expected of me." Her lips parted, her teeth flashing almost threateningly. "I look forward to the challenge."

I snorted, and we laughed for a moment before finishing our meal, and I went into the portal after undressing. "See you in a little while."

"Have fun." Mom smiled at me and went back to cleaning as the portal counted me down to get back in.

———

"Again!" Ori barked, and I tapped the same spot. "Harder, hit it harder!"

I growled and turned my anger on the spear beneath my hammer, beating it into the shape that the Aether impressed upon my mind and vision.

"Smithing weapons is as much a work of passion as anything in this world, Monami—you have to feel the heat of the forge working through you." His waxing poetic about the art had been a new one for me, and as much as it could have been a helpful lecture outside in the cool air, it was destroying what precious little focus I had. "The hammer is your will incarnate, and you must use it to exact your desire on the canvas before you, with the Aether as your muse. So help me, if you strike the damned anvil again, I will see you polish every blade we have!"

Clang! "God *fucking shit!*" My snarled cuss rang out around the square, other people stopped to stare at us.

"Get out." Ori sighed tiredly.

I set the hammer down and looked at him, his disappointment apparent in his downcast gaze. "I can do it, I just need more practice. Please, let me keep trying."

"No." He shook his head. "I can only teach you the mundane way to craft, and that is not what you need. That parcel I gave you? Was a letter of introduction to the smith I had told you to find. He could teach you both."

"Am I really that bad a smith that you don't want to work with me anymore?" Biting anxiety nipped at my chest. If I couldn't work here, we would need to pay full price for Mom's gear. We could do it, but what if we needed that money for other things?

"Save the waterworks, girl." Ori spat. "You know bloody well that I'd have you in this smithy over almost anyone. Your talent and dedication are admirable—my concern is ruining you and your potential. I cannot bring myself to be so selfish as that."

So, he was trying to save me from making bad habits stick

or something? "Okay. If that's how you feel, I'll practice my trade with this other smith and then come back to help you guys, too. But what of my mother?"

"Twenty-five percent below is still your rate. Employee discount and all." Ori glanced my way and gave me a sly wink as the other smiths shook their heads. "Get going, girl. I want you to be the best. Understand?"

"Yes sir!" I barked, and he smiled. Each of the smiths came out to the cool air to give me supportive hugs, Alvor holding on a little longer than the others and whispering his gratitude for everything. After I patted his back awkwardly, he let go.

I turned dejectedly and decided that since nothing else was going on, I'd log out and get some extra sleep. An extra hour wouldn't hurt anything.

CHAPTER FOURTEEN

SETH

Blaring alarms went off, startling me from an already fitful slumber before I blinked blearily at the ceiling and dragged myself out of bed. I checked my phone and saw that Sondra had texted me back.

—*Yeah, I'm okay. Went through a lot, and I kind of want you to see it before I say anything. See you in there.*— she'd sent that an hour or so after I had logged off and left her a half dozen voicemails.

Stalking from my room to the kitchen for a quick bite, I remembered the delivery was supposed to have been dropped off and checked outside. Sure enough, two weeks' worth of healthy, nutritious meals had arrived at my door in an innocuous box that had to weigh at least sixty pounds.

I put the food away swiftly, nuked the breakfast meal, and scarfed it down with a godawful energy drink that made me question my sanity. Once I was done, I stripped and hopped into the portal.

Colors flashed past my head, and I returned to where I had

been watching for some sign that she was okay, only to realize that I had come face to face with Belgonna.

"Kyvir." Her warm gaze washed over me. "I had wondered when you might return. A whole twelve hours?"

"My apologies, time moves weirdly where I come from compared to here." I smiled at her, and she grinned, her sharp teeth peeking out from behind her scaled lips. I peeked around her to try and see if I could find Sundar, but she wasn't there. "Can I help you?"

"I am here to help *you*." Her hot breath blew my hair back before she backed away and shifted form to that of her elven one. "I am going to teach you how to cast summoning magic."

"Oh!" I grinned at the prospect of it. "What will I be able to summon? Can I summon creatures? Will I be able to control them?"

A rumbling laugh made me pause, and her mirth confused me. "What?"

"Yes. You will be able to do that, and much more." She stepped closer, her gaze shifting to my face. "You have aspected Aether, yes?"

I nodded. "Ice."

"Unfortunate." The heat in the room dialed up to a ten and suddenly, it was so hard to breathe that all I could focus on that. "You will be unable to maintain any sort of ice magic in my presence. However, summoning other things will be possible."

"What?" My eyebrows dipped inward in confusion.

"Ice magic can be manipulated and changed in many ways, can it not?" Her question surprised me. "You have seen many different things since coming here, many types of magic that can be used in many different ways. So why do you think that summoning magic cannot be used in the same manner?"

She held out her hand, and warm air rushed across my shirt. I felt my chest and yelped in surprise, only to be even further surprised by the fact that my armor had appeared in her outstretched hand.

"I can do that too?!" I cried joyously before stepping closer to her.

"Someday, perhaps." It was hard not to note the pride in her tone as she let my armor clank onto the ground. "You are much too untrained and undisciplined to do something so complicated. As a new summoner, you will have difficulties taking things that you cannot see, worn objects, and things being held. Adding aspected Aether will allow you to summon creatures and other things to your aid. There are other aspects to learn, but they are better committed to memory through practical training."

She waved to her throne and placed a single coin onto the armrest before turning to me to order, "Summon the coin."

I took a deep breath and fought through my excitement to work on the task at hand. I opened my hand and reached for the summoning Aether within me. It was finicky at first, difficult to grasp, and then slippery to control.

"Do not fight it, simply show the Aether what it is you desire and will it to you." She coached softly behind me. "Keep trying."

I rolled my shoulders then allowed the Aether to span the distance between myself and the coin, about thirty feet in total before another bar of my summoning Aether faded and finally touched the coin. Once it did, the coin disappeared, and a slight weight dropped into my hand.

"I did it!" I hooted and danced back and forth.

"Yes, you did." She seemed pleased. "Tell me, did you notice something?"

"The further away it was, the more Aether it required." She nodded, and I frowned. "Then how am I supposed to summon creatures if they aren't near me?"

"That is another thing entirely," she stated. Belgonna stretched out her hand, a roiling flame erupted there, and a figure made wholly of flame stood waiting. "Aspected Aether forms the rift that summons them, and if they aren't friendly to you already, Aether will collar them."

"So, they would be what, temporary allies?" I asked as I stared at what had to be a flame elemental, his large humanoid body made of flames with black holes where his eyes and mouth should be.

"We are capable of great thought, small one." The elemental flame's voice crackled. "I have partnered with Queen Belgonna since she was powerful enough to summon me and see her as a friend, as I hope she does with me."

"Of course, I do." Belgonna admonished the flame and relaxed a little. "You can think of them as allies. You are also capable of building a rapport with your summoning's and conserve your Aether. It cost me little to nothing to summon Pyre, here."

"I see." I blinked at them both, and Pyre flickered out of existence. The heat radiating through the room died down a little.

"Come, we will practice more." She turned and grabbed a dagger from her hoard and placed it in her palm. "Take this from me."

"You just said that it was too difficult to take something from someone."

"You paid attention, excellent." She smiled, and her perfect teeth flashed at me. "You would normally not be able to. If I held it in a closed fist, you would likely lack the Aether necessary to take it until you were a *much* higher level. But as it is loosely held, then it will be easier for you."

I clapped my hands together and rubbed them in thought. "That seems to track with everything laid out so far."

By now, my Aether had recovered, and I lashed out with it, summoning the dagger to my hand.

"Excellent work!" Belgonna bellowed and clapped loudly. "Excellent indeed!"

We worked for a little while longer, her coaching me on how to summon things from my enemies and from allies that may be useful, and it was steadily becoming more and more second nature as we went on. To the point where she began to consider me more carefully as time went on.

On a break, she sat next to me, and I was grateful for the company. By now, she had been praising me so much that it was hard to feel any sort of negative about what was going on. This was a huge blessing.

"Kyvir, where are your mother and father?" The question softly asked, caught me by surprise, and I just blinked at her in stunned silence. "I cannot smell them on you, and in your memories, they were gone fairly often. I know that the bond you share with the lioness, Monami, and her mother is strong, but why are you not with your family?"

I chose how to answer carefully, not really knowing myself at times. "When I was young, I used to ask myself the same thing. Wondered why I had to stay with Monami and her mom at times when I could have gone with my parents. They had a mission in life, and though I was their greatest success, they felt they owed it to Monami and me to make the world a better place for us to be in. That it was their duty to change the world for me. Their visits were the best, and when we went home to see my family, we would party and eat and have a great time— but it never really could have lasted."

"The world you come from needed their aid so much?" She tilted her head to the side and watched me steadily, a slight expression of disbelief somehow clear in her eyes. "So much that it took them from you? Were they powerful?"

I had to laugh at her call on that one. "No. just really smart and ambitious." She nodded to herself, looking forward. "You know, your hoard isn't so impressive as one hears of in legends of dragons. Why is that?"

She smiled to herself as she stared at the piles of gold behind her throne and toward the rear of her room. "Because my children are my hoard. I value them and their lives more than my own. My city as well. All that I have, I give back to my beloved people. But even I, in my great power and might, know that I cannot change the world."

Her large hand engulfed mine, I was sure it was meant to be comforting, and it was. But at the same time, I didn't think that was right. "You may not be able to change the world as it is but changing someone else's world can lead to greater ripples all over. I think that was what my parents wanted to impart to me. If you can show someone there's a better way, give them the tools to better themselves and show them how—you've changed the world in a small way that will grow exponentially."

Her hand tightened, and I felt warm breath on the top of my head. "You are very wise, Kyvir. I am proud to know that you choose to take lessons from loss. You remind me of my son, Balfour. Wise and courageous, leading our forces on the front lines where his sister and I cannot be."

"I don't know about courageous, that's my parents."

"I do, they seem cunning, and ambition is a desirable trait among dragons." She looked down at me then, her glowing golden eyes ensorcelled me. "While they have admirable traits, I cannot condone that they left their nestling in the hands of another and that their inactivity has caused him confusion and pain."

I frowned at her, memories of the times I'd had to do for myself because they were gone. Parent-teacher days at school. Take your child to work days. My first kiss with Shanae Gretnie in third grade. Shaving for the first time without knowing how and cutting myself so badly I looked like I should have been in a bad mummy movie. Trying to tie a bow tie for prom and screwing it up so badly, I had nearly choked myself with it.

Christmases and holidays spent with Mona and her family.

Never feeling like I really belonged. Knowing that my parents loved me, but their way of showing it had sucked when I was young and how I had lashed out by cutting my hair and dying it crazy colors. Now I just did it because I liked the colors.

"You remember now." Her hot hands cupped my cheeks tenderly and stared into my eyes once more. "It is no longer hidden from you by wishful thinking and rationalization. You deserve to be treated like the gift you are. The gift you always should have been considered."

"I appreciate that, but I don't know what I would do with it." I shrugged at her and laughed at the absurdity of it all. "Does this mean you want to adopt me as well? Would that mean I have to renounce my parents?"

She chuckled throatily. "No, dear Kyvir, your mortal parents would still be there, it would just allow all the world to know that you are one of my dearest children. But yes, I would be honored if you would allow me to become your surrogate mother."

Do I talk this over with Mona? I wondered to myself.

"You are skeptical?" She had to have seen the indecision on my face, my knit eyebrows and bit lip likely giving it away. "You would have power, station, and love. *My* love. I may not be mighty enough to change the world on my own, but I would change *your* world for you."

"It's so hard to believe you get nothing out of this." I found myself laughing, and she let go of my face, seeming hurt. "I don't mean to be insensitive, it's just that everything I know of dragons has seemed to be moot with regard to you."

"I get a chance to prove that I am a capable mother," her muttered response was almost lost against the crackling of flames all around us that had suddenly burst to life in sconces I hadn't noticed before. "That I can give life and keep my city safe by choosing those who might be able to assist in its protection by becoming my children. I serve you, so that you may serve the greater good of my people. *This world,* as you have so sweetly put it."

I should wait to talk to Sonny before I pull the trigger on deciding—see if it's worth it. I frowned some more, thinking that was a good idea and looked back to the queen.

She walked toward her throne, then stopped ten feet from it and turned to motion to herself before me. "I know loss, Kyvir. I know pain and suffering the likes of which no parent should bear, and I have born it as well as I can. Aid me, my people, and the world by becoming something greater. By becoming mine. Let me help you, sweet Kyvir, as you should have been."

She held her hands out to me like a parent reaching for their child to pick them up and give them a hug. "Allow me to hold you and call you my son."

Power, a soft voice whispered through my mind, and suddenly, my mouth dried out as I remembered what she had given to Sundar.

Her *blood.*

My body moved almost mechanically, the lure of it too much to fight, and I stepped toward her. Her almost frenzied look of victory turned to tears of joy as she picked me up into her arms and cradled my body against her chest.

"My son." She turned and walked with me toward her throne, where she cradled me in her strong arms like a newborn for some reason. She lifted her right arm above me and slid a long sharp nail across it before lowering the bleeding appendage to my lips.

Crimson touched my tongue, sweet and spicy like peppermint that flared down my throat as I drank greedily. Notifications that should have populated in my view automatically slid to the side and cascaded out of view while pure fire filled my veins. My whole body seemed to pull the delicious nectar into it, my sudden avarice confusing, but the need to sate my sudden desire to consume overtook it.

My hands, claws, and even legs wrapped around the arm above me tightly, finally I felt hands, gently pulling me away. I felt stronger than I ever had. But as swiftly as I had found that strength, it had been taken from me, and now my body bucked and screamed, agony filling my stomach and every fiber of my being until finally, darkness surrounded me.

Welcome to the Void

The darkness swirled around me relentlessly, the pain gone, but I could finally see lights in the distance that swooped closer to me in a myriad of shifting shapes and colors.

"Confusing, is it not?" Mephisto's sinister voice echoed

around me. "The void is where you will come to play a *delightful* game of chance. Though Belgonna's interference was not foreseeable, it will be interesting to see what her blood does to you."

"What's with the special interest, demon?!" It was hard to keep the fear I felt at bay.

"Special?" His maniacal laughter echoed loudly around me, shaking my body as it bounced off everything and nothing discordantly. "Because this is fun! And I am no mere demon—boy. You would do well to remember that."

A large wheel that reminded me of an old game show wheel popped up with four options, then a fifth. The largest of them were Fire Aether, Level Up, Three Points, and Lose a Turn. The smallest sliver of an option was Death and had a small skull over it between Fire Aether and Level Up.

"See? Won't this be so much fun?!" Mephisto's hands appeared on either side of the wheel and hovered there, unattached to arms. "Would *you* like to spin the wheel? Or should *I*?"

As he presented each option, a single word floated above each palm **You? Me?**

"I will." I declared, and his hands popped up to the top of the wheel and his finger dipped down onto the fore like a stop stick, and a lever appeared for me to pull. I grasped it, and electricity passed through my whole body. I fell forward onto the lever while Mephisto howled delightedly.

I watched upside down as the wheel spun until it was all one huge blurry mass.

"Round and round the wheel will go, where it stops time will show, you'd better learn and do it fast if you stay weak, your future becomes the past!" The demonic visage of my malevolent benefactor peeked out from behind the wheel and grinned with his overly large mouth.

Finally, after a full thirty seconds of spinning, he seemed to grow bored, and he grinned again. "This one!"

His too-long fingers speared into the wheel, the momentum stopping with a sickening crunch and grunt from him.

His pinky finger, twisted and mangled, had struck Death, while the three others had landed in Fire Aether.

"Almost fun; still this shall be interesting." He stepped out from behind the wheel and pointed a broken finger at my face. "Also, don't expect to reach a hundred percent on an Aether source like this unless you plan to go around draining blood from highly powerful creatures."

He turned to walk away, then stopped and looked back at me with a wink. "Or do that. Go, create chaos!"

His cackling laughter chased me out of the darkness and back into a different sort of dark.

"Ah, finally awake!" Belgonna greeted me warmly. The warmth seemed to be mild, even with her fully draconic body pressed against my side.

She shifted, and I groaned at the light blinding me as her wings moved. "Oh, you look quite dashing."

I frowned at her and tried to stand, then promptly fell. "Careful now, you're still weak from the transformation."

"Looking good, Kyvir." A rough sounding voice greeted me. I turned to see someone who had to be Sundar. Only, she looked different.

Six inches taller than she had been and much thinner than before, she looked more like a muscled Amazonian warrior than the huge body-building orc she had been before. Her tusks were a little longer and sort of curved out of her mouth to the side. Her green skin had a slight blush to it all over, and the markings on her body that had looked painted on, now looked like they were made up of tiny scales.

"You look… different!" I whispered softly. She grinned, and I pointed to myself. "Do I look different?"

"Yeah, you do. If you pull up your status screen, you'll be able to see it." She smiled at me and made a shooing motion with her hand.

I opened it up, and sure enough, I looked very different. I was much beefier than I had been before, small red scales smattered my cheeks leading up past my ears and into my hairline.

My horns were thicker and longer than they had been before, as well. And my eyes.

Orange with slits in them. "Oh, that's cool." My stats hadn't changed at all to reflect anything other than the fact that I knew I had Fire Aether now. Which left me at three of each and one gray Aether.

That would be a pain in the ass to manage. I'd have to be careful with my magic use and Aether consumption.

"You are both my children now." Belgonna stood proudly now in her elven form. She held out a similar signet ring to Sundar's and dropped it into my hand. "And as such, I expect you to fulfill your duties to your people. Find whoever is killing your family and end them."

Quest Received – Find and kill whoever it is that is harming the people of your beloved city.

As a direct order from your blooded mother, this quest cannot be denied.

"Is this why you blooded us?" My eyes narrowed at her, she looked hurt at my accusation, but I pressed on. "We were committed to helping you even before this all. You didn't have to do this."

"I have blooded you so that we could be *family* Kyvir. I only order the two of you to do this because you two are my only hope as of right now." She stepped closer to the two of us, concern clouding her features. "You two working together have uncovered more in a matter of days than my people were capable of in *months*. This must stop, I fear that something is coming soon. While the two of you rested, the dwarf you captured was brought before me, and I found that the next planned murder is on the night of the full moon. Two days from now."

"We can try and sniff them out, but with the two of us alone there's no way." Sundar crossed her arms in front of her chest. "Is there somewhere we can go to gather some experience? Fight monsters and level up?"

"You may go with Blothl into the mines or the plains,"

Belgonna stated, her eyes closing. "I would suggest the mines because the plains have insect pods that roam and hunt. There is no telling how many will come, and they are exceptionally difficult to kill. The worst things you may find in the mines are goblins, spiders, or the occasional rock golem."

"Thank you, Your Majesty." I bowed my head, and a deep reverberating growl echoed around the room. I glanced up to find her disapproving glare aimed at me and changed my statement of gratitude to, "Sorry, thank you, *mother.*"

She raised her chin, and a soft smile graced her lips. "You are welcome. Do this for me, and I will reward you again. Experience that you crave, monetary reward—whatever I can do. Just try your hardest to foil this plot against my people. *Our* people."

I nodded. Sundar, and I turned to head out into the world, I slipped the signet ring onto the index finger of my left hand.

Nildy wasn't sure where Blothl would be this time of day, and she didn't have the extra people to send one to look for him, so she sent us toward the guardhouse at the city gate. They said that the Herd had some sort of training today outside the gates, so we stepped out and watched as a formation of dwarves on large goats stampeded by with spears drawn and jabbing forward in unison.

They maneuvered and barked orders for more than half an hour before someone finally noticed us.

Blothl came over on his surly-looking steed, the goat almost ramming me even with his evident control, "Ye better nae do that again, lad, I'll give yer apples to the nag!"

The goat bleated angrily and stomped the ground while Blothl just snickered at him, he nodded to us. "Royalty now, the both of ye?"

"I wouldn't say that." Sundar grinned, and I just rolled my eyes. "Mom—gah, that still feels weird to say—said that we can go into the mines to fight and get some leveling up under our belts before the group of traitors tries to get another sacrifice in a couple days. You in?"

"Aye, there be no dungeon in there that I be aware of, and I can have Nildy's husband come along with us." When Sundar and I both stared at him silently, he explained, "He be a miner. Well versed in what be under the mountain in there."

"Oh, okay then, sure." I shrugged, and we moved along the path back up to the gates and made our way toward the direction of the inn. Rather than going inside and speaking to Nildy, we walked straight to where the entrance to the mines were a little more north toward Belgonna's home, on the northern side of the city. The air here was much warmer than any other location I'd felt in the city so far, and I fanned myself a little.

We came down a path toward a large, open area, and I realized it felt more like the entry to a quarry as there was a huge hole in the side of the mountain with several layers leading up, and then a working area below with small huts and covered shed areas.

More than forty miners dotted the area along the walls of the entry to the mine—rather, what I thought had to be the entrance—on varying levels. They moved with picks and weapons belted to their waists.

"There a lot of action in the tunnels?" I couldn't help but feel a little excited at the thought of going in there. I could also see being able to put the pickaxe I had obtained from Ori to good use. But that would depend.

"Sometimes." He motioned to the area before the gaping hole and pointed to the building that looked more like a garrison than somewhere for miners. "Better question for the miners themselves an' the mettle brigade who watches over the tunnels an' entry point to the mine."

"Well, then let's go take a look and see if we can find our miner." I began down into the area along a path that several carts of stone and ore passed us on. The miners and their mules a stoic lot, quiet and contemplative as they strode by. Some of them watched us intently, obviously not of their ilk, and some others still muttered, "Bloody normies, think ta poke 'round our tunnels…"

After five minutes of trying to find someone to talk to, Sundar finally bellowed, "Where can we find Nildy's husband?!"

Several miners stopped what they were doing, and we heard the door to the building behind us fly open, "Who the bloody fook be harrassin' me miners, callin' after Nildy's man and INTERRUPTIN' the damned work we be doin' fer the war?!"

A bulbous halfling waddled out of the building, his face as red as the scales on my face and sweat covering his shirt. He pointed squarely at us, and screeched in a high-pitched voice, "You! What be you doin' here? Sabotagin' me worker's day? Fookin' up me productivity? I'll wring your necks—*fook off goat-fooker, I'll fix you too!*"

It was then that I chose to summon my first creature using both summoning and flame Aether in unison, not really knowing what would come through the rift. But maybe a show of power like this might keep him from trying to fight us. Once something came through, a small mote of fire that bobbed up and down for a moment, another bar of both summoning and flame aspected Aether drained, then another flame and finally the grey Aether too.

"I await your orders, Summoner!" the mote bellowed in a high-pitched, squeaky voice that sounded feminine. I blinked as it fluttered closer to me, and it looked like some kind of red, devilish looking pixie.

She grinned at me with sharp teeth, the horns on her head bobbing in time with her hovering movement back and forth. Flames decorated her body like clothes, and blazing blue wings flapped behind her like a demonic butterfly.

"Keep the little man from harming myself and my friends, but don't kill him." She blinked at my order, then turned at the waddling halfling whose gate hadn't slowed in the slightest and pointed her thumb at him with a raised eyebrow. "Him."

She glanced at him and shrugged. "Let him walk some more, it'll likely kill him anyway."

Howls of laughter made me flinch as Sundar and Blothl,

along with several of the closest miners, cracked smiles that they tried to hide behind their hands and coughs.

"Why I ought to flail you too!" The little man snarled and began to run, panting heavily. Genuinely concerned for his safety, I nodded to him again, and the hellish pixie rolled her eyes and flew toward him. Her wings and legs flared out like she was attempting to appear larger than she was.

"Stop!" She blared, her sudden rage making her light voice deeper and more commanding. "You come any closer, and I will *burn* you."

"Piss off!" The little man shrilled at her, but she held her ground until he went to swat her away, and she snatched his hand up in both of hers.

"I said, stop!" She wheeled around with him in her hands and the man swung bodily toward us, landing on his back, with a loud thud and cry of pain.

"Well, she didn't kill him," Sundar observed lightly as she stepped forward and flashed her signet ring. "Official business of the queen. We're here to explore the tunnels and fight some monsters if you have 'em. Please don't make me step in. I'm not as nice as the faeries."

"I'm a pixie!" She stormed closer to Sundar's head, stomping on the air as if it were solid ground.

"And you're an awesome one at that!" I placated her from where I stood, hoping my raised voice would bring her away from the woman who would likely crush her. It worked, and she floated my way. "What's your name? If I can ask."

She squinted at me hard. "I'm not giving you my true name —I don't know you like that. But you can call me Flicker. You gonna let me actually fight something if you summon me again?"

"Well, that depends on if you'll be the one to answer my call, is that how it works?" She blinked at me as if I were thick.

"I'm your first?"

I nodded, and she squealed delightedly, fluttering over to land on my shoulder and stare at me hard. "Never been anyone's first before. The less initial aspected Aether you use to summon a creature, the lower on the power scale they are. So, you spend one, you summon little old me. You spend twenty? You may summon something as strong as a djinn or something else. Whatever feels like answering the call."

"But, if that's the case, why did you take so much of my flame Aether?" It had taken all of my flame and the one grey I had for her to come.

"I didn't see a fight that looked interesting, so I fought the call until your Aether made me stay. Gotta keep that in mind for the future." She tapped the side of her head with a wink as she explained that last bit and giggled at the surprise on my face. "If you're not very strong on your own, most creatures will try to run from the summoning and fight you for control. So, you gotta bulk up, Summoner."

"Is there a way for you and me to become friends?" I lifted a brow at her. "Like the queen and her elemental friend?"

"Well, yeah if I trust you, we can be all buddy-buddy, but you gotta earn that." She looked at me then, a smile flying onto her face. "You're kinda cute, with all the red. Tell me, you planning to summon me more often for some fun?"

Sundar's face flew up at the last remark, and I shot her a look so packed with violent anger that she actually flinched and let the low-hanging fruit of the joke pass by. "Yeah, we may be fighting some stuff here soon, and I want to practice my magic. You down?"

She stood up on my shoulder and grinned with her hands on her hips and legs spread wider than shoulder-width apart, "Yup! I'll be there lickity split! So, you better call on me. All you have to do is think of me when you use your magic, and I promise not to run unless it looks super boring. 'Kay?"

"You got it." I grinned back at her, and she vanished. The cool thing about it was that my flame Aether had recovered by then, and my summoning Aether returned as soon as she was gone. Interesting.

The halfling had entirely quieted by now, with Sundar's fist and ring in his face. "You understand where we stand and lay now?"

"Yes ma'am." He growled, his eye darting from her face to mine with a scowl. "Didn't realize royals had any interest in the mines. What do you want?"

"Exactly what I just said—we want to fight whatever monsters you may have in those there tunnels, and we want them *bad*." Sundar grinned and leaned closer. "Any reports of critters or crawlers inside that we can take care of for you and dear ol' mom?"

The halfling snorted, and rolled his eyes. "Sure, she *finally* sent in the damned cavalry after three o' me miners go missin'? Feh, whatever. Take your damnable guide and see if you can stand a chance against whatever it is killin' me workers."

"You want to give us a quest?" I raised an eyebrow at him expectantly.

"You come bargin' in to me business, distractin' me men, throwin' me about and disrespectin' me in front o' me subordinates an' then *demand* a quest?" His corpulent face went a shade of red I wished I could make a dye from as he stood to his feet and pointed at us. "You can piss right off the lot o' you. Only reason I'm lettin' you in there in the first place is to keep you *damn lazy royals* in your place! Hope you don't die, *prince and princess.*"

He spat on the floor, and Blothl made to lunge forward and clobber him, but both Sundar and I grabbed him and pulled him back with a shake of the head. Much as I hated to admit it? He had kind of been right.

A quest would have been nice, though.

"Well, that were jus' 'bout the funniest thing I ever did see." A deep voice that almost sounded like the old Texan accents that some cowboy movies seemed to embellish so much brought my head around toward some of the miners. The dwarf sported a pickaxe and grinned at us. "Y'all know Nildy? You said something 'bout heading into the tunnels, need a guide?"

"This her husband?" I asked Blothl, and both he and the stranger nodded.

"Blothl, good to see you again, old friend." They shook forearms and nodded to each other before the newcomer turned toward us. "Name's Jimson, I'm Nildy's man."

"Is that some point of honor here?" Sundar scratched her head and held her hands up in confusion.

"It is when the woman who claims you is well known, likable, capable, and one of the best-damned fighters you've ever known." Jimson grinned; he winked at us and turned to Blothl. "History's always been your thing, and she's your friend, you wanna tell this part?"

"Best be believin' that!" Blothl grinned back before turning to us. "Dwarves look for their partners in traditional ways by a lot o' the same standards as other cultures be lookin', but it be the ladyfolk what do the courtin' aye? So, we as men have to be sure we're lookin' fine, well bathed an' worthy o' bein' considered. Well, Nildy be damned near runnin' that inn by now an' her prospects be linin' up 'round the block to come a showin' for her attention. She'd have not one other poor bastard but the one what never showed any mind."

"Jimson?" I pointed to the handsome dwarf, and he nodded his head with an obliging smile.

"Yer right." Blothl took a breath and held out his hands and motioned broadly, "Lasses from all over the lands came to the city to find 'em a man and ol' Jimson here had him a mess o' potential wives lined up, but it were Nildy what won the marital brawl."

"Marital what now?" Sundar's grunted with an astounded look on her face.

"Brawl!" Blothl insisted, almost angrily. "We dwarves settle things civilized in one o' three ways: makin', drinkin' or fightin'. Now, Nildy can drink, but her strength be in her fists an' gods help the poor crafters what saw her lay waste to precious materials. So, she knocked every single other lass on her gob to get to her man. An' then she socked him for good measure."

"Knew then and there that I was her man." Jimson shook his head. "We better get on into the mines afore y'all get to growing beards yourselves. I'll lead y'all to some fun."

We turned toward the mine entrances and trudged on after the dwarven miner and noted all the eyes on us keeping tabs. It was an eerie feeling, walking into a dwarven mine.

CHAPTER FIFTEEN

MONA

"All right mom, come on, you can do it," I whispered for the seventieth time since posting up at the newbie quest board. It had been hours since mom had said she would log in—not hard with the time differential at play, but it would have been about two hours real-time since she had actually logged into the game. Which had to have been terrifying for her since she went in under my watchful gaze after the workers had left. This blond guy had keyed her in with a huge grin on his face the whole time.

Seth had told us about Wilhelm after the call; I had *not* wanted to leave her alone with him, and I was glad I hadn't. Though he had found me fascinating as well, and I couldn't quite pin down why.

The liquid that acted as our sort of buffer into the game filled the portal and I watched the fear enter my mother's eyes, she slapped the door, and I put my palm on it speaking loudly so that she might hear me, "It's okay, Mom. It's going to be okay—try to relax, it helps!"

The fluid had covered her and barred my sight to her, which had been new to me, but then again, by the time my portal was fully filled my eyes were closed, and I was in the game. It was probably normal.

Waiting now, I couldn't help but wonder if it had been. Crowds of wanderers and NPCs moved past us in a blur as I waited for something—anything—that would tell me my mom was here.

As I was getting ready to log out and see if she had stuck it out, Albarth put a hand on my shoulder. "She'll be here soon. Stop working yourself into a tizzy."

"My mom *hates* video games." I sighed and looked up at the sky. "I'd be lucky if she makes it through the tutorial in one piece."

"If she's anything like you, she will be fine, I'm sure."

—*Mona?*— a whisper from an Emerald Fire took my attention. —*I think I'm here, I see a large tree?*—

"She's in the main area with the tree?" I blinked over at Albarth, and we moved instantly as I sent back, —*Albarth and I are coming mom, just stay there.*—

"How did she end up there?!" Albarth huffed as we ran toward the center of the city. People moved out of our way, cursing us as we moved through and around others.

"Well, the game puts you where your affinity is, right?" He motioned to me. "You popped up in the Earth Square for your metal magic and me in the Wind Square."

"Kyvir came up in the Wave Square as well, but why would she pop up there?" I was racking my brain, trying to sort it out when I remembered Sundar. "Animal magic! That has to be it!"

"Then let's go!" Albarth huffed and moved ahead of me in stride.

We turned through the alleys and streets before us with abandon, skirting people and stalls around the roadways with sometimes a mere couple of inches to spare. We shouted apologies and hoped for forgiveness as we came to the large circular area with the single largest tree I'd ever seen in person.

In the daylight hours, the huge trunk glowed amber, as the rays of golden sun shone through the dark green leaves up above. Under the tree sat a figure with several large animals gathered around them. As we approached, they looked up, and I saw a Kitsune much like Ünbin's wife, her furred body the same red as her hair in life, her eyes the same color as they were at home. The only thing different was the vulpine features and the tail.

"You went pretty far outside what I had thought you might choose, Mom," I observed; the animals around her stared from her to me. "An elf, or even Kin, I could see, but a Kitsune?"

"You had suggested an attempt at trying something new, and while I love all animals, dogs especially—foxes are cute." She shrugged and reached up to pet an elk on the snout. "Besides, I have innate abilities with this avatar that the person who walked me through the selection process was all too delighted to explain."

"Like what?" Albarth asked curiously, and held a hand out to a small dog that yipped at him happily.

"Shapeshifting, for one." She shimmered, and the animals around her bolted, a small fox standing where she had been stared up at us. I noted two tails just before she shimmered once more and stood before Albarth and I. "Besides, I read a book when I was a child about a character who had been a Kitsune, and it seemed fun."

"That old book?" I raised a skeptical eyebrow. "There were enough swear words in there that you wouldn't let Kyvir or me touch them until we were sixteen, and even then, it was with the understanding that if we repeated any of the vulgarity in them that we would be beaten and fed to the pack! Which I still don't understand, because you hate gaming."

"Fucking-A right, you would have." Emerald snorted. "And I don't *hate* gaming. I hate that it can take the wonder out of a good story because it's so heavily reliant on what you see as opposed to emotion and narrative. Much less that I hate gaming and more that I enjoy reading a good story instead."

"I *adore* your mother, Monami." Albarth almost groaned as he stepped forward to shake her hand. "I'm Albarth Remell, lovely to make your acquaintance."

"I suppose that's not your real name, then?" My mom's eyebrow arched at him, and he shook his head. "I suppose that is also why you haven't called... Kyvir by his name either. Very well. I am Emerald Fire."

"Why does that sound so familiar?" I frowned deeply at hearing the name out loud.

"Your father used to call me that." Her smile showed slightly sharpened fox teeth that made me smile in return. I remembered that.

My dad holding her at night with me playing on the living room floor with dolls and dogs while he stroked her head and whispered sweet nothings to her.

"Well, we have a good amount of work to do and a short time to do it in." Albarth clapped his hands, and we glanced at him. "Do you know what your magic is?"

She nodded, held her hand out in front of her, and a katana appeared, made of pure silver energy.

"This is what I have, for now, I guess." She motioned to the blade. "The ability is called Soul Sword. I can summon it at will, though I've never been one for using a sword, so I'm out of my element."

"That's okay, the first thing we're going to do is introduce you to some of our friends so you can start learning how to fight and level up." I looked to Albarth, who nodded, and we headed toward Gage's place. The walk was fine, though watching my mom observing everything intently was interesting, to say the least. She would reach out and touch everything she could, frowning at the sensations and gasping at the visuals before her at times.

"So, who is this friend of yours?" Mom asked quietly as she dodged a particularly irate looking woman with four kids in tow.

"His name is Gage, and he's pretty awesome. He's a weapon

master that we've learned from, and he's offered to teach you in trade for something we acquired recently," I explained cautiously as we moved through the city streets with people so closely around us.

"What did you acquire?" She looked around curiously before glancing at me again. "Speaking of acquiring things— where can I buy a dog?"

I stopped walking, and both she and Albarth plowed into my back before I turned and raised my voice, "Leave the dogs at home! Can you seriously not do something without the dogs?"

"I can, but I choose not to." Emerald eyed me steadily. "Animals are a part of my life, Mona. I'm in an environment where I know little to nothing, and nothing is familiar. Having something familiar to me here would help me cope with the newness of it all."

"Just where did you come up with that crock?" I sighed, tension just behind my eyes making me rub my forehead and eyes with the palms of my hands.

"My therapist, when I told him I was attempting to come to terms with all of this." She grabbed my hand and stared into my eyes. "I'm new to it all, and despite having read about it in my spare time, I'm vastly out of my element and have no control. I need something of my own to ground and center me. A dog to train and assist me will help."

I rolled my eyes. "Fine." Heaving a sigh, I stepped back along the street toward Gage's. He might know where to look for a dog my mother could train to her content. Fifteen minutes later, we stood outside Gage's door and knocked noisily.

No one answered for a minute, then Gage's head popped up over the fence for a brief second. "Please, be patient a moment longer!"

"What was that creature?" Mom whispered loudly.

"That's Gage, and he will be teaching you how to fight." I grinned at her and put a hand on her shoulder when she looked at me in concern. "I know he's big, but he's a usually gentle giant."

"Usually?" My mother looked taken aback. Just then, a large, horned head entered my peripheral vision.

"Yes, usually." He smiled at us as he stood up fully. "I am quite the brute when it comes to protecting my friends and my subordinates. Albarth, Monami, good to see both of you so soon. Who is this lovely person?"

Gage bowed at his waist and nodded toward my mom, her eyebrows shifting up and her mouth not seeming to want to comply with whatever it was she was trying to say, so I spoke for her, "Sergeant Gage Toomgarak, I would like to introduce my mother, Emerald Fire."

"A Kitsune for a mother? You wanderers are an odd sort indeed." He rubbed his chin and looked over her. "Ah, yes, I am the *former* Sergeant at Arms for the city of Iradellum, a pleasure to make your acquaintance madam."

"Oh, no." Albarth frowned and stepped forward. "You didn't get fired, did you?"

"No, nothing like that, my friend." He smiled and waved a warding hand at the nymph. "I am simply being reinstated as a sergeant within my platoon and am en route to my duties on the front lines with the rest of my soldiers."

"I see." I frowned at him. "Would you still be able to help train my mother? At least until she gains initiate level with the sword?"

He glanced up at the sky and looked back at her, "I haven't much time, but if you are the studious type and promise to heed my tutelage, I will take you in."

"I swear I will learn as best as I can." Emerald nodded once and looked like she was ready to attack him then and there.

He grinned and waved us into his house and through the back. Mom stopped to admire his garden while he caught up and ushered us outside to his training circle.

"Inside here, I will show you forms and motions, and then we will spar." He reached into his inventory and withdrew two basic-looking swords. "When we spar, I will come at you slowly at first, then pick up my pace so that you can develop a rhythm. You need not worry about being too hurt, though you will develop bruises, bumps, and small cuts if you do not block me properly. Do you understand?"

"Yes sir!" My mother answered in a surprisingly loud tone of voice. Gage must have liked the look on her face because he grinned and beckoned her into the circle. "This is an overhead chop, do it like so."

From there, he went through the motions and showed her every sort of swing and jab that he could, muttering how they could be strung together and used in better ways.

She practiced each stroke with minimal need for correction, which was surprising to me.

"Your mother seems to be a natural athlete," Albarth observed as Gage and my mom worked through how to block and parry. He saw me shoot him a questioning glance and motioned to her before explaining quietly so as not to disturb their work. "You can tell that she's held a weapon of some sort before, and the way she moves is adept. If I were to have had her in one of my classes for fencing as a youth, I dare say it wouldn't have taken me to sixteen to become Olympic level."

I tried to see how she moved, judging whether it was any more different from the way that I did, and I couldn't really tell the difference. "How do you know?"

"Professional athletes can sort of tell, after a while." He made a vague motion toward her. "Sort of how Gage and Sundar were drawn to one another because they could recognize that they had being soldiers in common. Law enforcement can sometimes recognize each other in a manner of speaking. You develop a sort of sense about it. Like how you could tell a gamer from a poser."

"Hate posers," I grumped and watched as my mom took a sword to the backside for lunging too far forward.

"Again! Do *not* overextend," Gage roared at her. I could see that there was sweat glistening in my mother's fur, and it made me smile. She thought gaming had been a waste of time. Here she was suffering as we had.

She corrected her footing and grunted as she failed to block the next strike, corrected again, and succeeded.

"Excellently done!" Gage clapped and drew her attention. "Now, to put the necessary pain into your body that will allow these motions to become second nature. Prepare yourself!"

Mom didn't even wait for him to move before she pushed herself forward into a roll and came up by the Minotaurs left flank with a jab that he parried and countered immediately. "Sometimes, it is okay to wait and suss an opponent's skills before attacking blindly."

"Sometimes, it's better to go for the kill before giving them the chance!" Her snarled response surprised me, and my concern only grew as her attacks became more and more desperate.

Gage moved and parried every swing and stab of her blade with growing confusion on his bovine features. "If you wish to wear yourself down, fine. I will be pushing you harder now."

And he did. His blade whipped in and out of range in heartbeats, his weapon battering her where her sword simply couldn't be. One such strike went for her neck, and as I cringed, knowing it would likely knock her unconscious, the blade stopped with a resounding peel of metal on metal.

"Ah, so this is what you had in mind?" Gage rumbled at my mother. The real sword protected her neck and shoulder from his attack, but her Soul Sword was pointed directly at his exposed thigh.

"I wasn't sure if I would be able to stop your weapon with this one, and it happened more on accident than on purpose. Forgive me." Mom seemed contrite as she moved her weapon away from her body and dismissed the magical sword.

"If that is how you must fight, so be it—if that would save your life or another's, I would implore you to do so." Gage rested a hand on her shoulder, and she nodded at him. "Steady yourself, and we will try once more. This time, I want you to be calculating and calm. Tell me, what do you do?"

Mom paused for a moment too long, and Gage held his hand out in front of him, "Forgive me, I know that is an odd question, but you have an air of being able to give instruction and do so well. You also seem to understand a student's role."

"I am a dog trainer by trade."

"Ah, a master of hounds, then?" Gage's eyebrows rose appreciatively as he looked my mother over again. "So, then you can understand how there is a need for precision and planning? It is the same for the sword. The patience that you implement with a hound is very much like that required to master the sword, and yourself. When you face an opponent, do so as the hound would—find an opening and use it to take them down. Forgive me, I do not know much of hounds to give more advice than I've seen on the field of battle, but I do know battle. You seem capable. Show me that you can learn, and this time, be more cautious."

"Yes sir!" Emerald lowered her stance, and watched the sergeant moving around the circle toward her, circling the opposite way that he did.

"Excellent," Gage muttered and bolted forward with his sword raised and clearly telegraphed his movements to give her a chance. She struck the sword aside as it should have sliced into her right shoulder and kicked at Gage's leg with her right foot.

Her kick missed, but only by an inch and Gage used that opening to whirl and shove his blade toward her face. Mom dropped into the splits, one leg forward and one behind her, her sword flashing toward the Minotaur's nether regions.

"Oh, no!" Albarth howled, grabbing himself as he watched. "Sundar would kill her if she injured him like that!"

I snorted and had to cover my face as my mother glanced my way. They exchanged blows a few more times before Gage increased his speed once more.

Mom held her own, though I could tell that she was a little

irritated for some reason. Was it because she felt she wasn't fighting the way she was meant to? We could sort that out later.

After another ten minutes, they stopped, not because they were tired or anything, but because Gage had taken mom out with a leg sweep that put his sword next to her throat on the ground.

"Have you earned your initiate level?" He asked as he bent down to help her up. She nodded, and he smiled at her. "Good. I am glad that you will be safe, Emerald, and you are very adept."

Albarth and I grinned at Gage as he took his swords and put them away.

"Gage?" Emerald spoke softly at first, uncertain it seemed, then cleared her throat and stood to her full height and addressed the sergeant firmly, "Thank you for your assistance. Would you happen to know where I can find another master of hounds? I feel... exposed without a dog at my side."

"It's surprising that you would trust someone you just met with that kind of information, mother." I stepped closer to them both and crossed my arms. I saw Gage gave me a weary glance, and I added, "It's best it be you, Gage, but this isn't normal for her."

"It is not so rare for those who cross swords to feel closer to someone whom they have just met, Monami." Gage offered sagely. "Many a soldier on the battlefield, amid the throes of battle, has found a truer soul in the face of his enemy than even some of his closest friends at home."

My mom nodded at me, her face blank as she added, "Not to mention, he may know where I can acquire a dog."

"The Master of Hounds might know where you can get one, though we do not have much in the way of a rapport, and I will not be able to take you to them." He shrugged and motioned to Albarth and I. "Monami and Albarth have been to the castle grounds before, they will be able to take you to them."

"Do we have time to get there before starting our power leveling?" I glanced at him, and he shrugged.

"We don't have much of a choice if she wouldn't be comfortable on her own out there." He looked over to Gage and offered a hand. "Thank you again, Gage, your time is greatly appreciated. Please, do stay safe on the frontline and come back to us."

"I shall endeavor to do so. Please, give Sundar my best and tell her..." he looked bashfully at the ground, and then to his garden before hurriedly adding, "Tell her that her flower blooms well here. And that I will return to care for it once more."

I smiled and rushed over to give the big lug a hug before patting his broad back. We left him then and made our way toward the castle grounds. It was midday by now, and the soldiers had likely finished their training and would be off to doing god knows what.

The front guards at the gate stepped forward and made to stop us when the elder of the two stopped him. "Y'all helped with that damnable dungeon in the crypt, didn't ya?"

"Yes sir, we did." I nodded to him and he smiled.

"Get back here, boy—thems the ones what prince Klemond said can come in any time." He grinned at us and winked when the other guard shrugged and returned to his place. "Though I ain't too familiar with this 'un. What's your name, miss?"

"I'm Emerald," she smiled sweetly and put a hand on my shoulder in a motherly way. "And I am this one's mother. We're here to speak with the Master of Hounds, perhaps you could tell us where to find them?"

He eyed her, then me, and raised an eyebrow, to which Albarth motioned toward us. "We wanderers are an odd sort, we know."

"Well, y'all are welcome in, and since she's with ya, well, I reckon I can't rightly keep her from heading on in too." He pointed toward the back of the sprawling yard. "Master of Hounds keeps the kennel toward the rear of the yard. You'll find 'em."

"Thank you." Mom smiled at them, and we stepped into

the area. She turned her head slightly toward me and spoke softly, "You'll have to tell me all of your exploits over a pint. Well, over a drink, at least. Everything I've read points to that being the way to share this kind of thing. And turns out my little girl is a hero of sorts already."

I could hear a treading edge of pride in her voice as she spoke and couldn't help the flash of warmth in my cheeks. "We just did a quest anyone would have. No biggie."

"They don't seem to think so, and I'm not inclined to either." She winked at me and turned toward her purpose and strode on.

With there not being any sort of training going on, the yard felt almost barren—though there were maintainers and grounds men aplenty taking care of the grounds and plant life, they seemed content not to eye us too much more than as a passing interest.

Soon enough, the barking and baying of dogs echoed in the distance, and we came to a small compound of buildings next to the castle wall on the left side of the structure. A small house stood next to the kennels, with a fifteen-foot gap between them, a figure sitting with an animal in front of it on the porch. A large, grizzled-looking human man watched us approach quietly with a small brush in hand, passing it over the large dog's fur.

"Hello, we were hoping to speak with you about a matter of great personal import. Do you have a moment to talk?" Emerald called out, stopping a good twenty feet away and putting an arm out to stop us from approaching too much closer.

The man continued to watch us for a moment, likely sizing us up before calling out, "You can come closer, he's harmless, though he's large and looks mean."

The dog had short fur and eyed us even more warily than the man. "What'd you want to discuss?"

"I would like to inquire about purchasing one of your dogs. A puppy who has been weened for at least a week?" Mom looked hopeful, but the man shook his head and she looked suddenly defeated. "You don't have anything then? I see."

"I never said that I just shook my head." He patted the dog and muttered a word, and the dog raced off toward the kennels. "Only the kennel master can sell the dogs, and that's only with the approval of royalty, which is a long and drawn-out process that only the queen can expedite."

"So, you aren't the kennel master?" Albarth said, confused. "What about the Master of Hounds?"

"Same thing, I'm just a worker." He pointed toward the kennels where the dogs had been baying inside. Just then, the same dog came back with a figure mounted on the back like it was a horse—saddle and all. "That's her now."

"Thanks for entertaining Leiland!" The thin gnomish woman hollered over the din. Her soft blue hair and purple highlights almost shimmered in the light as she paced the dog toward us, his huge jowls flapping as he trotted. She sat him down in front of us and stepped over the saddle onto the ground before patting the dog's head lovingly. "There's a good boy, thanks Morn."

"Good afternoon, ma'am," my mother greeted and stepped forward, offering her hand to the smaller woman.

"Don't rightly care for shaking hands, messes with my scent, but I respect you for trying." She grinned up at us all as my mother stood back up to her full height with an understanding smile. "I'm the kennel master here in Iradellum, Emmabreth Permaton, but you lot can call me Emma—assuming I like you after this."

Her sly wink at the end of that statement made everyone gathered laugh, and she put her hands on her hips and blinked up at Emerald. "So, what can I do for you? Can't say as I get too many visitors who aren't here for a hunt of some sort."

"I can imagine not," Albarth grumbled as one of the nearby dogs snarled in its enclosure, and the barking around us went up a decibel.

"They aren't too bad once you get used to 'em." She chuckled and continued to pet her mount.

"We came to see about acquiring one of your dogs." My mother paused to let that sink in as the smaller woman's light brown eyes flicked over her appraisingly, the two earrings in each pointed ear jingling as her head moved. "I'm a kennel master in my own right back where I am from, and I find that I would like to have at least one dog here to calm my nerves."

"I can respect that, she any good?" The woman glanced at Albarth and me. I nodded once, and she seemed to think harder. "Tell you what. I can't sell you any of mine, one because I don't know you, two because I don't know your skill, three because it's as much a pain in the ass as people using my full name, and four because I don't wanna separate my pack. No offense."

"None taken, I feel the same of mine, though I am a breeder of sorts as well." My mother inclined her vulpine head understandingly.

"However, I have to know." She ran a hand through her hair with a soft smile. "Anyone brave enough to come up to a complete stranger in their place of business and say that they can do what you do needs to be vetted, in my opinion. So, how about a little challenge?"

We looked at her steadily, I wasn't sure I liked her tone, and we were running low on time as it was since this seemed to be necessary.

When we didn't answer quickly enough, she motioned to us. "You're all wanderers, right? How about I make it worthwhile for you. I'll give you experience for it, and if you prove yourself capable, I'll even help you how I can."

Quest Received — Emma, the kennel master, offered one of you a professional challenge. Should you succeed in what she has in mind, you'll prove yourself worthy of her attention, and she may help you. Reward: 200 EXP and Emma's assistance.

Accept: Yes / No?

"Before you accept it, know this—if you cannot prove your-self at least my equal, you'll not be able to purchase a dog in this city without my approval, and you *will not receive it.*" She lifted her chin and crossed her arms in front of her chest. "Am I clear?"

"Crystal, show me where you want my assistance," Emma responded, and I saw that the quest had been accepted already. Two hundred experience? That was a good amount right there!

Emma marched us into the kennels to one that was sepa-rated from the rest that had a single dog in it. At first, I worried that the woman would sic a massive dog on my mother and call it a day, but as soon as we reached the kennel, we could hear the whining and licking sound coming from inside.

"She's pregnant and about to give birth." Emma looked over at the woman. "What can I possibly do here other than wait this out?"

"You're to help her give birth." Emma motioned with her chin at the dog. "This is her third whelping, and if they all die like the last two, I have to put her down."

My mother and I gasped at the thought of that, I was about to start in on her myself when Albarth grabbed my shoulder and shook his head, looking pointedly at my mother's hands. They had balled up so tightly I thought they might never open again.

"Believe me when I say that I don't want to do that," Emma stated quietly, her saddened gaze toward the cage made me take a deep breath and relax a bit. "If she does, I'll have to step down as kennel master, and there's no one here who'll care for these dogs the way I can. Leiland knows it sure as I do."

"What were the complications in the past?" My mother rolled her sleeves up and look into the kennel. "I see you have a large basket in there with sheets and blankets? Good. I'll need warm water in a clean bucket to be brought in as well as an empty bucket and a towel."

Emma snapped her fingers, and her assistant was off at a sprint to collect the items, I assumed. "She gives birth, but whenever she does, the umbilical cord is usually strangling the puppies. I've kept her confined with only supervised exercise to be safe, trying to see if that was the issue, but I can't know for certain. She's had the best chow and all the love I can give her. Otherwise, the puppies don't seem to live long enough to get on well."

"I see. Have you been in here with her for the last two births?" Mom inspected the dog, her concern outweighing her sense of self-preservation as she went to the door then seemed to recall herself. "I'll need you to go in first while I help. You'll be at her side near her head to give her praise and care, distract her from us, and I will see about saving these puppies."

They both went in, the gnomish woman first, muttering soothing words to the dog who whined and tried to stand, "No, no, you stay on down girl, we're gonna get them pups out of you sugar. You wait and see." She placed the dog's large head on her lap and stroked her neck and ears lovingly before answering Emerald's question. "The first two I stood and watched, I feared that my fiddling around behind her would make her stop."

"That was a stupid thing to do, you should always be right there with them," Emerald groused, and I shook my head. She had been there for *every* birth when it came to her dogs and even the majority of the births that Caesar had sired. She took what she did *that* seriously.

Emma scowled at mom but remained silent, her hands never moving from her dog. Mom felt around the dog's stomach surely, but gently—careful not to harm the precious cargo beneath the distended belly of the beastly dog before us. She made Tialca look malnourished, that's how obscenely large she was.

Shadows crossed the bars to my left as I stepped into the kennel, Leiland having returned with the items we needed.

I took the bucket and passed it in to my mom, and she took it and dipped her hands into it like she was a doctor prepping for surgery. She lifted her hand and felt around the dog's rib cage, "Good, breathing isn't too labored, but she's definitely ready. Here's how this is going to go."

She looked at Emma. "You have your role, I require unquestioning obedience if this is to have a chance at success. I respect that this is your kennel, and if you want to berate me after, so be it, but this is my birth. Am I clear?"

The gnomish woman nodded once with a stoic look on her face. "Excellent, Monami, you get in here and prepare with a towel to clean the puppies. Make sure as little of your scent gets on them as possible. Albarth and Leiland, you will be our doers. I say—you do. Am I clear?"

They both stood straighter. "Yes, ma'am!"

We waited for about fifteen minutes before the dog began to pant and whimper, contractions taking hold of the poor dog's body, and pressing the puppies forth. The first came out still-born, and my mother sighed heavily, cutting through the umbilical cord with a knife that Emma handed her before she set it aside, nodding to the bucket before her and holding her hands above the empty bucket. I knew what she wanted without being told and lifted the heavy bucket to rinse her hands as she scrubbed a little to get the blood off her hands.

Moments later, another large contraction shook the dog, and this time mom had to actually reach her fingers inside the animal and correct the puppy's positioning so that it came out head-first. She snipped the umbilical cord and used her nails to open the membrane around the pup before checking it for life signs and handing it to me with a nod. I used the mid-sized towel to clean as much of the blood and birthing fluid off of it as I could. I set the puppy into the large basket in the blankets and turned back with a small victorious grin on my face.

Two more puppies came, this time with seemingly no complications, and we were hopeful for the rest. The fifth came out tail first, and everyone around held their breath as mom reached forward to stop it from falling to the ground, worried that it would tighten the cord and cut off all airflow. She used her nail to cut it, unwilling to trust herself with the blade close to both mother and pup. She picked the cord apart closer to the neck and then the membrane checking to see if the puppy would take air. It did, but it was labored and breathing harshly.

I took it and cleaned it gently, my mother stating, "more towels." The men hopped to and disappeared, the dogs whimpering seeming to be less pained and more from exhaustion. We tried to give her water, but she seemed to be too far into what she was doing now to take anything and began to push again.

We worked for another half an hour, two more puppies came, both stillborn. Our hearts hurt. My mother's grim face, as she washed her hands for the final time seemed more reflective than anything else and I knew that my face was moist from tears rather than the sweat that dotted her brow.

"Well, I'll take three healthy pups and a runt any day over having to put ol' Miss here down." She heaved a sigh and put her arms around the dog's massive head. "I love her to death. Leiland, get her food and water, best of the first and an extra ration of bacon and beef, then take her for a walk to expel this nastiness."

She stopped and thought about it for a minute, "You know what? Today's a day for celebrating—they all get an extra ration, but you get ol' Miss here the most, hear?"

Leiland grinned, his scarred visage brightening significantly. "As you wish it, ma'am."

He sprinted away, and we all stood outside in the sunshine as the new mother lay resting in the cool shade.

I received a notification of the quest having been completed and grinned. Mom had been at level two before coming here and now looked to have gotten to level three with that. She smiled at me and the gnomish kennel master stepped closer to us.

"I can't sell you one of my dogs, but there's a breeder in the city who trains his dogs well, and who we go to for breeding." Her explanation replaced the sudden look of distressed loss on my mom's face with a look of pure hope. "As payment, I'll take you to see him, and we will see if one of his bitches has whelped recently."

I was surprised at the language for a moment, then realized that was the appropriate kennel talk for a female dog who has given birth.

"What breed of dog are they?" Albarth asked quietly, looking into the kennel.

"Those pups are a mix of blood wolf and shadow dane. Ol' Miss is the shadow dane, and the pa is the blood wolf." Emma ran her hands through her hair. "Part of the reason she's had so much difficulty is that breeding them hasn't been done before, and the other is that blood wolves are notoriously dangerous. They hunt by blood, but they also need it to survive. It's why our best hunters and trackers use them rather than our shadow danes."

"You think when they mixed, they were somehow devouring each other and Miss?" I blinked at Emma, and my mom reached out to grasp my hand. "That's insane. Who would take such a risk?"

"The Queen would." Emma sighed and wrung her hands. "She wants to get them trained and sent to the front lines to see if they can be useful in hunting demons down. If they can, we might have a mass breeding on our hands here, and we need to know what to expect. Emerald, you reckon you might have a suggestion to help the bitches and whelps survive?"

"Foods that are high in iron and good for the blood, I would imagine." Mom thought on it for a moment. "I would recommend a heavier diet of raw meat, fresh kills, and possibly even getting a chef in to see that their nutrition is worthwhile. They're mixed breeds, so their needs may differ slightly from their parents. Other than that, I couldn't tell you."

"Based on how you handled yourself in there and what needed done—I'll see to those suggestions personally." She bowed her head respectfully before looking up. "Thank you. I owe you a great deal. You saved a life today, and I can't know how to repay you other than what I have. If you would, I'd love for you to join me for a drink some time. We can discuss work, dogs, and other things?"

That last bit seemed mighty hopeful, and I had to laugh at the thought that screeched into my head next. *Did my mom just get asked out on a date?!*

"I would like that, perhaps another day?" Leiland had returned by now, walking past as mom spoke to Emma. "Seems we are free to leave now. Shall we follow you?"

"You shall indeed!" Emma grinned and hopped into her saddle on the back of her dog before looking to her assistant. "You've earned a dollop today, my man! You and I will share a few shots of that firebrand in my cabinet this evening over supper. I'll be back in a few!"

With that phrase, we set out, jogging behind the joyful gnome and her dog-steed. Leiland looked pleased as punch and went about his business with a little pep in his step.

She took us out the gate, three streets to the left and on for more than ten minutes to a large fenced-in compound. Low stone masonry built upon by long wooden slats surrounded an otherwise beautiful off-white mansion. The roof had four corners protected by pillars sat upon by gargoyles, grotesque figures that looked ready to spring into action should someone try to get in uninvited. They looked nothing like I thought they should have.

"This is the place, hold on." She pulled out a thin whistle and blew until her face was a shade of maroon and stopped. Her own dog having gone mad as soon as he heard it, snarling and baying at the air in front of him. She patted his raised fur and muttered to him for a second, which calmed him signif-icantly.

After three minutes of waiting, she put the whistle back to her lips and was about to blow again when a man howled, "Don't you dare blow that damned thing again!"

A hulking man with graying hair and a beard that would make most men jealous threw open the gate to our left and leered at us. "You know, one of my dogs damned near bit my damn hand off because of that thing—*again*. We have a damned doorbell!"

Emma grinned at him. "You leave me waiting ten minutes or more because you can barely hear it, but a dog nearly snatching a limb off? Now that will get your attention." She jerked her head toward us. "I made a friend who saved our experiment today. I told her I would introduce you. Emerald, a fellow kennel master in her own right, meet Huntsman Rogelio Bermudos."

Mom stepped forward and offered her hand to the man, who reached out and looked her over with interest. "You say she helped save our pups?"

"Yes sir, I played a role," she explained on her own. "I was told I couldn't purchase any of the crowns dogs, but that you were a private breeder with your own stock. I was interested in purchasing one of your pups if you had any older than weening age?"

His eyes narrowed, and he shot Emma a look of pure surprise, "You tellin' people about my stock again? The danes or the...other?"

Emma grinned. "She had no idea about the danes, but she does the other. Good going, mouth."

He sighed tiredly before turning back to my mom. "I have two litters just a week off weening that we've begun to work with. If you have the coin, we can strike a deal."

"Would it assist this process if I were to tell you we were the ones who helped the prince and my best friend helped to save the prince's cousin and her family?" I asked the question sweetly, but I activated Allure as I did so; warmth flooded me, and I could see that it had worked as he smiled.

"Good friends with the Lord Foster since I was a pup myself," the man harrumphed. "We hunt together occasionally, and my boys and his play all the time, and since your friend saved them, I think I could probably cut some sort of deal for that. Come on in, the lot of you."

We all made to enter, and he stopped, his gaze landing on

Emma. "You better leave that damned whistle out of your mouth, Emma—or I'll shove it down your throat."

"Tough talk, old man." Emma grinned back and raised her left eyebrow at him. "Have you grown so gray in the beard that you forgot the last time I whooped you?"

"You only won because you're a century older than me and can thus hold your alcohol better!" Rogelio barked and made a hysterically rude gesture at his apparent friend before stomping into the grassy yard.

He led us to a small hovel that had a latch to the outside and was hidden from sight by the wall and the house. He looked about and eyed us each. "You tell anyone about what you see in here, and I'll be forced to kill you. I know wanderers don't care —but it's the principle of the thing. Do you understand?"

We all nodded, then he asked, "None of you are bleeding, are you?"

We checked each other, mom found some dried blood under her claws, and we cleaned that thoroughly. Rogelio checked her again then nodded to himself.

He touched the door, then turned and stared at us hard for a few heartbeats before opening the door and walking inside down a set of steps that swirled around in a circle heading into the darkness. I could see my mother's eyes glow eerily in the low light, like an animal watching the shadows, then she was down the way.

I was so elated that she was here with us. Both of us actively looking for dad, trying to get to the bottom of it all.

We came to the bottom and piled closer together than any of us truly seemed comfortable with. Luckily, Emma had left her steed behind, or we would have all been crushed as Rogelio fiddled with something I couldn't see. Then a large door opened, and we all but fell through it into an almost deafening silence.

"Don't make any sudden movements," Rogelio warned, and I could hear Emma snickering where she stood behind us. Rogelio left us and walked into the room before a single torch burst to life, then another. Finally, a whooshing of air and fire filled the room, and dozens of bloodshot eyes fixated on us.

Dozens of dogs—wolves—with reddish-gray fur flared at us, their very beings rigid and ready to pounce.

"Rex!" Rogelio snarled, the one closest to the door on our left turned away and ran *behind* the other wolves to get to his master's side.

"Oh, they are *very* well trained," Mom almost purred. I noted an edge of respect in her tone even as I could see Emma nodding next to my knee with her arms crossed before her.

"Rex, command, heel." The wolf sat on his haunches and barked three times in short bursts. The entirety of the pack backed away and sat while the wolves closest to the doors sprinted over the earthen floor to sit behind and slightly to the left and right of Rogelio. And then the process repeated until more than thirty wolves sat fanned out behind the old man. "Rex, command, down."

The wolf at his side laid on the ground and growled, then yipped once. The wolves laid down and watched us still. The fur on my body stood on end while I bore witness to this well-oiled machine. If mom could have pulled this off back home—no one would have ever been able to compete with her.

Guess that's what coding and AI can do. I shook my head slowly with a wry grin. *Almost cheating.*

"This is my pack, I have to keep my blood wolves and shadow danes separated because they will try to mate and it's just messy, as you've seen." He reached down and snapped his fingers, Rex immediately sitting tall to reach his muzzle toward his master's hand. "And I don't want these ones learning bad habits from the less trained ones."

He stuck two of his fingers into his mouth and blew, a shrill, piercing note ripped through the room, and all the wolves moved to the open areas at the sides of the room in pairs. Once they'd arrived, they turned and sat, then after Rogelio made a shoving motion from his body, out, and they moved back into the little cave-like enclosures.

"You can come in now, they won't move out of there unless one of you is stupid enough to attack me." He turned and moved toward the rear of the room, it had to be more than fifty yards long and about half as wide. Toward the back right of the room, there were larger enclosures where several pairs of eyes peered out, and these ones had thick bars spaced across the bottom like a gate that stood little more than hip height so you would have to straddle it to get inside.

"These are my whelping pens, inside I have the puppies of one breed, siblings stick together, and I train them one at a time. It's slow going, but my boys are picking up the trade as well, and they enjoy helping."

He motioned my mother forward so that she could peer inside the room beside him, as she did, she frowned. "What am I looking at as far as loyalty, intelligence, strength, endurance, and difficulty between both breeds?"

"Good question, I can speak to the shadow danes." Emma took the lead from Rogelio for a moment. "They're loyal to their masters, for sure. They've been known to attack hell cats if they're too close to their masters, and will die for them if necessary. Intelligence is all right, they're stubborn and will be relentless in their pursuit to protect their masters or mates. As for strength and endurance, they could haul a grown human for a mile and only tire if they haven't been fed for two days. They wouldn't be *too* difficult to train for an experienced hand."

Rogelio nodded. "She has the right of it. Excellent tracking animals that can move through shadows in near silence, some of the more powerful of the breed being able to move *through* them from one place to another as if they were connected."

"And what of the blood wolves?" I asked excitedly, wondering what cool ability they might have.

All three dog trainers turned and glared at me, so I shut up with a muttered, "Sorry."

"Blood wolves are special trackers, they can smell blood better than almost any animal on land and can track it for hundreds of miles," Rogelio explained as he lifted one of the dark-furred dane puppies from the other side of the pen for my mom to inspect. "That's why I ensure that when they are used, we have a blood sample of the prey and that whoever is in the area when they are used is uninjured. Otherwise, the scents will confuse some of them."

He handed the puppy to Emma, who placed it on the floor and showed Emerald what to look for in them. Explaining how this was a good puppy because of his sturdy body, his gums being nice and pink, and the fact that he nipped at their fingers playfully was a good sign too.

I'd seen mom do the same thing over the years but never taken an interest.

"And how about the wolves as far as the same criteria?" My mother patted the puppy and stood from where she had been knelt down.

"They aren't quite so large as the danes, but they are much faster and as you could likely tell, highly intelligent. They are malleable and quick to learn, but they tire quickly if not cared for, and aren't quite as sturdy as a full-grown shadow dane. If I were to place one of Emma's dogs against my Rex, Rex might be in a predicament on his own since he's only just become strong enough to awaken his sanguine prowess."

"What's that?" Emerald frowned as the trainer lifted a wolf puppy out to be inspected. This one wriggled and writhed fiercely in his hands, his fat little belly protruding from an otherwise thin frame.

"Sanguine prowess is what a blood wolf awakens when they reach a certain level, they can bite prey and take the blood as more than just nourishment." He placed the puppy into my mother's arms and rolled up his left sleeve until a large, blackened bite mark was visible. "Depending on the wolf, it can be a necrotizing, stunning, draining, or even elementally enhanced bite. This was a necrotizing bite from Rex's sire. If you don't kill the animal quickly, the bite won't heal."

"So, it could be a potentially double-edged blade, good for a fight against someone, but if it happens to me, I have to kill the dog." Mom sighed and closed her eyes. "They seem to be highly trained and obedient, but they might be more pack oriented, and I don't have the necessary time to train up a new pack. The sturdier animal may be more suited to my needs in the long run, though they both seem to have added benefits."

She opened her eyes once more before looking at Rogelio, "I think I'll take a shadow dane puppy, if you have one you're willing to part with?"

"Wouldn't be showing them to you if I didn't." He grinned and pointed to the one on the floor before her in a separate enclosure. "He's pick of the litter, and with a *very* generous discount, will run you about sixteen gold pieces."

I whistled low and all three trainers just grinned, they were used to this kind of reaction, but my mom turned to me. "Forgive me, I'm sure there's something that I don't know concerning funds as I haven't purchased anything yet, but that *doesn't* sound like much to me."

"Let's put this into perspective." I motioned to all of my gear, "All of this cost me in the neighborhood of two gold pieces and protects me. That's a lot—matter of fact, that's more money than the three of us have together. Right?"

Albarth held up two fingers. "Little over two gold here." Mom held up one finger stoically.

I shrugged. "And I have three gold that I could add, but that would barely get us to half if we put silver into it too. We could try and get the money from Kyvir, if we really need to do this, but that would mean one of us having to go and find him before we could pay, and we have some serious work to put in to get you up to snuff. I'm sorry, but it looks like we won't be able to get it right now."

"Him." Rogelio corrected me sternly, a glint in his eye. "Referring to animals as 'it' is disrespectful."

"Quite, I know I raised you better than that." My mother's stern reprimand joined his.

I threw my hands up, and a chorus of menacing growls rang out around me.

Rogelio snarled, "Hush!" Every growl in the room stopped, leaving the puppies mewling to sound like a bulldozer.

"Tell you what." Rogelio reached out and took the puppy back from mom as she gave him one last pet. "Maybe not the pick then. Check the other puppies and see how you feel, if they take to you, and I'll give you a week to pay me for the one you choose. I'll even let you take it with you to begin training to save me the space, feed, and time."

"That's wonderful!" Mom looked as surprised as I felt, but the old man held up a hand.

"Under the stipulation that if he's been maltreated, malnourished, or killed by the end of the week, you pay full price as penance." His word sounded almost like iron bars slamming shut because I *knew* mom was going to agree to the terms. She nodded, and that was that.

I swore under my breath as he helped her into the pen and waited patiently. He turned to us, and I had to ask, just to know the depth of the dog-bomb we had just been shoved into. "How much is that?"

"Twenty-five gold per puppy." His answer drove a spike into my gut that nailed me to the floor. As mom played in the pen with the puppies, I contemplated the amount of questing we would have to do to make that up. It was way too much. I sighed and turned to walk out the door, the smell of dogs being way too much for the first time in nearly twenty-five years.

———

An hour later, Albarth, me, mom, and her new shadow dane puppy Zanjir walked down the street.

"Why do you pick the weirdest names for your dogs?" I rolled my eyes for the umpteenth time as the little dog strutted along beside us, a collar around his neck, and a lead in my mother's hands to help guide and correct him as they walked. She took her time, ensuring he knew to stay beside her, and spoke to him constantly, speaking his name any time she addressed him.

"I pick names that sound powerful and have history, or meaning to them. His name is Persian and means 'chain.' He is what will keep me grounded enough to find your father." She guided him back to her side since he had tried to wander closer to a small child who reached out pitiably for him. "*Fuss* Zanjir. *Fuss.* Not to mention your name, firmly rooted in history."

"I'm named after some creepy lady's smile," I scoffed, and we walked on, my mother smiling. "What?"

"Yes and no." I looked askance at her and she decided to explain, "You're named after her, but only because of the significant event that happened when I saw her."

"I'm dying woman," Albarth cried, startling Zanjir, his indignant high-pitched yaps at the nymph ignored. "I have to know this, please?"

Mom snorted and looked back at me. "I had been looking at her when your father surprised me with a wedding ring."

Albarth chuckled at my surprise, and I had to laugh when she continued, "He had saved all summer for it, and it looked like a piece of candy, but I swear he was so proud of it. I still have it…it's locked away."

The smile faded from her face, and she cleared her throat loudly after a moment. "Where is it that we're needed to question at?"

"'Quest' mom, and Albarth has them all." I glanced his way, and he had already pulled them up.

"We have a quest from Codgy, who could use some ram hides, so we will need to kill the sheep to get to them." Albarth shared the quest with her, and we all moved toward the newbie area. "I do wonder, have you spent your free points for leveling up yet? Also, what are your stats?"

"I haven't spent anything at all, and if you'll show me how, I can allocate them."

"Better wait on that." She frowned at me, stopping her from doing that, so I motioned that we keep walking as I spoke, "We need to get you leveled up swiftly, and there are nuances to that process that we need to truly pay attention to if you plan to really play."

"I'm not here to *play*, Mona—I'm here to find my husband," Mom groused angrily.

"And we don't know how long that may take, and we can't be stuck taking care of you if you make the wrong choices in leveling up," I shot back at her. "In the real world, you have a great deal of knowledge, experience, and influence—you have none of that here. This is where I reign, so if you want to be able to keep up and not hold us back, you need to listen and learn. Do you understand?"

"Now see here, Miss priss!" Albarth went on the offensive, going so far as to round on me and stop our walking completely. "You shouldn't speak like a totally entitled wanker to your mum!"

"No, Albarth, she's absolutely correct." My mom put a hand on my shoulder, ignoring Zanjir for a moment. "I got what I needed, and now you have to have your needs met in order to press on. You're right, and I need your help. Train me so that I can be part of the group and not a detriment, and I appreciate you taking the time to educate me."

"Love you, Ma." I smiled at her and she grinned back. "Now, let's go kick some ass!"

Her slap against the back of my head made me grunt. "Language!"

After that, it was a sheep and ram gorefest. Codgy had stated he would pay us a silver per every ram hide, and take a bulk price for the sheep hides we had if we wanted to go through him.

With Zanjir tagging along, fighting was a bit more difficult, but he did seem to understand that when a hostile creature came, he was to hide for now. We did the age-old newb grind ritual, and it was amazing how well it worked. Albarth and I partied up and coached mom on how to fight with her Soul Sword.

Lvl 2 Sheep – Friendly

Mom had Zanjir, who growled and lunged forward, tugging at his lead and biting the wool on the sheep's side for a moment to see how he would do in a fight. Not too bad if I'd say so. Though the sheep *baaa'd* at him almost in confusion before Zanjir nipped again and mom swooped in to stab it directly in the eye.

"Oh!" Albarth exclaimed at the sheer brutal efficiency of it. "Dear god, your mother is a sodding barbarian!"

We weren't in her party, so the notifications weren't visible for us, but with the critical damage, there was no way the sheep wasn't dead. When she looted it, she claimed the prizes and even found some raw meat in it.

"Will this rot if I store it in my inventory?" She held up what looked like a foot-long raw steak. Zanjir bounced off her leg, trying to get to it, but she scolded him firmly, and he flopped onto his butt.

"I don't think so; in most games, it stays raw, but this one is pretty realistic, so I'd say you have a little time but not a whole lot." I thought about it, then smiled. "But Albarth might be able to help get it cooked for you, maybe? Or we can later. Let's try for later."

Albarth scowled at me, grumbling, "My magic isn't a bloody oven," and we turned back to our duties.

After the customary three sheep, a ram would appear, and we would instantly get its attention with my Allure.

"Try not to take a direct hit from the horns and go for the vitals!" Albarth instructed loudly as mom just managed to roll aside and miss a horn. She growled in frustration. Luckily, I had grabbed Zanjir from her, or he might have bolted off. The little pup attempted to bark menacingly at the ram while it chased all three of us. Eventually, Albarth had to step in and use his wind magic to blow it onto its back so our trainee could stab it in the chest and facial area.

Once she was done, mom wiped at the blood on her face, her legs, wrists, and just generally smeared it all over tiredly.

"This is quite the challenge. I can see why you like this so much, and why your father talked it up as much as he did."

"It's fun." I smiled sweetly, then asked, "How much experience are you getting per kill?"

She seemed to be looking at something and frowned. "Only fifteen for the sheep and double that for the ram."

"So far, you've gotten nearly enough to get you to level four!" Albarth clapped and smiled. "I knew this would be a good quest for us!"

"What happens now?" Mom's raised eyebrow made me smile as I waved her toward another sheep.

"Rinse and repeat. We move on when you're level five, and we turn the quest in." She frowned at me, but I just shrugged.

And so, we moved to work once more, fighting until it was time to turn in the quest to Codgy, and then moved to the western side of the city where things would hopefully get a little more interesting.

CHAPTER SIXTEEN

MONA

"Get your sword out!" Albarth grunted as he moved toward the second large bear that had come at us since we'd started this quest.

The hulking, brown-furred animal raised up and swatted at him, only to miss as he whooshed by thanks to his wind magic. The tip of his sword disappeared into a small hole in front of him, only to burst from nothing and stab into the grizzled grizzly's ear.

CRITICAL STRIKE
33 dmg to Grizzled Grizzly
Disoriented Debuff — 24 hours
Lvl 9 Grizzled Grizzly – Enraged

It roared angrily and tottered where it stood, paws raised, and turning when mom sprinted closer with her Soul Sword held close to her body, the blade out toward her enemy. Level six had come easily enough after we took down the first bear thanks to the experience she got from Codgy and fighting our way here, but that had only been two levels above her at the time. This bear was an absolute beast compared to her, and we wanted to kill it bad.

Because if we didn't, it would eat all the honey we were trying to gather, and we would fail our quest. It stumbled forward slightly, and mom hopped onto a log next to it. She'd been going for the same ear, only to be swatted aside by a massive paw, and since we weren't in a party, there was no way for me to get a reading on her health.

"What's your HP bar like?" I snarled at her, activating Allure and hoping that the enraged status of the bear would make it more stupid.

"Three quarters," she groaned, and the bear turned toward her again.

I rolled my shoulders and pulled my chakrams from my hips, calling, "Roll away... now!"

Using my metal Aether, I threw both of them as hard at him as I could and began to dance toward the bear. Mom rolled aside in my peripheral vision, but I kept my eyes on where I wanted the whirling discs to strike.

A tempo thrummed through my body as I moved, swaying back and forth to it as my weapons slashed and returned.

12 dmg to Grizzled Grizzly

9 dmg to Grizzled Grizzly

Reaching out with my fingertips alone, I merely changed the chakrams' direction of travel to send them toward the bear again.

"Just try to go low!" The thing lurched toward me when Albarth's rapier, blazing with his Flame Dart ability, pierced a shoulder.

Ignoring the damage notifications, I watched in stunned horror as another lumbering figure came out from the shadow of the trees and joined the fray.

Mom was suddenly up and slid by the disoriented and brutalized bear, stabbing it in the thighs, both of them, before rolling out of the way of the second furred figure.

The big bear roared, blood gushing from its wounds, and

the legs weakening. The Grizzled Grizzly fell where it had stood, and suddenly, Zanjir crashed into its head, his paws scratching at the eyes a second before the massive paw reached up and fell aside. Mom panting as she stood over it and thrust her Soul Sword into the barely living creature's eye, killing it.

"Emerald!" Albarth snarled as he moved around the next grizzly that had joined the fight. "Get the bloody honey!"

Mom whipped around and slashed at the bear in the same manner as she had the old one before breaking away and sprinting toward the buzzing beehives behind me. The bees had left well enough alone since we weren't too close, but as soon as she got close enough, the buzzing grew louder. Which would likely attract more bears than it had to begin with.

My chakrams flew some more and we were whittling it down fairly effectively when I heard my mom cry out in what sounded to me like victory.

Bee Queen summoned

"Shit!" Emerald swore vehemently, and she flitted by me with her sword arm pumping at the smaller bees swarming around her. "I almost had enough!"

A plan hatched in my head, and I hoped it would work. "We can do this, put the bear between us and the hive!"

We cautiously made our way around the bear as the hive swelled against the tree and a large bee, roughly the size of a baby, shot out of it into the air.

Lvl 10 Bee Queen – Hostile

It buzzed angrily, two slightly smaller drones with stingers that looked like spears joined her from the hive. The bear bellowed its rage into the air, flecks of spittle buffeting the three of us as the bees moved in behind it.

Two giant stingers impaled the beast, and a globule of greenish-grey liquid splattered across the bear's broad shoulders. Its jaws yawned wide in agony as mom's sword whipped into the opening and sank into the roof of the mouth like a knife in warm butter.

The bear fell back toward the Queen Bee, and the two drones stabbed it again, likely thinking it still alive.

I moved on the drone to our left immediately as Albarth stabbed the air in front of himself in a similar fashion to before, the rapier stabbing through a small tear in space to pierce the queen's throat.

The free drone shot forward with his spear raised to strike at the nymph, and mom slashed it away.

"Don't worry about us—get that *honey*," I snarled at her before pulling out one of my daggers and settling into a fighting stance I hoped Cälaos would be proud of.

I threw one of my chakrams at the Queen with some metal Aether to drive and control it. This was my first time going hands-on while trying to control my other weapon, and sweat built on my brow from the concentration of it. She dipped and dodged out of the way, the drone spear jarring my arm as the dagger blocked a strike. I spun and used Allure once more to gain their attention as my dagger pierced the drone in front of me through the wing, dropping it onto the ground with a satisfying thud.

23 dmg taken.

A thudding sensation burst across my right shoulder and made the arm go numb. The familiar slicing sound of my chakram returning, coupled with my Aether awareness, signaled the weapon returning. Instead of catching it, I ducked just beneath it, it skimmed my hair before a slight crunch.

I rolled away from the enemies and turned, charging my dagger with metal Aether and launching it forward. With my will to set it straight and add a little extra oomph, the weapon pierced the soft flesh of the drone.

12 dmg to Drone Knight

Mom's Soul Sword swung down and hacked into its neck. Once, twice and it was dead, her breath coming in bursts of panting.

"Do you have the honey?" Albarth called his question as he dodged under a flying poison glob from the queen.

"Yes, but we should kill them!" Her eyes were wide, and she looked a little more bloodthirsty than I had seen her in quite some time. "Free experience!"

When she's right, she's right! I agreed and paced forward to retrieve my thrown weapons. So far, I had used two bars of my metal Aether, so I had plenty more that I could use to assist us.

We turned and looked at the queen, barely any damage done despite the hit from Al earlier, which was odd. Then I noticed a sort of gooey honey-like tether from her to the drone and noted that his health was much lower. She was draining his health to stay alive.

"We need to kill her first!" Albarth startled me. "She's a boss of some kind, and can probably spawn more mobs. If we drop him without damaging her, she will probably summon more. Focus on her."

"I'll take the rear." Mom growled and stalked around the queen's left side. "Stay safe."

I bared my teeth in a confident snarl and started forward with my daggers drawn. If I were to use my chakrams for this, it could prove dangerous for the group.

The Queen came forward, another globule of poison at the ready when the drone beside her had its health drained *heavily* from the hack job my mother put on the bee's backside. Wings slashed, and then healed draining the drone to a husk that dropped dead and left her alone to deal with three exhausted wanderers and an adorable puppy who had no qualms about goring an eye or two.

The globule fell and sizzled against the grass beneath us, and then she stilled for a second before her droning buzz grew louder and louder.

"Kill her!" I roared and bolted forward with my daggers poised and stabbed, piercing her abdomen.

11 dmg to Bee Queen

10 dmg to Bee Queen

The hive behind her writhed and shook, but the searing heat next to me drew my attention back as Albarth slid his rapier into the queen's chest, and then mom stabbed down into her back with everything she had.

This continued as the buzzing intensified, and a pulse of something hit my thigh, and I screeched in agony a heartbeat before the pain dulled.

I glanced down at the thin, pointed stinger protruding from between her legs that had slid into the flesh above my knee.

I ground my teeth and stabbed her twice more, her health bar depleting more and more and more until finally, just as the hive grew large enough to expel whatever was coming, it stopped.

Secret quest completed – You have taken part in usurping the Bee Queen from her hive. While the bees raise another queen to take her place, you have access to the hives in this area for the next two hours.

400 EXP earned

Loot Reward

Stinger Spear

Queens Wings

14 gold, 6 silver, and 9 copper

Level up!

"Woo!" I wiggled a little as I read through it all. "What's a stinger spear? How's your leveling, Mom?"

"I'm level ten now!" She smiled at me, her cheek slightly bloodied, and her legs reddened as well. "I am not used to this."

Those bears were some damned fine experience and the boss and her lackeys too… we should have just come here to level up. Damn it. Imagining Kyvir screaming about bees was a funny sight to behold in my mind's eye. That would have been nice.

A pang of hurt and longing rolled through me at the thought of him. I'd have to talk to him soon. I shook my head and refocused since both Al and mom were still chatting.

"You wouldn't be, you're also severely underdeveloped as a fighter because you need to spend your points." Albarth explained kindly. "Now, you're in greater danger than ever though—if you die now, you'll have to earn all of your experience back to start earning it at all if you do."

Mom looked confused, so I stepped closer and whispered, "If you have three hundred experience toward your next level and die, you'll have to earn that three hundred back so that you can start at zero. It's a hefty penalty. So, try not to die now unless you *just* leveled up."

"Understood." She frowned and turned back to the still hive. "What do we do now?"

"We loot the absolute... crap out of the hives that fall within the dead queen's realm and then sell it for a premium to pay off your debt." I grinned at her and turned toward our next goal. "Then, we get you properly leveled up."

We collected our honey, conveniently converted into pots inside our inventory for some reason since we had received a magic one from the quest giver, a sweet old lady who likes sweets and baking. Thirty-six extra pots than needed was lovely, and we also managed to grab thirty-seven honeycombs that we might be able to sell to someone else. Who knew, but by the time we were done, we had come dangerously close to the end of the two-hour mark, and snuffling grunts and growls came toward us.

"Let's get!" Mom hissed, and we hoofed it out of there as swiftly as our legs would safely carry us. We kept low to the ground, watching the limbs of the trees above us for anything that could drop down onto us, pausing at times to let massive birds pass above as we crouched in bushes.

It was hard to keep Zanjir quiet in those instances, the puppy wanting to bark at almost everything. Mom had to lift him into her arms and clamp a hand around his muzzle and whisper to him to please be quiet.

After another hour of keeping the dog quiet and in the shadows, the gate to the city was in sight, and we could almost relax. We walked into the city and finally relaxed, taking some time to get to the bakery for the nice, little, old lady.

She took the honey we had to give her for the quest, which

earned mom two gold for that, and then she bought twelve of our honeycombs for three silvers apiece. The honey heist had seriously been a good haul for cash. And levels.

Once we left, I stopped and gave Albarth a huge hug. "Thank you for being so good at getting quests."

"Honestly, I had another two lined up, but this means we can get out of here faster, and I am all for that." He grinned at me knowingly but took pity on mom and snorted at himself. "Sorry, Kyvir and Sundar are both terribly rash at times and can get themselves into trouble if we aren't there to manage them."

Mom laughed out loud. "Oh, I know how reckless he can be at times. So excitable and full of wonder, but his good intentions can get him into trouble. Now, teach me how to level up so that I can help you all."

"Well, it honestly depends on how *you* want to do this." I shrugged, thinking of how best to relate this to her. Finally, I just decided to go over the basics. "Normally, a party has four members, and those four members fill different roles. Tanking, healing, and damage dealing—it rhymes I know. I'm not that clever, it just happened. Stop smiling like that."

Emerald shook her head and motioned for me to continue.

"Kyvir is our tank, his ability allows him resistance to magic, and Sundar is our de facto healer because her totems heal and buff us." I motioned to myself and Al. "The two of us have abilities that allow us to deal damage and distract our enemies. Like me using Allure to gain attention and distract while Albarth stabs the hell out of an enemy. So, with your ability and your stats as they are, you may already have a role, but we should check your progression tree to see what you have available to you."

She blinked and muttered, "Status, and… ah! Tree."

She hit a couple things and frowned, tilting her head. "Interesting. Is there always something so odd?"

"What is that?" Albarth leaned over and motioned to her

invisible screen. "You can share it with us if you like. We can help you."

"Share screen," and no sooner had she said it than a screen flooded my view like my friends had when we first started playing.

At the top at level one was **Soul Sword**, which I had expected, under that for level three, was **Variable Soul** and **Assassin's Blade**. I pressed them and couldn't see anything, so I looked over at her and motioned to the screen. "Tell us what they do."

"Well, Soul Sword allows me to do damage from one to my maximum Knowledge stat. From what I've seen, that's one point to nine points of damage plus whatever stats add to that. I think the most I've done has been ten?" I nodded, and she pressed something then read aloud, "Variable Soul allows me to change my Soul Sword into weapons that I've seen. The damage doesn't look like it will change that I can tell, but it adds one point to Strength and Skill. Assassin's Blade allows for me to use either the Soul Sword or a new Soul Dagger, but I have an added critical damage modifier and chance depending on how I fight. It also gives me a point to Skill and Knowledge. After that, it appears to be bonuses to stats, and then at level five, I have affinities?"

"Types of Aether that you can use like magic, Albarth has wind and space Aethers, and I have metal." I used a bar of Aether to lift a dagger from my hand a little then let it fall back into my grasp. "What are they?"

"Animal and plant?" She blinked in confusion. "I'm confused."

"Why?" Albarth scratched his head and crossed his arms. "That's bloody brilliant, I know exactly where to go to get those both unlocked."

"Because there are question marks under that for level ten. Is that odd?"

"The system for the game may give you something based on your choices in leveling up, so you just need to level up. You have to use those points now, Mom. All nineteen of them. Do you know what you want to do?"

She thought for a moment, looking at me, then Al. Finally, her gaze fell to Zanjir, and she smiled. "I think I have the makings of a stealthy, or agile fighter now if I use Zanjir as a distraction. Training him well to protect me and 'tank' for me to keep the enemy's attention will allow me opportunities for better damage. I think I will pick the Assassin's Blade."

"Perfect!" I clapped and then reached down to pet the bored-looking pup. "Then, that means it would likely be a good idea to spec yourself into Knowledge, Skill, and Heart."

"Because Heart gives me health points?" She blinked at me, and I nodded. "Very well. Allow me to place them as follows: ten points into Skill, five to Heart, and four to Knowledge. That way, I can still dodge and attack well, and my critical chances should grow, right?"

Albarth whistled, and my heart pounded, *Momma wants to min/max?*

"Is that a bad idea?" She seemed concerned after having spent those points.

"Not particularly, no, it's just those are very bold decisions and well thought out." I smiled at her. "We made the choices to add things as we went because we had to. So, you having the opportunity to do that kind of thing is just awesome. Those are big bumps since you only get one point to spend per level unless you use the tree to add some. Which you'll do when you make your choices, so go ahead, and we will get you to the dryad to get your magic awakened."

I watched her clicking, a frown on her face. "Go ahead and think out loud, Mom. That way, we can help you."

"Thank you, dear." She didn't bother to look up and stated, "Assassin's Blade selected, adding one to Skill and Knowledge. After that, there is an option that gives me... two times damage to my Soul Sword or Dagger. I'm choosing that outright."

My eyes widened, and I glanced over in time to watch Al muttering a string of curses under his breath. Why did it seem like my mom's ability and stats were so damned broken? Luck? Beginners luck? Geez. Wish I had been so lucky. I would have *killed* to have those abilities and awesome skills, and I took it from his scowl and begrudging acceptance that Albarth would have too.

"There, it is done." She smiled up at us, then shared her status page and tree.

Emerald FireLevel 10 Race: Kitsune
HP: 180
Strength: 6
Skill: 20
Heart: 15
Knowledge: 14
Serenity: 7
Presence: 8
Unspent Stat Points: 0
EXP to next Lvl: 0 / 1000

"Wow, mom, can't argue with them stats." I smiled at her. Her tree stumped me though, since the level ten branch was still hidden. "Maybe we need to get your magic unlocked? What do you think, Al?"

"That could be it, maybe the system needs more data to give her the branch?" He scratched his chin, and closed his eyes. "Mona, why don't you take your mother to the dryad to get her power unlocked? I'm still a little freaked out by the last time I was there in his presence, and I don't want to be that way again. I'll go to Rogelio and pay for Zanjir, with the money from the quest, and then we can get our new lady assassin kitted out before heading back to Belganna's hold?"

"Sounds good to me, mom? Pay the man." Emerald rolled her eyes and counted out seventeen gold, insisting that a four-gold tip be given for Rogelio's trust on top of the thirteen he had charged. Once Al turned to go, so did we. "How are you feeling about all this?"

She was quiet for a block or so, content to observe the things around her, and before I could ask if she'd heard me, I found myself surprised. Tears fell down her cheeks. "Mom? What's wrong?"

"Nothing, dear." She sniffed and pulled Zanjir back to her side, barking for him to heel before looking over at me, "It's just that I can't believe how much you and your father did together and now that I'm here, I can't seem to get over how much I missed out on with both of you because I was so obstinate."

"You didn't know, it's okay." It was a little hard to see her like this, but if I was being honest with myself, having her here was so nice. "I'm just glad that you're here to help me find out what happened to dad."

"I wouldn't be anywhere else." She smiled at me comfortingly, and reached out to take my hand. "I love you so much, my dearest baby."

"I love you too, Mom." My cheeks almost hurt from smiling at her as hard as I was, but it was a welcome pain. "I don't know where I'd be if not for you. You're my rock. I'm glad that you no longer have to worry about the… uh.."

She quirked an eyebrow up at me and chuckled. "The big C?"

"Yeah." The high of our closeness sort of fell, and I turned my thoughts toward my map and finding our way to the center of the city once more.

I found myself wondering if my dad was watching us. If this was his plan all along, or if this had been the last thing he would have wanted. If he cared at all. We would have to figure that out once we got there.

After a while, we stood underneath the gigantic tree, and a creaking built through the boughs and branches as the large dryad stepped out of his own accord. The bark-like skin covering it, breaking away from the trunk as the creature's eyes fell on us.

"I recognize you, young one." He pointed at me, and I bowed my head. "This one is not familiar, but I *feel* you."

"Hello," my mother's lame, uncertain greeting surprised

me, but this creature was massive, and she had no idea what it would do to her.

"She came here to have her magic awakened," I offered, and both of them looked to me. I shrugged and stepped back, their attentions going back to each other.

"I see that you have a person who is guiding you, has she told you of what it costs to have your Aether awakened?" My mom shook her head, and I could have sworn I had said something, but then again, that wasn't entirely impossible given what we'd had to do since she got into the game.

He motioned her toward the base of the tree and sat next to it. Mom took a second to worry about whether she should or not, but he patted the ground, and Zanjir tugged her toward him and the spot where she sat.

"In order to awaken your Aether, I must exact a price, and it is typically something very precious to the awakened." His light voice flowed through the air around them and over to me, and that made me wonder what had been taken from me when I had gone to the metallic golem that stood in the Earth Square in a corner. I had touched it and lost some blood, but other than that, I had no clue what was taken.

"I can sense what you value most of all, the little one over there, and your love of animals is almost as supreme, but you seek something." He heaved a sigh. "I will awaken your Aether, but the cost will be great. Though you will pay it in the future, and I hope that you will hold no ill will toward anyone for it. I will understand if you do, for I loathe that I must exact this price."

"Can you tell me what it is?" Emerald asked hopefully.

The great, bark-covered head shook side to side. "Alas, that is a part of the price for awakening both types of Aether. You will be extremely powerful when it comes to nature magic, and it is that power that will take from you. Do you wish to continue?"

Mom looked to me, and I shrugged, giving her an encouraging thumbs up and a huge grin. "It can only help us on our quest."

She heaved her own sigh, then looked to the dryad and nodded. "I am prepared to pay."

The dryad leaned close to her, the bark crackling as he separated once again from the tree and touched her forehead with his own, then her chest just over her heart with a long finger.

Mom's back arched as if she had been struck by lightning. Her eyes glowed green for a heartbeat, then she leaned against the tree behind her and closed her eyes.

"She will rest for a time." His voice rose to me once more. "She loves you. And I hope that you find what it is that you seek."

I watched him in uncertain silence as he simply sank back into the tree where he had been sitting. His legs becoming as the roots next to the ones around him just before my mother woke back up to me and Zanjir licking her hand.

She stared at him almost in shock, lifted her hand from the ground then looked to me. "Did you hear that?"

"Hear what?" I walked closer to her as Zanjir trotted around her and consumed her attention again. "Hello?"

"He spoke to me." Zanjir sat and wagged his tail at her delightedly. "Zanjir spoke to me."

"Well, that's cool." I grinned at her, remembering all the slightly dirty looks I had given the puppy when mom hadn't paid attention. Now I had a dog that really could tell on me.

CHAPTER SEVENTEEN

SETH

"How the hell did this happen?!" I growled and slammed my fist into a goblin's jaw as we backed down the tunnel we had come into behind Jimson. The dwarf had been adamant that there were moles down this way that tried to eat people, and here we had stumbled upon a camp of goblins, the little green freaks surging toward us en masse.

I summoned Flicker with a silent prayer, and she appeared in a tent with only a single summoning Aether bar gone with two of my flame blinking out.

"Finally!" She stretched and looked around, her presence suddenly almost blinding in the darkness of the tunnel. "Oh, goblins! Gross. Want me to kill them?"

"Yes!" Sundar and I bellowed as the creatures moved forward a little more warily. Blothl grasped Jimson by the shoulder and guided him back as the dwarf swung his pick and gashed one of the goblin's arms before another lashed out at him with a crude spear of stone and bone.

Flicker cackled as she fluttered forward and began to spew

flames, punching and kicking at faces and dodging spears and thrown rocks with jeers at her enemies, "You throw as well as you are cute—not at all!"

The goblin she had taunted likely couldn't have been able to understand her, but her tone must have given the idea of an insult because he shrieked and pointed before a small burst of sickly green light flew from his finger at her.

"Woah!" She ducked and clobbered a goblin in the nose, and looked back at us. "A little help here?"

I shook my head and glanced about. "There's a choke point twenty yards behind us, keep them distracted so we can get to it and then let them come!"

I turned and sprinted toward the point I had spoken of and prepared myself as the others joined us. I cast Ice Armor (full) on myself, the spell sucking me dry of my three ice Aether, in exchange for a boost in defense for half an hour. Weather and damage permitting.

I took out my short sword and shook myself out as I hollered, "Now, Flicker!"

She shot back toward me and then behind me as the wave of twenty goblins charged forward. The ten-foot-wide tunnel funneled to a three-foot-wide entrance, and I stabbed the first goblin that approached in his wide-open mouth. The sword passed through the back of his head, and I stepped forward and yanked my blade to the side of his head, the top portion of it falling to the ground with a squishy thud that made a little bile rise in my throat, but the smell of the blood was intoxicating.

CRITICAL STRIKE
22 dmg to Goblin Raider
24 dmg to Goblin Raider
Lvl 7 Goblin Raider died
37 EXP

"They don't seem very hearty!" I called back to the others as I stepped forward and grabbed one. "I'm going to try something, don't let them hit me!"

Sundar stepped forward with Blothl slashing and stabbing

with their swords as the Goblin Raider in my grasp struggled. That only seemed to excite some part of me even more as I whipped it around to face the other goblins and dropped my face toward the delicious warmth flowing through the side of its neck. Fangs pierced flesh, and warmth flowed into my body. It was the sweetest concoction I had ever tasted outside of the delicious offering I had taken from Belgonna herself. I could almost hear Mephisto chuckling somewhere in my soul, but I didn't care. Warm red filled my vision, and suddenly, I was aware that this one goblin was no longer going to satiate me, and only one of my bars of ice Aether had returned.

Aether stolen – Earth affinity at 2%

"What the hell is he?!" Blothl grunted under the onslaught of the goblin raiders, but they seemed to be a little warier of me.

I cracked my neck, growling, "Hungry," in reply before I rolled my shoulders, and for the first time, I felt so much more alive. More... *me* and I wanted more.

I surged forward, coating my blade in fire Aether as Flicker slipped over my frost-covered shoulder and into the face of an unsuspecting raider. My blade dipped and stabbed into the goblin on my right as I snatched another one closer to me with my left hand, my intent to drain more Aether from them. One of the other goblins jabbed a stone spear into my armor, the icy plate taking the brunt of the damage. I was so hungry I just couldn't bring myself to care with this veritable feast at my feet.

3 dmg taken.

A hiss of outrage escaped through my teeth, and my flaming sword whipped around and slashed the goblin along the shoulder and chest. The searing path of it making the air stink of cooked flesh, my nose crinkling up in disgust at the stench.

13 dmg to Goblin Raider

4 fire dmg to Goblin Raider

"Watch yourself!" Sundar bellowed, and I scampered back before a magical blast hit another goblin in the face, caving in its disgusting bald head.

The blast had come from my left, and I turned to see a

robed figure among them, a goblin hand waving a pattern in the air as its aura bled dark red with blackened streaks through it. "I got that one!"

Blothl and Sundar parted, my gait widening as I prepared to launch myself at the goblin caster when a blur of motion from my right forced me to drop or be struck down where I stood.

"Well, that's unfortunate timing," Jimson said, then spat from behind me. I looked up to see him standing there with his pick glowing the same sickly reddish-black color. "I had hoped to be rid of you all before they began to come to."

Blothl leaped over my body and slammed into Jimson with a grunt and a feral howl of rage at the betrayal. "Ye whoreson! Why have ye betrayed us?"

Jimson struggled with the enraged goat rider and managed to slip from his grasp with a couple scrapes and a bloody lip, he ran his hand across his mouth, and the blood smeared as he sneered, "The demons mean to free us from that manipulative bitch's influence so that we're free to be as we were meant to be. They promised to return us to the earth and tunnels of our ancestry."

"It's all lies!" Blothl cried as he came to stand, the goblins backing away from the fray. They even backed away from us as the two men circled each other, another fiercer aura moved toward us. A clacking and dragging sound made the hair on the back of my neck stand on end, then a scratching of something sharp against stone made a thrill of primal fear and uncertainty drop through my spine like a runaway elevator.

"We try to keep our promises sometimes, especially when the people we make said promises to are as efficient and cunning as this one." A husky, breathy-sounding woman's voice echoed pleasingly down the tunnel toward us, glowing embers for eyes watched us from the darkness. "Though I do wonder, why would you bring them to us before we're ready to take this city and its pretender god to task?"

"Because they had plans to come in here anyway," Jimson

shrugged, and Flicker moved herself as inconspicuously as she could, being a glowing beacon of magic in the tunnel, making her way behind the traitorous dwarf. "I figured them dying once or twice at our hands would dissuade them from interfering."

The clacking and dragging sound continued until the goblins ducked their heads, and she stepped into view. The light of the sword flickered and faded where it was in my hand. Her body came into view, tan and red-scaled sections of flesh unadorned by clothing swam into the light. She was beautiful even as she exuded the same disgusting aura of power that the caster and Jimson's weapon had, her large, leathery wings flared over the goblins, making them cry out in fear and awe, then settled once more against her back.

I'd seen demons like this before in other games, her horns lifting from her forehead and rising into the air half a foot above her, her black and gold hair flowing provocatively over her chest and to her navel, just covering her ample chest. Her waist swayed as she stepped toward us, the long, pointed tail behind her swaying in time with her swaggering. "See something you like, handsome?"

I blinked and shook my head, finding my way to my feet, I didn't want sex—I wanted blood. Flicker launched a wave of fire at the back of Jimson's head, and Sundar cast her Totem with the Hell Cat buff on me. I pulled a goblin into my grasp and bit into its neck, draining what I could as I slashed with my slightly burnt sword at another.

9 dmg to Goblin Raider
Earth affinity at 4%

A wave of fire Aether burst from my hand toward the succubus and the goblins, the notifications blurring by, letting me know that I had set most of them on fire. That sickly-looking aura swept toward us. I shoved the goblin in my bloodied grasp toward it, and as soon as he touched it, the goblin crumpled to dust along with every other goblin in her way. The notifications careened past my vision as I moved back as swiftly as I could.

Level up!

I almost cried out in relief when the energy hit me. Muscle fibers screamed and screeched in my body as they snapped, bled, then the blood leached from them. Everything I knew in that minuscule second had been fire and anguish, and suddenly, I could hear her voice in my mind. "So delicious. I can't wait to play with you some more, handsome."

You have died.

———

I came to, looking at my experience bar, it showed a big fat zero and that I needed to get eleven hundred experience. The relief that flooded into me made me actually lay down where I was, finally taking my surroundings in. We were in Belgonna's throne room.

"Fuck!" Sundar swore and made me jump. I turned in time to see her thrashing about angrily.

"What?" I stood and made my way over to her, she had tears of rage streaming down her face. I saw that she was level eleven too, so it couldn't have been that. "We leveled up, what's wrong?"

"She killed Blothl!" Her gasping, angry sobs punctuated by her meaty fist smacking against the stone floor. "He shoved me out of the way, and she grabbed him and sucked his fucking *soul* out, Kyvir! Then she shoved her clawed hand into my chest and pulled my heart out with a damned grin on her smug-ass face!"

A chill ran down my spine again as I imagined that. The loss of the dwarven man—a good man and good friend—dropping my heart into my stomach.

I closed my eyes and selected Mona's avatar name and sent her a whisper, —*We have a demon problem within the city. We need you guys here, now.*—

—*We're here and so is mom, where are you?*— Her immediate response went a long way toward easing my troubled heart.

—*Belgonna's throne room, get here ASAP and speak to no one that you don't have to. We don't know how many of them have infiltrated the city and where.*—

—*Coming*—

"Mom!" I roared as loudly as I could, my voice echoed around us, growing impossibly loud as it did so until the door off to our left that the children had gone out previously swung open and Belgonna strode through it in her elven form to see us standing there.

She went to smile but seemed to take in our distress and frowned at us. "What has happened."

"Blothl is dead, we've been betrayed." Sundar stood, and her fists clenched so hard at her sides that blood dribbled down her fingers onto the ground beside her. "Jimson was a plant and showed his hand. They've been plotting on you and the city."

"No!" A wave of fiery fury seared the air around us, and suddenly, Belgonna's draconic form reared into view as she blared her rage everywhere. The mountain rumbled around us, her pieces of golden armor rattled and tumbled as the heat continued to thicken the air until it was almost too much to bear.

"Where are they? Where is this 'Jimson', and why is he not dead?!" Her long fangs came into my view, where I had fallen to my knees. "Do you fail me as well, my beloved children?"

"A demon was there!" I wheezed, and the heat tripled, then vanished, the relief instantaneous, the cool air chilling me, and the sweat that had sprung from my skin.

"A demon?" She lifted me gently in her clawed hand. "You saw a demon in my city? Where?"

"In the mines, Jimson had lured us there with a promise to take us to things we could fight against. She showed up after he played his hand, but she said it was too early for them to be ready to make a move against the 'pretender god.'" Sundar shook her head as if trying to clear it. "Do you know what she might have meant?"

Belgonna thought on it for a moment, her eyes closing as she quieted, though her tail continued to thrash behind her loudly. "I hold no illusions of being a deity. However, my subjects do worship the god of making as all dwarves and crafters do. I think the name they use for him now is... Falgrun?"

"Why would they attack a church?" I rubbed my eyes; it was closing on time for us to log out to sleep, and I was beginning to truly feel it.

"A group of demons bent on creating as much discord and strife as they can, would benefit greatly from it, wouldn't they?" Sundar ran her hands through her hair and sighed as the door behind us opened, and Sinistella joined us, followed by Monami, Albarth, and a kitsune woman I didn't recognize until I saw the puppy plodding beside her. It had to be Ma.

"Mother, I can feel your rage from here, if you do not take this medicine, you're likely to cause the land around our home to change more than what your mere presence has done already." The dragon's daughter held a large bottle up, and the queen growled angrily at her but sighed and transformed her shape once more into the elven beauty.

"My people are in danger from outside foes, and I am all that stands against them; my experience is needed and as I continue closer to my end, I find that I have much to leave to you, daughter."

"Nothing that I do not already handle the majority of for you, for our people," Sinistella stated as the queen stepped forward.

"Maybe you should take this time to train her to take over the more intricate things?" Mona asked so that she would be heard. Belgonna looked over at her, not with the disdain that I thought she might have, but with genuine curiosity. "It took being together doing the same thing to help my mom realize what she was missing. Why should you, someone so wise and mighty, allow something like death to steal what little time left that you have with your children—all of them."

"Say what you mean, child." Belgonna stepped forward until she was almost close enough to touch her chest to Mona's face. The new person stepped between them, pushing Mona back to stand before her. "And who are you?"

"I'm her mother, and what she said was right." She turned to look back at Mona and pulled her into her arm, protectively. "Since coming here, I've realized how much I have missed out on because I was too stubborn to be there and try something new. To let someone new take over for me so that I could make my children a priority."

We all remained silent in the wake of her realization, and she squeezed Mona and shook her head. "I missed out on so much time with my whole family. And I wonder, in the light of my folly, if I had done so sooner, would my husband still be here? So, I implore you—don't wait to try and care for what you have."

Belgonna stared down at Emerald with open amazement until finally, she turned and looked to Sinistella. "Consider this your trial as queen. Using your new brother and sister, their friends and this woman, I would like for you to protect our people. How you decide to do so is up to you but know that this is to decide whether you are fit to reign."

Sinistella perked up immediately, then remembered that the rest of us were in the room. "I will not fail you, Mother."

Belgonna shook her head and sighed as if she had already failed some test. "It is not *I* you need worry about failing, but our people. Protect them, and do so as I would have. Or better." She turned away from the now-scowling Sinistella to regard Emerald again. "Tell me, who are you?"

"I'm Emerald Fire." She stepped forward and held her hand out, Belgonna blinking at it for a moment until she dropped it to her side. "But my friends can call me, Em."

Belgonna smiled then, the grin splitting her face. "Do you wish to be *my* friend?"

"That's why I said that my friends could call me that." Emerald raised her eyebrow back and a grin of her own quirked up her cheek slightly.

"Very well, Em." Belgonna held her hand out, and Emerald shook it firmly. "You may call me Bell. Let us go and speak mother to mother while our children discuss matters. I simply must have you meet my other children."

"Oh sure, can Zanjir come along?" She motioned to the dog as Belgonna ushered her toward the door, nodding that the dog could come.

"The children will adore him." Her smile seemed genuine, and we waited until they were gone again to breathe fully.

"Well, you heard her, let our planning commence, you all seem to be quite tired." Sinistella glanced at all of us. "We will conclude here as swiftly as possible and prepare how we can. I need to know everything that you learned."

I could tell that both Albarth and Mona were both dying to ask us what the hell had happened to make us both so vastly different, but they would have to wait.

It only took about ten minutes to relate what had happened, long enough for her to ask questions on things that I had spaced on, or couldn't answer, like if we suspected anyone else.

"Not off the top of my head, but the miners all seemed heavily interested in us or as though we were intruders." Sundar looked askance at me, and I shrugged.

"I just hope Nildy wasn't a part of it," I muttered. I had really liked her, and I didn't think she would take the news of Blothl's demise thanks to her husband's demon girlfriend very well.

"I will have that taken care of," the queen-in-training replied in a cool tone. "How would all of you suggest we proceed?"

"They might expect us back in the mines if the four of us went in, but I'm thinking that their final plan is to do something to the church, and we can't let that happen." Albarth rubbed his chin thoughtfully. "I think it will be best that we lay a trap for them there. Let them think they've scared us off or confused us, then surprise them where their plot is unfolding."

"And what of spies?" Sinistella pointed out a little harshly.

"We go to the church and have the queen read their minds, then go back with them under the guise of help or something to lay the trap." Monami motioned to the stanchions around the outside story of the room. "We check the guards and other people we smuggle in as cargo, before it all goes down and lay in wait."

"They're likely to have the church under watch, and if they notice something out of the ordinary, they might call the attack off." Albarth reasoned, and I had to admit that made sense. "Is there another way for us to get there? Or have them come here?"

"There is rumored to be an underground passageway—built well before my mother had come to this area—that spanned the bottom of the city and led to the church among other places as a route of escape. It would stand to reason you might be able to utilize it as a means of stealthily gaining entrance to the church to take the priest there and bring him here. From there, we could question him and then set our trap."

"Great!" Mona grinned and looked to Sinistella, the dragon princess almost beaming at her in return for some reason. "Where is this entrance?"

Sinistella's face fell, crestfallen. "The royals all parted ways with this realm long ago and well and truly before anyone was blessed with that knowledge."

"Well, it has to be in here, right?" Sundar shrugged when we looked at her. "Think about it, if you wanna escape some big bad who could have invaded, you put it in the most easily accessible room, so you get out sooner. So, it stands to reason that it would be in this room and or the former king or queen's rooms just in case."

We began to search the walls and everything closely, behind the throne and over the treasures that had been piled up along the walls to the rear of the room. As we did, I couldn't shake the feeling that the room felt familiar somehow. Not just because I had been here so often, but because I had seen it before.

Before!

"Mona!" I cried out hurriedly, scrabbling down a pile of golden coinage and baubles, displacing them noisily. She turned toward me, and the others halted their search to look excitedly my way, but when I wasn't standing near an entrance, they turned back to it.

She rushed over to me her eyes narrowed in concern. "What is it? Did you find something?"

"No, but I remembered something—does this room feel familiar to you?"

"Of course, it does, you lummox, we've been here before!" She threw her hands up and made to turn away, but I stopped her by grabbing her arm. "What?! We're trying to search for something here."

"We are! And it looks familiar because I remembered where we had seen it before!" I grinned and clasped her shoulders in my hands. "Your dad's hidden room. Come on!"

I grasped her hand and ran toward the far-right wall next to the armor that had been standing there before falling over under Belgonna's rage and the doorway to the right of that. As soon as we were there, I began to grope and feel the stones that had been laid there, looking for anything that might work as a lever or entryway. I couldn't believe that I had been so dense and hadn't seen it before.

"This doorway is pretty far back from the entrance, is it not?" Mona observed from next to the door. The wall leading to the door stood about four feet from the wall I groped, to where the door was. "I feel like we're onto something here. I touched one stone about four feet off the ground where the walls met, and the stones meshed and gave it a tug. A grating, churning sound came from the wall by the doorway, and a passage opened up, dark and covered in cobwebs and dust.

"We found it!" I hollered, and all of the others came to join us.

"What do we do?" Sundar asked, looking to all of us. "I'm pretty wiped at the moment, and the time for this thing to happen is still closing in."

"According to my mother, she found that the time for this thing to occur was going to happen in two days?" Sinistella looked at us in confusion. "That was this morning."

"Yes, but we also can't trust that something hasn't changed in their plans since we ran into them, and the sooner we get things taken care of the better." Sundar motioned to the darkness leading into the depths before us. "We have no clue what's going on down there, and if we *go home* before then, it'll be a minimum of twelve hours before we're back. That leaves little time to broker the kind of plans we need to have."

"Then, you will have to trust that I know my people and my forces well enough to ensure that they will be capable of mounting a suitable attack and defense." Sinistella insisted almost with a hiss, her eyes narrowed at Sundar. "I am centuries old, *little sister,* and have been assisting in the rule of this city for more time than you have been alive. While you are home, I will interview the appropriate forces and have them readied in secret for an attack, and then you will go to the church, with my blessing, to retrieve the priest and return so we can vet his compliance."

She turned and walked toward the center of the throne room, waving her hand, and a large oblong table appeared there with a map of the city stretched across it and several pieces resembling dwarves.

"You may retire for your twelve hours, I will plan and prepare. All of you are dismissed save for Monami—I must have a word with you."

Mona looked to the rest of us and shrugged before mouthing, *"Log out."*

Sundar and Albarth went after that, but I remained a second longer to stare daggers at Sinistella's shoulder before Mona made to shove me away and mouthed her orders again. I rolled my eyes and logged out of the game, finding myself staring out the front panel of my portal.

I rinsed off real quick, ate one of the meals I'd subscribed to —surprised at how bland it was for what had been advertised— and passed out with an alarm set for four hours from then.

———

Darkness so thick it could cloak the world and devour everything in front of you, including your hand, to hide it from sight. I just opened my eyes, and it was everywhere.

The world around me seemed muted, no sound as I stepped toward... well, nothing. Strangest dream I'd ever had, and I'd had some bad ones.

Whispers echoed around me, coming from somewhere, then nowhere as I looked around. Then the void-covered spaces before me grayed and lightened slowly until shapes formed. Trees around a small pond, and some ferns next to it. Suddenly parched, I moved closer to try and slake my thirst.

Finally, the area seemed to find a comfortable gray hue and stayed there; the shapes darkened and black, but somehow, I knew what they were easily. The water stood still, my reflection in it, colorful highlighted dark hair, mixed Hispanic features, and my tired eyes staring back. I reached into the visage of me and cupped some water to my mouth. It was warm to the touch, and on my tongue, it tasted sweet and savory all at once. I had to have more of it, craved it because it made the thirst that clawed at my throat subside.

Eventually, my hand wasn't fast enough in getting the water into me, so I dunked my face in and pulled the vividly sweet nectar into me until I thought I would burst from it or drown and came up for air. But as the ripples stilled beneath me, the droplets of warmth flecking the water beneath me, the ripples revealed color. And in that color was my avatar, face drenched not with water, but blood, staring back at me with a wretched grin—fangs peeking from my lips and crimson pupils gazing into mine.

Then the *hunger* set in and cramps knotted my stomach, and then the creature's hand rose and plunged out of the water toward, me and I cried out as the blaring bleating of what I thought had been my alarm banished the baneful dream. It wasn't though, it was my heartbeat pounding and something in me crying out.

Air whooshed past my ears as I launched myself out of my sweat-drenched covers and collapsed to the ground in a pile of sore muscles and fear. Something wrapped around my leg and I cried out as I looked down to see my shorts had slipped down around my knees in my flight from the bed and struggling with the covers.

Panting, unable to return to sleep, I grabbed my sheets and took them to the laundry room and set the cycle to start. The washer and dryer thankfully one unit, so once the wash was over, it would dry the load inside automatically. Another amenity I loved dearly because it made life so much easier. My parents had teasingly groused that I was spoiled by it, and I agreed wholeheartedly, but that didn't mean I wasn't going to enjoy it.

I blinked blearily around the house, I had time to kill before going in. I could eat again since I was actually hungry right this second. I pulled out another one of the meals, glaring at the fajita instructions, pull out the flour tortillas and microwaved the fixings. Peppers, steak, and chicken with pinto beans, corn salsa, and jalapeños. I put the bowl in and nuked it for the required four-and-a-half-minute time and stared as it cooked, not willing to watch anything at that moment. My hunger was just... there in a way it had never been before.

I pulled a skillet out after a couple seconds to warm the tortillas one at a time and transferred them to a plate before following up with the ingredients for the meal and a generous helping of Tapatio and sour cream. The hot sauce helped a little bit, but otherwise, everything tasted *lackluster.* Like something was just missing. I growled to myself, had an energy drink that I thought had always tasted like crap, and then hightailed it into the portal.

CHAPTER EIGHTEEN

MONA

"You made that remarkably fluid," The dragon-in-elf's clothing observed over the table at me, her sort of sharp teeth flashing in a grin at me. "How did you convince her to speak so candidly?"

"I didn't." I motioned to where I thought they could be outside, Mom and Belgonna. "Truth be told, I think your mom is crazy, and I wouldn't have known where to begin explaining her. But apparently, my mom saw something of herself in yours and went for it. Plus—she's never been one not to stick her nose into other peoples' business before, so it wasn't so surprising that she stuck it into a queen's."

The sorceress snorted and thumped the table before covering her mouth. "Forgive me, but your mother and mine sound very similar in that regard." Her smile only widened. "I told you I would reward you, and I will. Here are the stones that we discussed. This will allow you to attune to other spots around the globe to make teleportation easier and fast travel simpler. These ones are better and are personalized, unlike those ones I gave you before. These stay on your person and will take you anywhere you have been as long as they've touched another stone. Not to mention, a little added coin for the ease with which you managed to do this."

She placed a sack of coins onto the table and then put four stones right beside it. "When you return, I will have another made for your mother as well. A gift."

"Thank you." I thought for a moment. "Can you tell me what happened to Kyvir and Sundar?"

"My newest brother and sister?" She raised an eyebrow at me curiously. "They've been adopted and blooded."

"What does that do?" I rubbed my face, recalling the curiosity that I had pushed down when we first saw them both. "They look so odd now."

She frowned and looked about us before speaking, "A dragon offered her blood to them. This makes them akin to family, changes them fundamentally, and gives them a few perks racially, but what it really does is make them more under her control. Children cannot refuse quests from their mothers and fathers unless they are of age or given the option."

"But Kyvir is twenty-five and Sundar older than that, how —" she stopped me from continuing and motioned to herself. "What."

"They may be of age in mortal years, but this applies to a *dragon's* idea of maturity, which is fifty years to become a young adult."

"So, your mother basically just enslaved two of my best friends?" The fury singing through my veins was astounding and made me want to march right outside to Belgonna and strangle her.

"They made the choice to submit to the blooding, and my mother *does* try not to give quests in that manner." She sighed heavily, fatigue making her look a little less held together. "This is why it was so important for me to take the throne. So that she could be out of this predicament, and we would be able to act better on more sound judgment."

"Don't enslave anyone else," I ordered flatly, and she just rolled her eyes at me.

"I have no desire for children the way my mother does, though I will blood those I find worthy and those whose wills align with mine."

A clicking drew my attention across the room, mine and Sinistella's conversation halting.

"You two seem to be getting along swimmingly," mom observed as they entered the room. I took my rewards and grinned at her.

"Time to go get some rest. We have a long day coming up." I smiled and nodded at both the queen and Sinistella before hurriedly logging out.

Back in my bed, my consciousness fading, I set my alarms and dozed off—dreams of finding my dad plaguing my slumber.

Someone popping into my room humming woke me before my alarm went off, and I howled angrily. "What good is raid sleep if you don't get any damn sleep?!"

A sharp smack on my shoulder woke me a little more, and the smell of coffee hit my nose. "Mom?"

"It's me, dear, you know, you should eat better. Here," she placed some food on the table and called me over with a pat on the couch. I got up and shuffled over to it and picked up a fork.

"You really should tell him how you feel, and soon," Mom lectured me as we shared the meal, apparently not feeling all that tired since she had gotten a full night's sleep and had her probably-illegally-strong coffee soon after. When you have coffee that strong four hours counts as a full night.

"Why?" I grumped. I had been late logging out and only had three and a half hours to get some well-needed rest.

"Because I can see how awkward it's making the two of you —well, more you." She smiled knowingly to herself, and I tried to wrap my brain around what she'd said. I hadn't done anything out of the norm, had I?

"Bell and I were watching you both, she said that she could

smell the affection you held for each other. She said that since she was his surrogate mother now, she had a desire to know if you would be a good mate to him. Though she does have her concerns and wouldn't share them."

I rolled my eyes and tossed my fork onto the half-eaten food on my plate. "What is it with mothers and pressuring their kids to make these decisions?! Can I not even eat in peace without being told I should be pining for someone who's not noticed me and seen me in even a remotely sexual light until he was twenty-five?!"

"We meddle because we care, sweetheart," she chided lovingly with a glint of mirth in her gaze. "What is it that you have to lose?"

"I don't know, my entire friendship with him?" I stood and paced, suddenly not really caring all that much about sleep. I had been *perfectly* fine without her bringing this up.

"He wouldn't forsake you because you like him, Mona Lisa." Ugh, she'd used my middle name like I was a frigging child. "And besides, it's clear from your reaction that you like him, too. You said he asked you if you wanted more—that's a sign of its own. What's wrong?"

"I want to find my dad!" I bellowed at last. "I have a chance to see him again, and here I am thinking about a boy? What the hell is wrong with that?"

"Mona!" My mother tried to sound offended at my language, but I cut her off.

"No, mom. Just no." I sighed and grabbed the back of my couch more for stability against the wave of emotions I felt. Panic about not being able to find him, worry if he was okay, anger that he hadn't been able to be direct or that he hadn't said anything. Mostly confusion.

"I can't help you if you won't talk to me, dear." She came over to stand next to me, and suddenly, her presence was stifling. When I was quiet for too long, she sighed. "I tried going through his things again before coming out here. I couldn't find anything more to help us. Nothing whatsoever."

It felt like the room had begun spinning, and I took a deep breath. I needed to prioritize.

"I cannot do anything until I figure out what is going on with dad." I decided tiredly. "Nothing else matters until I know what happened and that he's okay."

"You shouldn't have had to worry about any of this," her statement seemed a little too late as it was. Had been for years, but gaming had been my relief, and this was far too much for me to truly let go. Because every time I would game, I felt like I was closer to my dad. Closer to what was meant to have been.

And now I had a chance to find him. To get that back. To be a family again.

I couldn't mess that up. Couldn't allow this chance to slip from my fingers. There was more to all of this than I was aware of, and I had to know what was going on.

I'll do what I have to, to get those answers. Everything else is just an obstacle. Even as the thought occurred to me, I knew it to be true. As much as that should have been terrifying, I found it strangely... comforting.

I finally had the resolve to do it after months of wondering what to do with myself if I should try to search his things again. If I should try and find him on my own. Things I had thought since I found out he wasn't coming home ever again. Since the second day he'd been gone.

Finally, I could do it.

"I'm going to take a nap," I announced groggily. "I know we go in soon, but I need like, ten more minutes just to be okay."

"What was it that Sinistella was saying to you when we rejoined you in the throne room?" Mom's question was a little unexpected, but seeing as though she had never played a game like this, I could see why it would be interesting to her. Sinistella was an interesting NPC, after all.

"She was thanking me for finishing up a quest for her so nicely." I smiled, and even I could feel it was the genuine article. "Gave me a pretty nice reward too, that I'll split with all of you when we log back in."

"Thank you." She took my plate and walked outside.

I replayed Sinistella's *gratitude* over in my head when I fell into my bed.

That went well. I hope she does good as queen someday.

———

Shuffling from my room to the living room a bit more rested than I was ten minutes ago, the first thing that hit me was the smell of my mom's special coffee, enough to put hair on anyone's chest and she had a steaming cup of it on the table for me. I was pleased to see the plate of food had been taken away, though the coffee alone scared me. Still had some time before we needed to be in, so we could sit for another couple minutes.

Mom nursed her favorite mug, her favorite green robe wrapped around her body and the pack lying at her feet. Tialca raised her head as I walked in, the other dogs turning to see what had garnered her attention. She stood and trotted over to greet me happily, and her cold, wet nose touching my hip made me laugh. She'd done that since I was a kid, and it never failed to make me smile.

"Still sorry, I had a part in knocking you out T-T." She chuffed and heeled at my left hip like all the dogs were trained to do. At this point, it was as much habit to her as training. She sat next to my leg, leaning against me as I sipped the potent brew. I fought the urge to scream as the caffeine hit my veins, heart, and brain like a Mack truck full of dynamite with boosters full of nitro flaring out behind it.

My whole body vibrated like a wire strung too tight, and that was just a sip.

"Don't worry, I weakened it with creamer for you." She raised her chin and her thermos simultaneously and watched me as I drank a little more. "What's the plan today?"

"We listen to Sinistella's plan, make it through whatever fresh hell is below that castle, and the city to get to the church, then we find the priest." I heaved a sigh as more caffeine spiked my heart rate. "After that, we plan a raid."

"A raid?" She blinked at me and the dogs perked up at her voice, eyeing her, then laying back down. "What's that?"

"Well, a raid is when a group of players goes up against a stronger enemy, typically in a longer and larger dungeon." I exhaled and tried to calm my jittery nerves a bit. "Since we will likely be teaming up with the guards, it counts as a raid. To my mind, since we will likely be fighting a strong enemy."

"I see." She nodded and stood before going toward her portal. "Then I suppose we should get started."

I nodded, finished the rest of my coffee with a grimace and involuntary shudder before heading to my own portal. Once I was inside, the usual countdown happened, then paused before a voice came over a small speaker next to my ear, her voice thick with concern.

"Hello, Miss Hart, my name is Ranhita, and I wanted to discuss a matter of your health." I blinked as her face popped up on the small screen before mine. "Are you aware that your heart rate is very high at the moment?"

"It's from coffee—I'm okay, thank you Ranhita." I gave her a good smile, I was embarrassed as hell from it.

"As long as you say that you are okay." She looked uncertain for a moment, then the feed was gone from my screen, and the countdown to log in began.

CHAPTER NINETEEN

SETH

Watching the stars like this had been interesting for the last few hours. It had been nice and all, but there was nothing to keep me engaged, and my hunger wasn't passing.

My stomach in knots, I stalked through the throne room and out into the hall before it. The guards let me out with a bow, and I offered them a smile that only seemed to unnerve them. One of them reeled back, hand falling to his sword before another was on top of him in an instant. Not wanting to find out what was wrong, I figured maybe he just thought I was a demon and made my way down the hall.

I found myself walking toward Nildy's inn and then behind it as I remembered who she was married to. The slimy bastard who had lured us into that trap. Voices drifted toward me where I stood in the shadows, but the blood in my veins chilled at the sound of Jimson's voice.

"Yes," he hissed quietly. "No, she has no clue, but listen— shut up and listen!—she can't know. She's been too ingrained with the royals and their antics to fully trust her with this kind of job."

I inched closer so that I could see who he was talking to behind the bar and in an alleyway. It was dark, and I couldn't make out both of the other figures, but one *did* stand out to me. It was the youngest-looking Talon, still wearing the plate armor of his station. I didn't know what his name was, though. Shit.

"Brave words coming from a nobody—I've been the one keeping the other Talons away from your trail while Vilarn funnels the necessary things to you, and then you do *this?*" The younger Talon snatched Jimson up by his shirt and picked the other man up. "Vilarn and I have been patient with you and our benefactors in moving through the mines and killing the occasional person who has what we need to move on to our next steps, but this is brazen. *Too* brazen. We need to know that you have this under control and that we aren't under suspicion. What did you tell them?"

"Nothing, they only died and badly at that," Jimson scoffed and slapped the hand that held him, and the other dwarf dropped him. "The only one that could have pinned any of this to us is—was—Blothl, and he's dead."

"How *fortunate,*" the Talon growled angrily, "that your wife's best friend and a source of your jealousy ended up in the cross-fire between you and two meddling wanderers. You know what I think?"

"You better shut your big mouth when it comes to my Nildy, or I'll shut it for you," Jimson threatened darkly, his voice lowering menacingly.

"I think you did it on purpose to get rid of him. She was ready to toss your arse back to the mines when she found out how worthless you are, and you worried she would go for the worthier man—admit it."

Jimson snarled and socked the Talon in the face for that, the two dwarves fought and beat each other until finally the armored dwarf backhanded Jimson and push-kicked him back into the stone wall. "I could have you arrested for assaulting a Talon."

Jimson snorted and spat back, "And I could have you arrested for high treason." Both of them stared at each other for a minute as a slow smile crept onto Jimson's face. "Except that you can still be useful to me and the demon who will help us reclaim our city and birthright. Go make sure those meddling imbeciles stay away from our work, and I'll ensure nothing goes amiss. We have the final ingredient, and all is prepared. Be gone."

The Talon growled and kicked dirt at Nildy's man before turning on his heel and retreating down the alleyway away from my hiding spot. I waited until the dwarf was alone, taking one heavy pull from a large flask he produced from his inventory.

While he watched the other man walking away, I made myself move as swiftly and silently as possible, tiptoeing my way behind him. I'd added another point to my knowledge, giving me three of each Aether type and two grey bars.

Using that and my stealth to my advantage, I grasped Jimson from behind, covering his mouth with my hand and slamming my fangs into his exposed neck. He grunted and struggled, but as I drank from him, I used my Aether to freeze where I touched, an Aether bar would disappear and then refill as I drank my fill.

The blood was like ecstasy and tasted bitter like liquor.

Aether stolen – Earth affinity at 10%

Aether stolen – Demonic affinity at 5%

Secret quest completed – Begin collecting at least five different types of Aether. Reward: Roulette.

Would you like to collect your reward now? Yes / No?

I opted for no for the moment and settled on lifting the dwarf, heavy and cool to the touch over my shoulder like a sack of potatoes. Then stopped and fished out my old rag shirt and tied it around his face so he couldn't see and that others might not see him either. In a fit of genius, I took the flask that he had dropped and poured some on him, then myself to add to the illusion I wanted to effect on curious onlookers.

I picked him back up, using another bar of Aether to keep him on ice and somewhat compliant while I walked the sides of the streets toward Belgonna's throne room while keeping as close to the shadows as I could. When I couldn't, I stumbled and swayed, and people just discounted us both offhand the majority of the time. The one time they questioned it was funny, though.

"Oi!" A slurred voice grunted as I crossed a small side street. I turned my head left and swayed precariously on instinct. "Wha's wif da bag on he's face?" That last bit said with a hiccup and a belch.

"Old lady said if she caught 'im drinkin' again, she'd box 'is ears, so if she can't shee'im she can't beat him." I tried to chuckle at my own ridiculous feigned and terrible impression of the gruff dwarven accent, but he seemed not to care.

"Das a good idea!" The dwarf turned back toward the wall he was taking a leak on and began to hum a discordant tune to himself. "Oughta do 'at meself."

I fled from there as drunkenly as I could manage without falling over and pumped another bit of Aether into my prize.

Time to go tell mommy what I had learned.

The guards ordered me to stop at the door and drew down on me while I was still a decent distance away, but I held out my ring and ordered them, "Open the damned doors—now!"

They scrambled to follow my instructions and moved quickly to open the door to the hall. The dimly lit corridor was exactly what I needed. By now, the others would likely be logging in, and I was ready to have this jerk in chains. Or worse.

I liked the or worse thought *very much*. Once I arrived at the end of the hall, I nodded to the door and grunted, "Open it." I must have sounded as impatient as I felt, because he didn't give me any crap as he followed my command.

Monami appeared three feet from the table where Sinistella, Sundar, Albarth, and the Talons all stared at me.

"What is this supposed to be?" Growled Qornath. "I can smell the sauce from here—be you marinated now, boy? Out o' all times?"

"This is a gift to mother, Sinistella, summon her now— please?" I added the last bit because me ordering her had put a glint in her eyes and a tick in her jaw.

She blinked and whispered something and motioned for me to come closer, the lights in the room growing brighter so that she might see me better.

Two minutes later, a whooshing gust of wind came from above us, and Belgonna swooped down in her hulking dragon form.

"This is twice you have summoned me with little word, my son." She sounded bleary and tired. "I hope that this will not become a habit that I must break you of?"

I dropped my head respectfully, and I slid the dwarf from my shoulder. "I hope it is the last time that I must disturb you so."

"What have you there?" She cocked her head and lowered her neck so that she could stare intently.

"A gift, one of many gifts." I leaned down and ripped the shirt off Jimson's head, and Sundar stomped forward to try and get to him, but the dragon queen held her back.

"This is the one who betrayed you, how did you come upon him?" She blinked her eyes at Jimson, and I could almost smell the fear radiating from him.

"I happened upon him during a secret meeting, one that *he,*"—I pointed to the younger dwarf who looked to have gotten a black eye from their tousle— "Happened to be a part of."

"Lies and slander!" The dwarf stammered, his brow broke out in a sweat and he clenched his fist. "These five have done nothing but come into our fair city and cause trouble and calamity. Demons in the city? Ha! How could they be?"

Qornath and Greldan both turned in unison to stare at the dwarf, and Greldan stated, "But Darengor, we only just arrived here—not one ut'rance o' the word 'demon' has been spoken."

To add the final nail to his coffin and another's, I asked a burning question, "And by the way, who is Vilarn?"

The dwarf next to Qornath blanched, his white beard suddenly darker than his bloodless face. He backed away before a being of pure fire burst from the air behind him and grasped his armor, the heat from the creature's grip heating it and turning it from red to orange, and it buckled as he writhed in agony.

"How can this be?" Belgonna hissed savagely as she regarded both dwarves with murderous intent plainly visible in her gaze. "No one should be able to hide anything from me mentally. No one!"

Her tail hammered the ground close to Darengor, his knees knocking loudly in his armor. "The demon! She cast a spell on us that sealed our minds except the thoughts we wanted you to know, please don't kill me! It was them; it was all them!"

A massive clawed hand speared through the dwarf's chest, armor rent and body gored where he stood. Blood burst from his mouth as he stared down at her knuckles, attempting to comprehend as his mouth opened and closed with no sound other than a low, gurgling, sucking sound.

Rather than being horrified at the extreme violence, I was more saddened I hadn't been able to drain him of the delicious crimson flowing from him onto the floor.

And good *god, what is wrong with me?* My stomach soured at the thought.

"You will tell me everything, Vilarn." Belgonna hissed, then remembered something and turned her gaze to Sinistella. "Forgive me, beloved daughter, I have taken over once more without meaning to. How would *you* handle these traitors?"

Sinistella stood quietly for a time, watching Vilarn coldly. "That one knows little, he's a financier. I had wondered why funds had gone missing from certain places, but it had been done too well to be simple theft. He was the money, and likely only aided the other Talons in covering their tracks." She pointed to Jimson, who had fully regained his faculties once more and leered at everyone. "This one is the doer of the group, as evidenced by his betrayal, though how it served him I'll never know."

She walked around the side of the table toward him, under everyone's gaze and lifted him by his shirt. He struck her several times in the face, which she never once flinched from no matter how loud the sounds of flesh hitting flesh were.

"I invoke my blood right, the right of the gold." Tinkling sounds surrounded us, my mouth quirked downward in a frown, and I turned to see several thousand gold coins shaking and shimmying toward where she stood. "I invoke my blood, the blood of the old."

The coins shot toward her her skin and disappeared into it, where they touched golden scales remained until finally her whole body was covered in shimmering gold that reflected the bright light in the room.

"I invoke gold, as is my right, stolen and taken by might," she snarled, a red forked tongue flicking from her mouth. "Heed my words and submit to my sight, tell me thy truth wholly and right!"

The coins on the ground roiled and lifted as if flung into the air, circling more than sixty feet above us around the golden sorceress.

"She cast the spell to keep us hidden, and all who wish our goal to fruition hide in plain sight." Jimson's voice was a droning monotone, his eyes blank. "We mean to summon a demon capable of causing enough chaos to overthrow the god, so that we can return to our way under the mountain. Where all true dwarves belong."

Sinistella leaned closer, inhaling deeply as her forked tongue stretched across his face.

"Truth was spoke with life at stake, and so a life I cannot take." The powerful tone the sorceress had before sounded defeated, the coins in the air cascaded slowly to the ground around us.

The golden scales danced along Sinistella's skin then fell

away in a dusty shower of ashes. She swayed where she stood long enough for Qornath and Mona to stop her from fainting and hitting her head on the table.

"She will be out for a little bit," Belgonna advised, drawing our attention. "It costs her much to draw on her bloodline like that."

"She's part gold dragon?" Monami's voice sounded horrified.

"I was young, and not all the chromatic and metallic dragons hate each other." Belgonna smiled sadly, "But that is a story for another time. My children, as you were the ones who suffered at this dwarf's hands, I will leave his punishment to you."

Sundar and I looked at each other, and as our gazes met, I could feel her fury mount all over again.

She nodded to me once, and I understood what she wanted. What *I* wanted.

"As prince and princess tasked with the dispensation of justice by your Queen Mother in the trial of Jimson, traitor to the city you were blooded to help protect, how do you find the accused?" Belgonna intoned loudly for all to hear.

"Kyvir, this is weird, what's going on?" Mona grabbed my arm and tried to pull me away from Jimson and Sundar. "What is this crap? I know you were adopted, but what if he has a way to help us?"

I looked her squarely in her eyes and grasped her face in my hands, whispering, "It's okay, Mo. This guy is a lackey, and the only thing he knows is how to take. He killed Blothl in cold blood and for petty jealousy."

"Yeah, but this isn't you, Se—Ky." She pleaded, her insistence weighing on me. "Blothl was a good guy, sure, but he was just code. An NPC. What if Jimson knows something about my dad?"

"You know, for one of the most caring, and protective people I know, you can also be the most thick-headed and stubborn." I could tell that my words stung a little. But she needed to learn this. "Code or not, he was a friend and had helped us. This guy took us into a trap and got our friend killed."

I pried her fingers away from my arm and pulled away from her before stepping up behind Jimson and forcing him to kneel on the ground.

"We find the accused guilty," I growled, my blood boiling as I announced the verdict aloud.

"And what is your sentence?" Belgonna asked, her voice almost gleefully sweet.

Sundar stepped in front of him as I knelt behind his back, her lips pulled down at the edges, and her tusks jutting out cruelly. "Our sentence is *death*."

I wrapped my fingers into his hair and yanked his head to the side, my fangs sinking into his neck near the same bite marks I had made before. He cried out, and then a sickly *schunk* shook his body, and he gasped. I looked down to see Sundar's sword protruding from his chest, then she yanked it out. She snaked her hand forward, and dived up to the arm inside the dwarf's chest cavity.

"Oh my god, stop that!" Emerald cried, her voice growing near hysterical. "Stop that right now!"

I wanted to stop, but I couldn't control the hunger anymore. I needed all of this blood. I needed to taste his death. To feel his pulse stop.

A wrenching force pulled down, slightly ruining my hold, and I had to bite down and tear flesh to hold on, then I saw it, and a sickening glee fell over me as the life ebbed from our victim.

I'd had my fill and was delighted to find that my curiosity had been rewarded.

Earth affinity at 25%
Demonic affinity at 20%

So, my affinity would rise higher if I killed my target while feeding?

Good to know, I smiled and licked my lips, looking up to the horror-filled faces of Monami, Albarth, and Emerald front and center. The dwarves behind them at the table stood carefully out of sight and as quiet as could be.

I no longer felt as confident as I just had. Mona and Ma had tears streaming down their faces, and as I stepped forward, Emerald rocketed forward and slapped me fully across the face, blood splattering the ground.

"What the hell is wrong with you?!" Her sobbing caused her body to spasm. "I told you to stop. Why didn't you stop?"

"I... I couldn't—I don't know what's happening to me. Please." I looked from her to Mona, to Albarth who stepped closer to them both. "You have to believe me. I... I..."

Suddenly, it was much too hot to be standing there in front of them, and I had to be away.

I opened the previous notification I had received and selected yes. Then, I was whisked away to the darkness once more.

It was the same set up as last time, only the wheel now had six choices, death still being there but slightly larger.

"Oh, how delightful, I was worried that we wouldn't meet again for some time—but look at you! How did it feel to drink the life essence from someone and claim so much, my little *monster*?" Mephisto's delighted demonic voice echoed out from behind the wheel. "I decided to spice things up a bit since last time. Add a little more *flavor* to the pot. You like?"

I growled and sighed. So far, it was weird. Looking at the board as I did, it was a little odd. Again, death was there, a little larger than it had been last time. There was level up, rand aether, wishful thinking, pain on max, and Aether split.

"You wanna spin the wheel again, killer?"

The same prompt as last time burst into my vision, I selected yes and then stepped forward to grasp the thin sticks jutting out haphazardly from the front of it. I spun it as hard as I could, the words blurring in a mix of fantastic carnival colors.

"Bloody business, vampirism." Mephisto teased, his large hands unfurled from the shadows behind the wheel and waggled back and forth in different directions. "Everyone has to see your point sometime. Too bad about your friends and family, though. Thinking that you're some kind of freakish monster with no control—but hey!—that's family for you, eh?"

His cackling laughter sent chills down my spine and made my skin crawl as one hand went to the top of the wheel like it had last time just before spearing the contraption and bringing it to a grinding halt.

Four fingers entered, and three of them had stabbed pain on max, "Oooh. This one's a doozy! Hope you don't mind a little bruise with your bacon getting kicked, there, killer."

"Wait!" I cried just as his left hand readied to snap and send me back. "You like these games, right? How about we play again? Double or nothing?"

The hands sucked behind the wheel, and immense pressure bore down on my shoulders before piercing nails dug into the meat of my deltoids.

"That's a dangerous thing to say to a demon who just *adores* his games, boy." His voice a low growl against my ears. "But since you're the only one I get to play with like this, for now, how about I take you up on it with a new game I've just been *dying* to try. You up for a little spin on this game of chance here?"

My adam's apple bobbed in my throat before I nodded wordlessly, the pain in my shoulders flaring as he squeezed excitedly. "Excellent!"

A snap of his fingers, and suddenly, I was looking at him from the wheel where I was strapped in, like some kind of circus sideshow.

"Now, here are the rules." He reached up theatrically, above his mouth and dropped his fingers, hand and then arm up to the elbow into his creepy, widening mouth. Finally, he grasped something and slowly pulled out a long, shiny sword. "Phew, that was a little stuck in there. Anyway, here are the rules. Now, I've taken death off the board because *you* are the death choice, and obviously, I can't give you max pain again because that would just be ridiculous. I need you to struggle to not go bonkers, though that might be fun to see. So, whatever I hit is what you get. If it's you, you die. Simple as that."

He thrust the sword into the ground and strutted over to me, his ridiculous clothing switching with his movements until he could grab my face with his creepily-long fingers. "You sure you want to test your luck, Kyvir? I'm only going to be this generous once."

"Bring it on." I feigned confidence, and his eyes rolled back in his head as if he were loving every second of my heart pounding so hard it could burst any moment.

"Oh! And to make it a little, teensy tiny bit more interesting and not about me just killing you for daring to challenge me to a game of chance so selfishly, I'll be blindfolded."

"Wait, what?" I had enough time to mutter those confused words before a blindfold appeared over his eyes while I spun wildly, and he groped around his waist for the sword.

"Oh, where is that thing," he muttered, to himself and my heart did a little somersault when his fingers wrapped around the hilt, and he grinned, "Gotcha."

His grin only widened as he yanked it from the ground, and the sword sliced through the air toward me and the wheel. A sharp *chunk* echoed through my entire being, and the whole wheel shook with the force, but other than my shoulders, I felt no pain. I grinned and looked around me to see where the sword was, but I blinked and was standing. The room still spun.

The room tilted, and I landed on my side, violently spewing all over the floor as Mephisto cackled hysterically.

I looked up to see that the sword had struck wishful thinking. I could see that there appeared to be a subtitle beneath each other choice. Beneath death was a small bar that read: *Mephisto devours you slowly and your screams serenade him into a nap.* Rand aether: *a random type of Aether is given to you.* Level up was self-explanatory, and the final one Aether split: *Mephisto splits your Aether how he sees fit.*

"Well, you picked one yet since it's a wish?" Mephisto

popped out from behind the wheel and startled me a little. "Please tell me it's death."

I actually laughed at that one, and it seemed to confuse him. "Let's go with Aether split."

"You do know that I could choose to take your Aether and split it *from* you, right?" He suddenly stood right in front of me, his eyes narrowed at me.

"You could, but I don't think you will." He frowned, and it was a good look for him, the loon. "You want me and my friends to be able to fight against your demons, right? Well, if you take my power, it shows that you're not as unbiased as you say you are. And besides—where's the fun in that?"

His grin widened, and he cackled wildly for what felt like forever before he finally settled and stared. "Where indeed."

He reached toward me and up, grasping my Aether bars and snapped one end off. I groaned, as the physical pain of it was undeniably the worst pain I had ever felt in my life. He put the one back where it was supposed to go, then the other beneath it. But he wasn't finished.

"As a reward for challenging me and being a good sport, I'll give you a little bonus." He winked at me, then his demeanor darkened, and he grabbed my armor and yanked me toward him. "But this is the last time you get *anything* from me outside the games we play."

He reached out beside him and grabbed nothing before shoving it into my lower abdomen, and I had to reevaluate how bad that previous pain had been. I coughed up blood, and he only chuckled as the crimson liquid splattered onto his hand just before I passed out.

CHAPTER TWENTY

SETH

I slowly returned to consciousness, wondering what was going on. It was so still around where I lay on the ground, then Sundar and Monami's faces swam into my vision, Belgonna peering over them in her draconic form.

"Where did you go?" Mona asked quietly. I looked at her in confusion. "One second you were here, then you were gone. You've been gone for two hours, and we had no idea where you went."

I sighed and tried to sit up, my abs and solar plexus feeling like they'd been pulverized by a heavyweight boxer. Fighting for breath, I growled and stood on my own.

Once I was up and on my own two feet, the pain subsided, and I could breathe and think again.

"You know how I told you Mephisto took an interest in me?" Sundar, Al, and Monami nodded slowly, Mona looking like she had sort of caught on already. "I went there for another secret session with him. To play a game, only this time I lost. So, we opted to play double or nothing. Then I won. Although, I'm not sure *what* I won."

"And this sudden horseshit about you being a vampire?" Emerald crossed her arms and tapped her foot, a dangerous stance she was known to take when upset.

"It's true, but I'm an Aether Vampire. I didn't know that I was draining health to refill my Aether bars." I started to slide my hand through my hair as a nervous gesture but stopped when I saw the clotting blood still covering it. "I wasn't expecting the hunger that came with it or the fact that it would be so… well, so awesome. But I know you guys don't think that way."

"Of course, we don't, it's disgusting." Albarth grimaced as his eyes found my hands again, balking at the sight of them.

"But from what Belgonna has explained of the thoughts and emotions running through your mind when you were in the middle of *feeding* was that it sounds like it could be some sort of addiction?" Mona blinked at me in surprise when I rolled my eyes and asked, "Is that not correct?"

"No, it isn't *not* correct, but it seems like it's such a weak way to put it." I tried for the right words and thought of food. "It's like eating the best thing you've ever tasted and then making it even better. Any time I smell it, I feel like a starving man who just walked into a buffet with a for free sign out front. When I start to feed, even if it's just to replenish my Aether—which that's all it was at first—this feral mindset takes over, and makes me do things I wouldn't normally do."

"Like what you just did?" Emerald frowned, stepping forward to examine me closely. "Is there a cure? Can we help you?"

"I don't need help." I shook my head and finally could see what Mephisto had done to me. He had torn my Aether out of my body and separated it, then shoved it back in and added more. Right now, I had two Aether bars. One for summoning, and the other for my other two types of Aether. "This is exactly what I need to be able to protect the people I love. I have two

Aether bars now, you guys. Both of them are at ten bars apiece."

"How is this possible?" Belgonna blinked at me. "A second Aether bar doesn't become available until a wanderer or mage gets to level fifteen."

I rolled my eyes and growled. "Of course, he didn't really give me anything awesome." They all blinked at me, clearly waiting for me to tell, and I sighed. "Though I'm still reeling from the loss. I feel a little iffy."

"What was that?" Sundar asked excitedly. More so than I thought was okay.

"I feel pain the way we would in real life, my setting was upped to max." Emerald looked at me, same as Belgonna, as if I were crazed.

"You mean to say that wanderers do not feel pain as we do?" Belgonna gasped as four of us shook our heads, and Emerald just shrugged. "No wonder you all are so fearsome."

"We try really hard to be." Sundar grinned at her. "So, you'll be able to do a little more than we will, for now, that's good. We can use that. It's time for us to get down into that escape passage and try to get to the church. Time is wasting."

"Yeah, we should be on our way." Albarth stretched, and paced toward the darkness.

"Flicker?" A flex of will and a bar of summoning and flame Aethers brought the tiny flame pixie to our realm.

"Hey! Oh." She flew closer to me and stared at me hard. "You're stronger."

"Thank you." I smiled at her, and she grinned back. "What?"

"That means that you can either summon another creature stronger than me or help me grow." Her wings fluttered behind her wildly, and she dipped closer to my face.

"Uh, Mom?" I blinked up at Belgonna, her eyes on my summoning with approval.

"She's right, you can do that."

"But is there a benefit?" I felt a light sting on my face and turned to see Flicker glaring at me with a finger pointed my way menacingly.

"Yes, as I said before, if a creature has a good enough rapport with you, they will come when you call and will not fight you for control." Belgonna motioned with her head toward her blazing elemental friend. "The more they like you, the easier it is to keep them here and to summon them. If they see you as a friend, it is even easier."

"And if you give us power, it makes us like you more," Flicker explained with a smug look, almost like she expected me to agree. "All I'll need is seven Aether bars."

"Any kind?" She shook her head, and I guessed, "Flame or summoning?"

"Yup! Though summoning is stronger." She thought about it for a moment longer and shrugged. "You'll have to leave me summoned here for at least an hour, so any summoning Aether you feed me will be staying with me until I leave on my own."

"Is that bad thing?" I posed, then stopped and held a hand up. "Never mind, I think I get it. How do I do this?"

"You'll focus on me, and then there will be a prompt, and you can give me a little snacrifice." She bounced up and down in the air before me as I tried to do as she wanted me to do, but she kept moving too much to really try it.

"Hold still!" My voice was louder than I thought it would have been. She blinked at me and stilled long enough for the prompt to populate, and I sacrificed five flame and two summoning Aether to her.

The warmth left my body, and I felt a pull from my navel down my arm and into my hand as I offered her my power. The drain was familiar, but not too bad. She stretched and groaned in delight, her eyes flashing dangerously at me, then a grin split her face. "The next time you see me after today, I'll be different. So be ready."

I gave her a thumbs up and licked my suddenly dry lips before motioning toward the entrance to the underground escape tunnel.

"Let's skedaddle," I said, then grunted and moved away from them. I received an invite to party up with Mona, accepted it, and saw that all of the others were in it already. It was weird seeing Mom's name, but oh well. "Flicker, you're on shotgun with me."

"What's that?" Her inquisitive voice grabbed my attention.

"We got a lot to cover." I rolled my eyes, and we moved into the darkness below the castle slowly.

———

"Are you sure we're heading the right way, Sunny?" Albarth griped for the fourth time in an hour.

"Yes, according to the map, this is the area where the entrance to the church is." Sundar growled back at him and then punched him when he tried to take the small map Sinistella had given her. "Quit the macho bullshit and just help me find it."

We all rolled our eyes, she never had been the best with directions and was a little sore when anyone tried to help her too much. The dusty stone walls around us signaled that we had indeed come to the foundation of some kind of building, but we weren't sure if we were on the right side of it or not. There were twin alcoves built into the foundation, whereas the street view map we had didn't show them.

"This is such an odd thing to have here, is it not?" Emerald studied the same wall that she had been studying for more than ten minutes as we bickered and fought over the map.

Mona turned and stepped over to Mom's side and noted the thing she was talking about. "It looks like grout."

"Yes, but it's a different color, see how the rest of it here is all a dull grey, but this looks metallic?" She raised her hand, index finger traced the seam of it, and suddenly, the dust loosened from the wall as it shook and separated from the base around it, lifting above us with the stale air inside wafting out.

Just before several glowing red eyes flicked our way. "Get

ready!" I hissed too late as one of the impish creatures that resembled old cartoon devils rocketed out of the darkness at us.

"What are these things?" Mona gasped and spun away from one of them as it tried to latch onto her arm.

"What do they look like?" Emerald snapped and lashed out at one that attempted to herd her away from us with an almost spectral-looking dagger. "They have to be demons!"

"Imps," Albarth grunted as he stabbed the one in front of Mona and then whirled on the one next to himself, slamming it with a burst of wind from his outstretched palm.

Flicker bounced into view, slammed her fist into one of the little creatures, and it grunted, his jaw snapping to the side. He stood still long enough for me to pull out my half-ruined short sword and thrust it into his neck. Black and red blood spilled down the blade, and it actually made me gag to look at it until the scent hit my nose. It smelled almost spicy, like chili.

Critical Strike!
16 dmg to Harrier Imp
Bleeding debuff added.

"Keep it together, Ky!" Sundar said, her tone commanding, and slammed her fist into the one that I had stabbed. I snarled at the world around me and summoned my ice Aether into my hand and envisioned a sword. Two of my ice bars melted away, and I held an icy short sword in my left hand now.

I brought the weapon down and sliced the creature's wing and used the force to free my blade before stabbing it with both and pulling it apart. The combination of demon blood and their internal fire partially melted my ice blade, and the metal one looked chipped and slightly bent as well.

Lvl 6 Harrier Imp died
32 EXP (party size experience debuff active)

Well, that would have been nice to know when we made the party, but that was still some great experience for having killed a significantly weaker enemy. I wonder if it being a demon had something to do with that?

"Mona, time to dance!" My voice was low to avoid

attracting unwanted attention from inside, but I knew that she could hear me because I saw her whirling chakrams lashing out to my left and then she swayed into view.

Another one of the imps fell, and the other three grouped together and held their hands together while summoning a fireball the size of a basketball.

"Flicker, can you tank that?" The pixie dipped over my shoulder and shook her head.

"Demon fire is still potent to non-demons." She shook her head again. "You're cool and all, but I'm not willing to go back to my realm, taking that hit for you. Get out of the way, and fast!"

Suddenly Emerald stood behind all three of them where they flapped their wings and sliced into all of them at once. The magic surged back into their bodies and rendered them sputtering and shaking on the ground long enough for the rest of us to converge on their prone forms and stab at critical spots.

"Great work, Mom!" Mona shook her mom by the shoulders, and I grinned at them both. Then she turned on me and the sorry state my sword was in. "Making me use all my repair powder!" She repaired the worst of the damage and spent roughly ten minutes with it on a whetstone before returning it to me at nine durability.

"Thanks, Mo." She just shook her head and checked the rest of our weapons before we all piled into the dark basement of the building.

Inside we saw all kinds of books, wooden signs, and other things decorated in what I had since begun to recognize as the dwarven script. I couldn't read it, but it was a start that I could recognize it. In a dwarven city, I'd take that.

We traversed the room carefully and slowly until we found a set of stone steps that led up into a decently-lit chamber. We opted to let the stealthiest among us go since she seemed to have some sort of ability to stealth that none of us did.

She was gone for all of forty seconds before we had to stop Mona from tearing off after her. Seconds later, she returned. "I couldn't figure out the whisper thingy, so I came back, the coast is clear, and I found a couple of people praying and two priests."

"Two? I thought there was only one?" Sundar hissed and looked at us before turning back to Emerald and asking, "The ones you saw, was one of them a gnome?" She shrugged, and Sundar rolled her eyes. "Too short to be a dwarf with a beard and pudgy belly?"

Ma seemed to think for a minute before nodding excitedly, "He was alone in his quarters while the other one oversaw those praying."

"That's Caltross; he's the one that they summoned last time to heal a dwarf, right?" Sundar's tusks flashed as she grimaced, her lips pulling away after that in disgust. "The other guy may be a plant of some kind."

"How do we know for sure?" Emerald looked slightly nervous. "He was reading from a book of some kind when I found him, though I couldn't read it myself."

"Then, we just have to trust that he could be who we were sent to get." I decided and moved to stand next to her. "I'll go up with her in case he struggles or if we get into any trouble. If we do, well, it won't be quiet."

Sundar snickered, and Albarth rolled his eyes with the beginnings of a grin spreading across his face.

Emerald led me up the stairs, slowly so my armor wouldn't rattle too much. I would have to see if there was a way to keep this stuff quieter for things like this.

The stairs wrapped around and then came to a hallway, went down that, and into another hallway where Monami's mother grabbed me and pulled me toward the side of the place into a small room. "Wha—"

"Quiet, someone is coming." Her breathless response accompanied by her hand over my mouth made me freeze and still as best I could. A dwarf with a salt and pepper beard walked down the hall, muttering to himself as he shoved open the door two down from us.

"Quit readin' that tripe and go about yer duties as a man o' the cloth!" The dwarf shouted, though I couldn't see what was going on, I could guess he ordered about Father Caltross.

"This *tripe* is the book of our Lord!" An older, wizened voice snapped back. "You have no power here, filthy creature, and you *will* be stopped."

"I ain't a damn demon, like I told ye afore, but they are hell-bent on helpin' us return to where we came from." Then the dwarf's voice soured even further as he spat, and said, "Not that a homeless, gutless gnome such as yeself would understand our struggle."

"I wouldn't stoop to consorting with demons for anything —they *lie,* and all they want is for you and yours to die!" I heard what sounded like scuffling and flesh hitting flesh and made to move, but Emerald only held me tighter and shook her head. Then a derisive laugh came from the older voice. "Awfully brave, beating on old me. Is that the dwarven way of old you cling to so much? They'll see all of us murdered, and for what? Petty ancestral pride? Get out, you fake worshiper. You snake."

The dwarf launched out of the room with the other man clutched in his grasp, then threw him into the wall. Spit frothed at the edges of the dwarf's mouth, his face mere inches away from the smaller man's. "Yer reservations be noted, and I be not in the mood for that shite. Do what ye ought an' stay out o' me fookin' way."

The dwarf spat in the tiny man's face and let him fall the two feet to the ground in a heap with a grunt.

Once the dwarf was out of earshot, Emerald whispered, "Father Caltross?"

The gnomes head whipped up toward us as we stepped out of the little room.

"Who are you?!" he hissed before wiping his forehead with the cloth of his sleeve. "You have to leave; if they find you here, you'll be in danger!"

"We're here for *you,* father," I corrected, then showed him my signet ring. His eyes widened, and he nodded. "We need you to come with us to the Queen. We need your help to stop this."

He turned back to the other side of the hall, biting his lip as he did and took a knee right there where he was. Parts of his whispered prayer louder than others, "...Father... right thing to do?... guide me... amen."

He stilled and finally breathed easily once more. "I don't think they'll hurt my flock as he's gone for now."

We started to turn when he grunted and smacked his knee lightly.

"You'll have my aid, just let me grab my walking stick." He stood and shook himself out before he limped into his room and came back with a mace that he held by the ball portion with his fist inside it like it was—looking at it when he turned it toward me showed that there was, in fact, a handle inside the spiky portion for him to hold onto.

He moved slowly at first, his back hurting from his violent exit from his room, so I picked him up and nipped around the corner and toward the basement.

"Mind the imps!" He warned quietly. "Evil little things like to play with fire and bite people. How they were allowed in here without my Lord smiting them is beyond me, but if it's his will."

He made a motion like he was saying it was out of his hands and almost smacked me in the chin.

"We killed them before we came to get you, so we should be good," I explained, then turned downstairs into the basement proper where the others waited nervously.

Sundar took the priest, and I led us back to the throne room. Through the small cave, we found the entrance, down a long and winding tunnel and across a river of flame that we attributed to Belgonna's influence on the world around her in her immediate vicinity. Traveling through here was easy since no monsters seemed interested in being near the lava flows.

The high roof of the cave stood high above us with low hanging outcroppings and stalactites resembling fangs fit to eat all of us. Otherwise, the journey up into the throne room, which now had a collection of guards that the queen must have vetted herself, had been as uneventful as it had been going out.

"You return, victorious!" Sinistella drawled sweetly, moving toward us with her mother's massive head swinging toward us, as well. "Did you encounter anything of note?"

"Other than lava?" Sinistella raised an eyebrow at that, then I added, "Just some imps that we took care of. But Father Caltross can explain everything that is going on there to you both."

"They've taken the church!" The little old man howled, all of us jumping slightly at his fervor. "Evil creatures, sinning dwarves consorting with demons! On sacred ground, no less."

"And you are not one of these members?" Belgonna's question was asked in a way that showed her skepticism, but also didn't sound accusatory either.

"I still have the mark of favor by my God, his love, see?" He didn't roll up his sleeve, or pull his shirt to the side to show anything—but tore the whole sleeve off in a single jerk of his arm so that the mark of a hammer stood out against his stark-white skin, the skin hanging and frail-looking.

It was seriously a wonder how he could use that spiked mace as a walking stick.

"I see." Belgonna looked him square in the eyes and took a deep breath, her gaze falling from his as she focused. "You carry the scent of demons with you, but it does not cloud your mind. And I do sense a divine presence with you."

Caltross looked proud as he strutted toward the table. "I take it that since you've rescued me from the damned, that you mean to use me to help you stop those bastards from doing what it is they're planning?"

"Yes, sir, we are." Sundar joined him by the table and grasped his shoulder gently. "We'll need you to tell us everything you can about their preparations and how we can foil their plans."

"They keep me out of their way and in the dark as much as possible, using my flock to blackmail me. If I speak out of turn

or go for aid, they threaten to hurt them. I cannot abide that."
He took his mace and stamped the ground with the handle
angrily. "Though I've heard them speaking about someone
special coming to the church to do the summoning. Someone
who's taken a part in the murders personally. Gathering the
necessary disgusting energy to give them enough to summon a
stronger kind of demon and desecrate the holy ground and
leave the city defenseless."

"You ever seen them before?" Mona asked, but the little
man shook his head. "Well, we're going to be bringing in a
strike troop, I think, would you be able to tell us where we can
hide our people?"

Sinistella stepped in then, unfurling a map of the church as
it was when it was first constructed millennia ago. "Preferably
by marking the locations here as you think necessary. And if, at
any time, you think of something we can do to sabotage this,
please let us know."

"I reckon I would, Majesty." He seemed content to put
figurines in different areas around the side of the room that had
been marked with a balcony, then several other places closer to
the altar itself. "The first thing we're going to want to do is take
care of that fake priest."

CHAPTER TWENTY-ONE

MONA

"Come on," Mom's voice made me flinch, but I recovered quickly and made my way up the stairs behind her. Our job was the simplest, but most crucial—lure the fake priest away somewhere and take care of him.

I shook at the thought of *taking care* of anyone, remembering the look of absolute feral ecstasy on Kyvir's face as he fed on that man's neck while Sundar pierced him with her sword. The execution and feeding had soured my stomach so much that I wondered if I would vomit then and there.

He's been affected by something Red, you know that. I coaxed myself into thinking on the task at hand and not the man I loved being in the beginning stages of some sort of comic-style takeover from the early nineties.

The dwarf we sought out needed to go, and it fell to me to lure him somewhere and... dispose of him.

"With extreme prejudice!" Father Caltross had insisted six times as he'd explained what the cruel dwarf had been telling his flock. "Making them doubt their craft, and then their god!

Ought to be drowned, he should. No dwarf should blaspheme so!"

His tirade had gone on for some time before we were able to calm him down long enough to get a word in edgewise. He gave us good positions to watch from, how to move through the area in a way that would keep ourselves hidden and out of sight from below and above.

It was disconcerting that a priest would come to think of these things, but the wily old gnome had made the journey with us to help protect his church and flock so I couldn't hold his fervor against him. Nor his willingness to take part.

Time to do your part, Mona. I took a deep breath and let it go after a moment more and rounded the corner to wait for my victim.

Ten minutes later, he came striding down the hall, and I activated Allure, willing myself to be seen, and he stopped, blinking at me.

"H... hello," he started as I wagged a finger toward me and stepped toward the room to my right. He stumbled toward me a little, then strode into the room where I waited, dancing for an added distracting effect.

He closed the door behind him with a foot and began to fiddle with his shirt, barely getting the top three buttons undone before crossing the room toward me. I used my quick slot to pull my dagger and plunge it deep into his chest near his heart the same time my mother struck with her Soul Dagger, sliding it into the priest's carotid artery and tracing it around the back of his neck to his spine. His body crumpled, and we drove our blades into him again for good measure.

58 EXP

Nice amount of experience even with the sacrifice for our five-man party. We'd have to try and find a workaround for that.

Whispers surrounded my head, something I could hear and not hear—promising fortune, fame, power, knowledge.

I shook my head and frowned to myself, then blinked at my mom. A shadowy figure reached around her toward me. My heart nearly burst as I lunged forward, dagger first to slice at the hand grasping at me through her, and she fell back.

"Mona, what in the world are you doing?!" she whispered, scrambling to her feet to glance outside.

"You didn't see that?" I hissed through my teeth, glancing around into the shadows for the figure who giggled around me *somewhere*. "It's still here."

"Monami, there is nothing here. Come on, we have work to do." She sighed, dismissing her weapon and turning to leave.

She's wrong, Monami, a breathy, husky voice whispered in my ear, *I'm very much here.*

The door closed, making me flinch, but I could see where the voice was coming from.

I can feel the desire in you building, so deliciously. You want something, and I know what it is.

"You know nothing about me!" My knuckles cracked, and the hilt of my dagger dug painfully into my hand as I stalked toward the door.

I know so much about you, the voice feigned hurt so well, it almost sounded like it was pouting. *I can help you find what you seek.*

"You won't lie to me, whoever you are!" Even though I was doing my best to sound like I couldn't care less, my heart thundered. Could she know something about my dad?

All will be revealed in time... the voice faded, and I was alone. Sweat had beaded down my face, and I wiped it away.

The door handle shook in my grasp. I bounced back from it and readied myself for a fight, only to have Kyvir open the door and motion me out into the hallway. He paused long enough to study my face before coming into the room, leaving the door open behind him.

"Hey, what's up?" His frown and concern touched me in a way I didn't know I needed right then, and when he stepped closer to me, I no longer felt so awkward and out of sorts.

"I think something's trying to tell me it knows about my dad." His eyes widened, and he leaned closer so I could lower my voice. "They said everything would be revealed in time.

Mom didn't see it when it was in the room with us, and I think I'm going crazy."

"Hey, it's okay." He pulled me close, and I could smell him, feel him thrumming over me like a taught string, and I was suddenly very aware of how I had almost *never* thought of him this way. *What is wrong with me?*

"We will sort this out, don't pay attention to whatever voices you heard, okay?" He smiled at me softly, his fangs peeking out from behind his lips. "It could be a demon."

Suddenly, I felt the urge to kiss him in a way that I never thought I would. Heart bounding behind my rib cage and butterflies doing loops in my stomach hard enough to make me feel feverish to the point where I clung to him.

He looked at me, curiously, but I didn't care. Mom had said I should tell him how I felt. He had asked me how I felt. It was time I showed him. Showed me. I could do this. Maybe if I could give him a reason to fight for his humanity then he wouldn't have any violent outbursts like he did in the throne room.

I lifted my chin. His breath tasted like cinnamon and sugar against mine. A soft, chaste press of lips that fed a fire I had never let grow beyond a smolder out of fear and concern burst, and suddenly, I wanted more. *Needed* more.

Hands on my chin. Pressure and a small slit of sweet fire as a fang pressed into my lip and moved as he tilted his head back.

I opened my eyes to a look of concern so profound that my heart stopped as he looked at me.

"Mo… I love you, but it's not that kind of love." He was gentle as he pressed against my shoulder and hip to distance us a little bit, and it felt as if the distance may as well have been miles and miles.

My mouth moved, even as my heart stuttered and stammered, breaking with the confusion and concern building in my chest. "But… but you asked me if I wanted more. *You* brought it up, you asked me if I wanted more, Seth. I wanted more! I was just surprised and panicked, why are you being like this?!"

Crack! "*Graaaaaaagh!*" A body flew by the doorway, one of the city guards bloodied and singed.

"We don't have time for this, but we can talk about it later—let's go!" Kyvir turned and bolted out of the door, a flame-covered figure bursting into existence beside him and following behind.

As he fled the room, my adrenaline dumped, and all I wanted to do was cry. I wanted to bury my head in the sand and roll over.

You will not, no man will ever hurt you again. The voice returned, sounding as angry and indignant as I felt.

"How do *you* know?!" I sobbed, tears flecking the floor.

I know. A stirring before the door showed me that same shadowy figure beckoned me forward. *Come. I will show you what I can offer you. What will keep anyone from hurting you ever again.*

My feet could move, and almost as if on its own, my body moved toward the door and out into the hallway covered in the blood of the NPCs that had come with us. Down the hall toward the commotion and chaos.

CHAPTER TWENTY-TWO

SETH

That's going to be a very awkward discussion, I blinked as I summoned Flicker, her pixie body much more robust and her wings more solid and definitely larger.

"Hey, Kyvir!" She greeted me warmly, her wings beat at me as she alighted on my shoulder, grinning from ear to ear. "What're we doing now?"

"Getting ready for a fight!" I ground my teeth and summoned my next companion. "Sprinkle!"

The sour-faced frost faerie kicked me in my earlobe angrily. "I was just about to get a date with one of the prettiest ladies in the cold realms!"

The three Aether it had cost me to summon him lent him some credibility in that. "Sorry, but we have a city to save, and I need both of you."

"Fine!" Sprinkle snarled and growled his frustration at me. "But the next time you summon me, you're feeding me more Aether to help me grow. No more freebies."

"Freebies?" I balked, rolling my eyes. "Just make sure that

we do good work and keep the bad guys busy. We can settle payment later!"

The two of them hopped off my shoulders and sped into the open chamber before us, Flicker snickering at Sprinkle, "Try not to melt, little guy!"

"A little stronger than me, and you think you're better?" I heard the smaller faerie's tone that sounded like his eyes were rolling. "Puh-lease, get in line, hot stuff."

A burst of elemental magic flashed ahead, and I growled, pulling my separable glaive from my quick slot over my shoulder and slashed at a hooded figure in front of me.

12 dmg to unknown dwarf

The hood fell, and a dwarf wearing leather armor colored brown like stones sneered at me and attacked just before several bolts, and an arrow struck him about the neck and shoulders. I slid my glaive into his solar plexus and twisted it with a brutal jerking motion before taking the weapon out and turning to survey my surroundings.

Chaos had broken out, and brother fought brother. Red-blooded dwarves decorated in their beliefs, the red of the dragon—order and faithful service—fought against those adorned by the stone of their ancestors—steadfast and sure as the earth we stood on.

Gone were the hoods of the rebellion, replaced by the same brutal surety on the face of every fang of Belgonna's law enforcement.

13 dmg taken

I gasped as a red-hot line of agony seared across my spine, my lungs emptied in a shout of pain so guttural I couldn't think.

I stepped forward and turned to find a smiling dwarf. "Yer late to the party, Kin."

"Fashionably so," I retorted and brought my glaive around to bear down on him, the weapon whirling and striking against the war pick in his hands. He was adept with it, more so than me, but I had tricks.

"Sprinkle," I muttered under my breath, and the small blue

being rocketed overhead, releasing a burst of snow above the dwarf's head as a distraction. His overhead swing passed through my now separated hilts just before the blades sang through his right arm, and then his throat.

A notification popped up, but I ignored it and moved on to find my next target when I noticed a single figure clouded in an aura so thick with demonic energy it could fill the room and suffocate us all.

Their movements were sure and steady as they walked a large symbol on the ground ten feet before the pulpit, where the priest would likely give his sermons.

Their glowing arms—looking almost to be surrounded by electrical energy with waves of heat—carved a glowing symbol in the air that hung there before moving on.

— *That's our target right there, we need to stop them,*— I whispered to the rest of the party, then called out, "Flicker, Sprinkle, time to rock!"

"I don't know if you're aware, but if I were capable of using earth magic, I would punish you for that," Sprinkle sniffed at me as he passed by and I rolled my eyes.

As soon as they were near the figure, several of the dwarves around us cried out and bled from their eyes and ears before their eyes shifted to black. They turned in unison and grinned, then bellowed and threw themselves at the two summoners.

A familiar voice rang out around us all, "You weren't ready for us last time, so you brought more toys to play with?" Laughter echoed around us. "I liked playing with you, but the rest of them? They weren't part of the guest registry, unfortunately."

A burst of green and black flames snaked out of the ground by where the two summonings fought bravely against their tormentors, and there stood the same succubus that had killed Sundar and me. She reached out and grasped the ice and flame beings, and they screamed wildly before dissipating in a wash of agony.

"No worries, I wasn't meaning to play all that much, I have

a message." She turned and grasped the shoulder of the person behind her. "Good work, Arglyn, don't stop now. Our friend is *so excited* to come play."

The figure just continued to mutter droning words and phrases as they made broad motions with their hands.

An arrow flashed close to them, and the succubus flicked it out of the way as Sundar made to join me on the front line as the dwarves that had been taken over turned and faced me.

"Don't worry, all I want to do is talk, but not to you." The air around her shimmered and shook like a mirage as her demonic aura crashed toward us, and rather than destroy everything in its path, it merely stole my ability to move a single muscle.

How can she make it so hard to move? What level is she? I growled and strained at the bonds holding me. A sickly red aura surrounded my limbs and those of my friends and the people we had brought with us.

"Besides!" She clapped delightedly with a grin at all of us, her sharpened teeth exposed. "I have good news for one of you!"

She looked out into the crowd. "There you are, Monami, quit sulking where you think I can't see you and come on down here for a second. It's okay."

Monami's body jerkily moved into my visual range. My drive deepened to get out of this damned bond holding me, but my body wouldn't respond. I could hear the others straining violently. Albarth howling where he watched from the walkway above. "You stay away from her, you bloody bitch! I'll kill you, I'll fuckin' kill you!"

"Now, now, play nice," the demon tutted at him, her arm draping over Mona's shoulders like they were old friends. "Remember how I told you that all would be revealed in time?"

She didn't wait for there to be any sort of recognition but paused to let the insinuation of them having spoken before sink in. There was no way. Mona wouldn't side with the demons. It was a lie. It was all a lie.

"Well, it's time. I know what it is that two of you seek, and we have *just the thing* to flush him out." She moved so that she stood in front of Mona and lifted her chin. "You can finally have what you want most. Well, *wanted* most."

The creature's gaze flashed my way, and her eyes narrowed as she bared her teeth, the aura around her flexed, and my body slid forward slowly. My skin hurt like it had two-day old bruises where the bands of her demonic power held me tightly.

"He *scorned* you," her voice was low, almost a whisper. "You told him you loved him, and he pissed it all away. You know, I would happily kill him for you."

She raised her hand, Mona's eyes widened, and she flowed pink where she stood, the succubus turning back to her with a sad smile. "Ain't love a bitch? See, I know why he refused you. And I know why you can't seem to get the old man off your mind. You wanna know? It's okay, you can speak."

Mona was released then, her body sagging dangerously close to the circle on the floor.

The person speaking whatever spell it was, Arglyn, had kept going all this time, and now had about fifteen feet to go before finishing the circle. More than twenty glowing symbols glowed eerily in the air around it, and they looked like they were sweating heavily with how damp their dark-colored cloak looked.

Monami's voice drifted to me, barely a whisper at first, but then her anger flared, and her head whipped up to the succubus, "Why?"

"Because it was *stripped* from him." Her satirical, sad pouting face made me want to punch her even harder than I did. "When you awaken your Aether, they *take* something from you. Steal something that is most important to you. To him, I could imagine that it was something hefty if he's able to use summoning Aether. Something as hefty as, say... his love for someone he's known for all his life?"

Suddenly the fetters around my mouth gagging me dropped, allowing me to shout, "I still love her, you're lying!"

"Well, see, that's one thing I won't do to her." The succubus laid a hand on Mona's shoulder, her sickly aura flaring wildly while she pulled Mona closer to her and the circle before I bellowed in outrage. "Men, all animals driven by such base motivations. Mona, I want to help you find your father because we're looking for him too. Help us, and you'll be united with him. You and your mom. Don't you want that?"

Mona's breathing almost stopped, and I called to her, "Mona, she's lying to you. All they want to do is make us suffer. We will find your dad together, I promise."

Her tear-stained face turned to me, puffy eyes glaring at me. "What if they take your ability to keep your word from you? What if they take your memories? I can't trust you. I can't trust anyone. But I'll find my dad, and I'll make them pay for taking you from me, and I know just where to start!"

She stomped her foot as hard as she could, and the succubus flinched with it, but only grinned when Mona snarled, "Right here!"

"Easy there, Kitty." The succubus giggled, covering her mouth with a nailed hand. "We have other things in mind for you. Momma too."

Another scraping sound and Emerald stood next to me, her face red with shouting, but her voice was gone. Her whole body looked to be covered in red flowers that bound her as tightly as the succubus' magic.

"Let me guess, they took something from her, too?" Mona looked defeated, gaze downcast and shoulders slouched as they were.

"Mo, look at me, you don't have to do this, we can do this together," I insisted, pleading with her, "Just help us out of this, and we can *fight!*"

She shook her head, anger replacing her tears with right-eous fury that burned in her eyes. "I've done all I can, Kyvir. I have to fix things. I have to find my dad. I have to fix all of you… this can't go on."

"You're right!" The succubus grinned. "And we're going to

start *right* now!" She grasped the back of Monami's arm and tugged her toward Emerald. "You, me, and momma!"

"Wouldn't it make sense to leave her where he can find her and make contact?" Mona posed calmly, and the succubus cried out with a look of ecstasy on her face.

"I like the way you think!" The demon patted Mona on her shoulder, appreciatively. "You'll make a good demon, kid. Well, everyone in this city is about to get *real* dead, so we should go ahead and get a head start."

"Mona, don't go—*no!*" I pleaded, but the two of them melted away into shadows, Mona looking at me as if I were so much broken junk. My best friend in the whole world vanishing in a dark, inky aura with nary a second thought.

"*Raaaaaaaaaaaaaaagh!*" I screamed my voice ragged, my vocal cords shredding as I did, but I didn't care. Mona was basically a willing captive now, and the ritual looked like it was almost complete. The magic was still intact, and I couldn't move, but if Mona had been able to use Allure, maybe I could…

The chanter, Arglyn, pulled out a large vial of crimson roughly the size of a football and made a show of drawing the last glyph, and the vial floated over the middle of the circle. The cork at the top of it dissolved, and I knew I'd have a single shot at this.

Luckily, Aether recovered when I was still. As the vial tilted and the crimson began to spill out, a large splash of it hit the circle, just as my summoning Aether wrapped around it, I poured everything into pulling it to my side, and as soon as the magic took hold, I pulled the container toward my mouth. The liquid poured in, power flowed through my veins. The bonds holding me weakened, and I burst from them, my hand grasping the vial and holding it steady so I could gorge myself on the blood.

It tasted like I had decided to upend a bottle of cinnamon alcohol into my gullet and chug it all down in a single go.

A woman's voice rang out from the other side of the circle,

"Kill them! Don't let them interrupt the summoning any more than they already have."

I tore forward and brought my glaive out of its quick slot and slashed the nearest enemy dwarf across the chest, then kicked him into the circle. The glyphs flared and blocked the body from entering and bounced it out of the way.

The others broke free, and I continued my assault until I could get to Arglyn, her hood had fallen now, and I could see her for what she was. Some kind of weird-looking kin with purplish skin, small horns just above her eyes, and red irises.

An arrow fired down at her, and she blurred, stepping out of the way and into my path. My weapon lashed out, the blade passing most of the way through her glowing hand before she stepped toward me with a smile that disarmed me for a moment.

"You're gonna have to work a little harder than that to get me, kid." She winked and smiled, then faded altogether. A rush of Aether through the room made me turn just in time to get tackled by a dwarf.

12 dmg taken

I groaned and hissed loudly, "*Agh!*" Looking down, I saw the dagger that he had slid into my abdomen. I yanked it from my body and growled, stabbing it into the man before I bit into his arm to replenish some of my spent Aether. A single bar of summoning Aether returned and another percent of earth affinity with it.

I'd look at my notifications after the fight was over.

The Aether that flooded the room stilled, swirling in hues of red and black like a cloud of dust particulates, then converged back on the circle. The glyphs burst outward in a rain of magical fragments like shrapnel that peppered the puppet dwarves and killed them where they stood, the one over me taking the majority of the damage for me.

Luckily my resistance helped further. Unfortunately, it was still painful.

47 dmg taken

A rush of blue healing energy overtook me, and I found Sundar standing next to me, her hands outstretched to help me stand. "We need all hands-on deck here for this one. You have to help us kill whatever is coming out of those shadows."

Emerald, still wrapped in the red plants wept openly, her voice finally having returned.

"*Greeeeeaaaaaaargh!*" A loud screeching echoed around us, the fog-like shadows thinning to reveal a lanky demon that looked like an emaciated gorilla with half-formed wings that tried to flap behind it. The mouth hung open angrily, sharp fangs pierced its tongue, and then it howled again. It raised its arms above its head and it slammed the ground as an arrow sank into its shoulder, the flames that covered it doing little to no damage.

Lvl 16 Balgrus Demon (incomplete summoning) - Hostile

"Get your lazy ass in there, Kyvir!" I glanced back. Albarth, his face a mask of blatant fury, brandished his bow.

Spitting toward the demon, I cast Ice Armor (full) on myself and trudged forward with my glaive ready. I hadn't healed fully, but I'd gotten a good twenty health back and was still in her radius for healing.

"Shaman!" Old Father Caltross called from off to my right. "Can you make things faster?"

"Yeah. I'm about to do that for Kyvir, why?" Sundar grunted and then took a breath that made me stop and stare at the old gnome.

He had taken his mace into both hands and shimmered with a golden light that made the demon shrink away from him.

"Glory to my god, his power of making, remaking my body in his image so that I might smite his enemies and those who threaten his creations!" The gnome stood taller now, his beard black and his body rejuvenated, muscular, and ready for war. "I am my God's hammer, and I will strike true!"

Golden light enveloped his mace, and both of us launched ourselves forward to attack.

I couldn't see his damage, but every single time he struck the weakened demon, it screeched in agony and its flesh singed from the holy strikes.

Fury mounted in me, but my gamer mentality still whooped over having stolen this creature's lifeblood from it before it became too powerful.

My damage was doing a little, bit by bit, but the old man's fury was bolstered by the Hell Cat buff that increased his speed by that much more made all the difference.

The Balgrus demon swiped for me, and I made a shield of flame that melted my armor slightly, but the claws didn't sink into it or pass through, and suddenly, Sundar stood behind it. Her hands grabbed the beast under the armpit and elbow before she swung her hip around and yanked it over her shoulder.

As soon as it was on the ground, Caltross leaped into the air and brought his mace down covered in divine energy. "Purify this fiend!"

The Balgrus demon tried to fend off the attack, but the mace sailed through the thing's arm and into its head like a missile, splattering the holy floor with blood and grey matter.

Several notifications flooded my vision, but I didn't care. Mona was gone, and the hole in my heart threatened to devour me where I stood. It was enough to consume any sort of victory that we had earned.

All the times we'd been together careening through my mind, the times we had laughed together. The times that we'd had our spats and then all the times that we had just been there when the world was too hard.

And at this moment, I wanted her by my side. Had someone taken my love for her? Had I loved her?

Crack! My jaw ached wildly, and I stumbled to the left, the world suddenly turning on its axis as I fell onto my butt.

"You absolute sodding wanker!" Albarth seethed, his teeth clenched harder than his fists. If it hadn't been for the two city guard dwarves holding him back, I knew he would have been on top of me beating the hell from me, and I knew that he thought I'd earned it. "All you had to do was just return her feelings. You love her too—why?! Why did you just piss it all away?"

"I don't feel that same way!" I insisted. "She kissed me, and all I felt was discomfort. Like a sister trying to make out with me, and all I wanted was for it to stop."

"You bloody arse." Spittle flecked my face as he strained to reach me. "Your damn pride got hurt once, and you think what—turnabout's fair play? You prideful bastard, you couldn't think about *her* for a single moment?"

"She's my best friend, of course, I was!" I was on my feet now, moving toward him until Sundar grasped both of my arms to hold me back. "All I wanted was for things to be what they were again. For all of us to get through all of this and to figure out what the hell is going on in this game and out of it—shit isn't right!"

"Of course, it isn't!" He shouted back, eyes bulging from their sockets. Finally, he shook his head and glared at me, then at Sundar. "I take it you're going to support this farce?"

"He's not wrong, Albarth." Sundar tried to get him to meet her eyes but stopped when he just shook his head again. "We need to figure out what's going on, and we can get her back."

"That you aren't prioritizing her being back with us shows just how little you both care." He stopped struggling and relaxed, the dwarves letting him go but staying near just in case. "I'll get her back myself. Goodbye."

With that, he turned and strode out of the church and didn't so much as glance back.

A hacking cough drew my attention from my sulking and the loss of two friends at the same time. Father Caltross sat on the steps up to his God's altar, leaning back, his muscles and body wilting before our very eyes. He hacked again, and Sundar pulled me toward him, casting her totem again to heal us, and any dwarf brave enough to stand near us.

A stifled gasp and soft sobbing behind me made me turn

and find Emerald kneeling on the ground next to the circle, tears streaming down her face.

I moved toward her instinctively and knelt down next to her. "Hey, Ma, don't worry, we *will* figure this out, okay?"

She shook her head and shoved me away, the shock of her reaction to my being close almost as jarring as Mona's kiss had been, but then I saw what she pointed to. A scuff in the painted circle that had broken it.

"She went with them to help us," Emerald sobbed, her eyes closing in a mixture of grief, pride, and worry. "She went with them so that she would leave, giving us a chance! My baby…"

My heart thundered, if that was true, then there was hope. We could get her back. We could save her.

CHAPTER TWENTY-THREE

SETH

Our dour trek through the throngs of citizens who had heard the fighting in the church and been kept away by the military and law enforcement of the city was slightly short-lived. Belgonna and Sinistella leaving their home under the mountain to meet us had seen to that.

"I see that our city is not on fire." Sinistella grinned triumphantly, her eyes scanning the group. "But where are your friends? The attractive one and the nymph?"

I looked to Sundar and Emerald, uncertain how to put it or if I wanted to say anything at all when Belgonna shoved herself forward and pulled all of us into her grasp. "My condolences for the loss of something so precious. If there is ought that we can do, I offer it to you, my children, and precious friends."

Emerald croaked, "thank you."

Belgonna touched all of our faces before turning toward the steadily growing crowd. You would think that the majority of the people had never truly seen their queen before. More people seemed to be familiar with Sinistella and that lent credibility to her being the logistical one running the city behind the scenes.

Once they all quieted, she raised her arms and voice, "My children! We have suffered the battle against the demons here on our very lands. In the heart of our fair city and for a time, we failed you in protecting you from harm. I ask you, how is a mother to remain in control of herself when her children are in mortal danger?"

Muttered voices cropped up here and there, confused faces upturned toward her, waiting for more information. "I did not. It was my failure that allowed this to continue for far too long."

Voices raised, shouts of disapproval, not for her failure, but rather for her having said she was a failure. One dwarven man close to me wept openly. "Ye gived our people hope, Majesty! We know ye were tryin' yer hardest to see to yer children. We love ye!"

Those around him assented and agreed with his outburst, Belgonna closing the distance between them to touch his face lovingly, like an indulgent parent looking into the face of her naïve offspring.

"I am unfit to rule you, but there is one with whom many of you are familiar who will take my place." The crowd looked near to rioting then and there, but as Sinistella stepped closer to her mother, the great wyrm's arm wrapping around her shoulder with care, they quieted expectantly. "I will spend what precious time I have left caring for all of my children how I can, and as I do so, I have abdicated my throne to a more capable and fresh-minded ruler. Sinistella will take my place, and she will nurture this city as I have with the hopes of fostering a better future for our people. For our *family*."

As she finished her speech, Belgonna summoned a crown made of pure flames that writhed and danced as she placed the symbol of status atop her daughter's brow. Belgonna turned back to the people and shouted, "Long live the queen, Sinistella!"

"Long live Queen Sinistella!" I hollered with the others so

we wouldn't stick out too much, even though the bile in my stomach and the roiling through me at everything that had happened was so much to deal with. We had to put up a front. *I* had to put up a front so that no one would suspect what had happened.

"Thank you!" Sinistella bowed her head slightly and raised her voice as she stepped closer to our small group. "My first act as queen is to celebrate these fine wanderers, my brother and sister fought bravely to ensure that our people could hold their heads high without the fear of demons invading our home. I would grant them a boon, but first, I offer them up to the fair people of this city!"

The crowd went absolutely berserk, surrounding us with words of appreciation and promises of food, and drink aplenty.

"We will hold a feast for them tomorrow evening, where I will give them their reward for protecting you, my beloved family." She smiled and came to stand with the three of us. "This may be a time of change, but this change is for the better. We will all assist each other through this—together."

After that, she turned to us. "You may all return to our home this evening. Rooms have been prepared for each of you so that you do not have to fear the repercussions of any of the remains of the defecting faction. I have also had your rooms at the inn searched and found these."

She handed us the stones that Mona had been given. "Binding stones, they will allow you to travel quickly to places you've been before. They are rare and hard to make, but well within my means. And no, they are not your rewards. These are stronger than the originals I gave you. These you will carry with you so that you may travel safer."

"Thank you." Emerald frowned at the rest of us. "I think I'm ready to go back to the... what is your place called?"

Belgonna and Sinistella blinked at one another, before the former queen answered, "Forgive me, I thought the guards had told you, it's called the Den."

"Then I'll return to the Den first, I need to go and check on something back home." With that, Emerald was off and on her way, the crowd parting at her dour demeanor, though some of the women in the surroundings moved toward her to speak in hushed tones.

Sundar shrugged, and we moved to follow her with our gratitude to both of the dragons and those in the crowd who wished to call out to us. "She's a strong woman, Kyvir. She knew what she was doing."

I blinked and kept my mouth shut for a moment too long, and she added, "It's not your fault."

"I know it isn't," I said and growled back at her softly, my voice still a little raw from screaming as I had. "What was my fault was that I wasn't strong enough to contend with that demon. If we're supposed to fight those things, we need to be prepared. We need to be ready and stronger, and with every-thing bad that has happened to all of my friends and the people we care about, the only way for us to do that is to play as hard as they are. Time to take the kid gloves off and get the job done."

"What're you talking about?" Sundar stopped me, forcing me to look at her with a hand on my chest.

"They made me out to be a monster for what Mephisto did to me, even after they understood, I could see the reservation in their eyes when I fought." A sense of knowing calm fell over me. The same sort of calm I found in my heart when I had brought Jimson to face his death for betraying us. "I'm going to embrace what I've become, and I'm going to collect as much power as I can so that we can take the fight to them and get our friends back."

I stared her straight in the eyes as I made my oath, to myself and the world around us. "You with me?"

"Someone has to keep you alive." She rolled her eyes, then her body stiffened, and she looked ready to fight. "But I agree. We have to get them back. I'm with you."

It had been about an hour in-game by the time we made it back to the Den, all the people stopping us to thank us and offer us words of kindness for our good turn took longer than we would have expected. We had just gotten into the hall of the Den when Emerald, wild-eyed and incensed, came screeching down the path toward us.

"She's gone!" she cried, "Mona's been taken from her portal!"

"What?!" Sundar and I both bolted forward to meet her, her panting breaths coming faster and faster as she fell into a fit of panic.

"Dogs...tranq'd." Her chest rose and fell as worry claimed her. "Portal open... she's gone. Seth—my baby's gone!"

I could almost hear that sick, demon bastard laughing in my ears as the realization of what had happened set in. If we could have been near her, she could have spied for us if that had been her plan. So, they took her to keep us out and to isolate her.

"What will we do?" Emerald clung to both of us, her weight barely registering against my body.

"We get stronger and we find her." Even I knew my voice sounded harsh as I spoke, but I needed to channel my outrage toward something tangible, or I would lose myself to the darkness welling up within me. Threatening the little control I had left after all the shit that had happened in the last few hours. "We have no choice but to move on and try to get ahead of them somehow."

Sundar and I comforted ma in the middle of the hallway, this mother who had lost her husband and her daughter and had nothing to lose.

Those demons had no idea what hell they had really opened up on themselves with this. But they would soon learn; we would bring it right to them.

ABOUT CHRISTOPHER JOHNS

Christopher Johns is a former photojournalist for the United States Marine Corps with published works telling hundreds of other peoples' stories through word, photo, and even video. But throughout that time, his editors and superiors had always said that his love of reading fantasy and about worlds of fantastic beauty and horrible power bled into his work. That meant he should write a book.

Well, ta-da!

Chris has been an avid devourer of fantasy and science fiction for more than twenty years and looks forward to sharing that love with his son, his loving fiancée and almost anyone he could ever hope to meet.

Connect with Chris:
Facebook.com/AxeDruidAuthor
Twitter.com/JonsyJohns

ABOUT MOUNTAINDALE PRESS

Dakota and Danielle Krout, a husband and wife team, strive to create as well as publish excellent fantasy and science fiction novels. Self-publishing *The Divine Dungeon: Dungeon Born* in 2016 transformed their careers from Dakota's military and programming background and Danielle's Ph.D. in pharmacology to President and CEO, respectively, of a small press. Their goal is to share their success with other authors and provide captivating fiction to readers with the purpose of solidifying Mountaindale Press as the place 'Where Fantasy Transforms Reality.'

Connect with Mountaindale Press:
MountaindalePress.com
Facebook.com/MountaindalePress
Twitter.com/_Mountaindale
Instagram.com/MountaindalePress

MOUNTAINDALE PRESS TITLES

GameLit and LitRPG

The Completionist Chronicles,
The Divine Dungeon,
Full Murderhobo, and
Year of the Sword by Dakota Krout

Arcana Unlocked by Gregory Blackburn

A Touch of Power by Jay Boyce

Red Mage and
Farming Livia by Xander Boyce

Space Seasons by Dawn Chapman

Ether Collapse and
Ether Flows by Ryan DeBruyn

Dr. Druid by Maxwell Farmer

Bloodgames by Christian J. Gilliland

Threads of Fate by Michael Head

Lion's Lineage by Rohan Hublikar and Dakota Krout

Wolfman Warlock by James Hunter and Dakota Krout

Axe Druid,
Mephisto's Magic Online, and
High Table Hijinks by Christopher Johns

Skeleton in Space by Andries Louws

Chronicles of Ethan by John L. Monk

Pixel Dust and
Necrotic Apocalypse by David Petrie

Viceroy's Pride by Cale Plamann

Henchman by Carl Stubblefield

Artorian's Archives by Dennis Vanderkerken and Dakota Krout

www.ingramcontent.com/pod-product-compliance
Lightning Source LLC
Chambersburg PA
CBHW031600240626
47153CB00002B/579